The Trouble

With Heather Holloway

CAROL TURNER

D1602761

Copyright

Disclaimer

This book is a work of fiction. All contemporary characters are invented. The ghost towns of Hellfire and Wolftongue do not exist. The town of Sugarloaf does not exist. The Colorado Frontier Museum and Colorado Western University are also invented.

With the exception of Alonzo Holloway, the Sand Creek Massacre and the names of persons who participated, those who tried to stop it, and those who were killed are real.

Acknowledgements

Thanks much for helpful feedback from Laura Manuel, Alison Turner, Laura Usselman, and members of my former critique group in Denver, associated with Rocky Mountain Fiction Writers.

Dedicated to the descendants.

One

Marshal Beth Mayo crept toward the woman, who huddled behind the cashier's counter, sawing at something. Her fingers were smeared with blood and she was muttering, "Ouch! Ouch! Stupid!"

It took Mayo a moment to sort out what was going on—the woman had a straight razor in her hand and was dicing her own arm.

"What the—" Mayo grabbed her hand mid-slash and pried at the small gooey fingers until the razor pinged across the scrubbed linoleum floor.

Her expression fixed, the woman dipped her chin and scanned the floor using just her eyes, which set off another alarm for Mayo.

The woman was petite, maybe mid-twenties, with a showy pixie haircut in platinum and copper. She'd be pretty if she didn't look so mental. Blood smeared her arms and legs. She wore an oversized men's Oxford shirt and apparently nothing else. Her mouth was a deranged red smudge.

"You're a pig," she said.

Mayo fought off a flash of annoyance, followed instantly by a familiar rise of jitters. This kind of shenanigans wasn't supposed to happen in the adorable little Rocky Mountain hamlet of Sugarloaf. That was the deal she made with that crafty old coot who called himself the mayor, wasn't it? She was supposed to spend her mornings chasing elk off the road and tucking the odd drunk into a smelly cabin somewhere. On slow afternoons, she'd leave a deputy in charge, round up her housemate, Monte, and his two hounds, and head into the woods to burn off some of her seemingly endless supply of anxiety. She really wasn't good for much else these days. She was sure she had explained all that to Mayor Davy. She had insisted on it, and he had promised.

Now, her third day on the job, this.

"What is going on?" Mayo tried to conjure some warmth into her tone but probably didn't manage it. Her own cousin had been rumored to be a cutter and she'd run across a few over the years. There was no reasoning with a cutter.

"Bad guys coming here, all the damn time. You think I made this up?"

"Made what up?" Mayo said.

"Is she okay? Is it Patty?" Deputy Roger McKern clumped through the door and tangled momentarily with a rack of potato chips that had been shoved out of place. Somehow, McKern's jacket and gear and all the rest of him always took up twice as much space as it should.

"Bugger him off!" The woman demanded. "Bad guys coming here, all the damn time!"

"What the f-f—" said McKern.

"It's not Patty." Mayo roused into action, poking McKern back, out of the woman's sight. It took more than a subtle tap to get him to budge. "Grab a blanket from the car," she said. "You see anyone in the area?"

"Nope" McKern craned his neck for another look before heading off again. "It's the new girl."

"Get the CSI kit," Mayo called after him. "And tape the front door."

"Someone came in and hurt you?" she quizzed the woman. "Was there a robbery?"

"He hurt me."

Mayo surveyed the scene. The cash register was closed. A few tins of snuff and cigarette packs lay strewn across the floor. The pleasant smell of eggs and sausage wafted from the counter, where two heat lamps warmed a pile of Dulce Salazar's fat breakfast burritos wrapped in foil.

Mayo found a box of tissues under the counter and dabbed the woman's lip. The woman gazed gratefully into Mayo's eyes, pushing her lower lip out.

"I guess you were pretty scared, huh?" Mayo said uncomfortably. That gaze felt too intimate.

The woman held up her left arm, apparently wanting that dabbed too.

Mayo found more tissues and patted the forearm. A tidy line of fresh cuts appeared, along with the pink shadows of older cuts.

What next? What next? Had she forgotten how to be a cop?

The woman had hold of Mayo's hand now and was crying. She had huge tears, Mayo noticed. How could tears be so darn big? Before she realized what she was doing, she was pressing a fresh bunch of tissues against those tears.

Gawd, how had she ended up in such a worthless muddle? She wanted to be far, far away from this, struggling for oxygen in the alpine zone, battling the scree and talus of a fiendishly indifferent peak. *That* was the distraction she wanted—not this.

She dragged her mind back to the situation. Nine-one-one call. Terrified woman. Nobody at the pumps outside. Blood and cuts inside. Bare legs. Potato chip rack askew. Stuff strewn about.

Something off about the whole thing. She had spent eight years on the Denver P.D. She had automated skills and knew what to do next. Just a bit of trust in herself, that's all.

"I meant I'm a stupid pig," the woman said. "Not you."

"How about neither of us?" Mayo suggested. The woman made a faint noise from inside her throat. Mayo looked for signs of injury, aside from the razor cuts. "You've got blood on your legs too. Were you cutting there?"

She woman licked her lips, shrugged. She couldn't have weighed more than a hundred pounds. Easy target. If she had been a target.

"What's your name?"

"Heather Holloway." Surprisingly, her tone was loud and sharp.

Mayo felt suddenly very calm, on course. Routine. "What happened, Heather?"

Heather gazed at Mayo again. She had the disquieting quality of seeming young and old at once—something about her frown. "A guy followed me into the store and raped me."

"Okay. Did you know him?"

"No." Heather rubbed her eyes with the ball of her thumb, smearing her eye make-up. Her skin looked smooth and well cared for. Expensive creams, Mayo thought, to go with the expensive haircut. Money somewhere, and not from a cashier's job at Zippy's Gas & Go in Sugarloaf, Colorado.

"Did you see his face?" Mayo asked.

Heather nodded.

"Could you describe him?"

"He was an Indian," Heather said.

"India-Indian or American Indian?"

Heather straightened up. "American Indian," she said. "He was big, with long black hair and only one eye."

"He was missing an eye?"

Heather crossed her skinny, abused arms over her stomach. "It was there but it didn't look at anything."

Great, thought Mayo. A sexual assault with no lab in town, and no help except for two novice deputies and another one on vacation. Worst of all, Mayo herself had been a drifting wreck for—how long had it been? Only about a year, not nearly long enough. She wasn't ready to be on the ball again.

"Okay," she said, digging up a professional tone from deep in her past. "How long you been working at Zippy's?"

"Patty just hired me a few days ago."

"Did the guy have a weapon?"

"A gun."

"Did he take it with him?"

Heather glared at her. "I don't know! I wasn't watching. I was busy being raped!"

"Okay, Heather," she said soothingly. "How long ago was this?"

Heather was back to her pleading gaze and she reached for Mayo's hand again but just pawed at it instead of grabbing on. Mayo let her do it. "Five or ten minutes, maybe. He ran out the back and I called 911."

"Did he come in through the front?"

Heather shook her head. "I was opening up the store and he came in the back door behind me."

"Did you see any unfamiliar cars around?"

"No."

"No one else here? Customers?"

Heather's lower lip came out again. "Of course not."

Mayo noted that the crazy mumbling cutting Heather had now been replaced by a competent and practical Heather.

"How long had you been inside the store when you were attacked?"

Heather used a fingertip to trace the fresh cuts on her arm, as though re-living the cutting experience. "Not long."

"One minute? Ten minutes?"

"I don't know. Not much time. I came in the back and unlocked the front door and got back to the register and there he was. It happened fast—"

"Where did he attack you?"

Heather gestured at the floor. "Right here."

Mayo scanned the linoleum. They'd need to run a blue light over the area to look for spots of semen—now that she'd probably been stepping in it. That was at least one screw up so far. If she didn't get her act together, there'd be more.

McKern pushed in through the front door again with a blanket, which Mayo took and wrapped around Heather.

"Crime scene tape," she reminded him when he hovered.

Watching her step this time, Mayo helped Heather up into a chair. On the floor underneath where she had been sitting was a jumble of clothing—jeans and panties. After getting her a bottle of water, Mayo scooped the clothing into a paper evidence bag. She took another quick look around the area. She still sensed something was off about the scene, but she couldn't pinpoint what.

"I'll drive you down to the hospital in Boulder," she told Heather. "We'll have a nurse examiner look you over. And then maybe talk to a sketch artist if you're up to it."

"I just want to go home," Heather said.

"I know it's hard, Heather, but it's what you have to do." A bit of a fib, since Heather could do whatever she wanted.

Mayo pulled McKern aside, out of Heather's earshot. "Keep the store closed while I'm gone," she said. "Take pictures, use the blue light to check the floor area behind the counter for semen. Dust for prints. She says he came in and left by the back door so focus there and behind the counter. And don't forget to wear gloves."

McKern tended to look elsewhere when she was talking to him but now he glared at her. "You don't have to remind me about every little thing."

"Good," Mayo said, "'cause I don't like doing it. And you've got paint all over your pants."

He'd been painting the office when they got the call—a project that had been going on for the entire three days since she had started, two days longer than it should have taken, in her estimation. This was her first call with McKern, who had reportedly squeaked through a four-month program in some obscure law enforcement academy. "Mayor Davy," McKern's uncle, had promised her that his nephew would work his butt off to earn her trust but she hadn't seen any evidence of that so far.

The other deputy on duty, Bernard Nutt, had an eager, cooperative nature but was even greener than McKern. Her one experienced officer, Rick Gumble, was camping at Mesa Verde with his family and wouldn't be back until Saturday—two days away. Still, Heather obviously didn't want to be around a male officer, so Mayo would have to leave the store in McKern's hands until she got back.

She escorted Heather out to the police SUV for the drive down the canyon to Boulder. Wrapped in the blanket, Heather climbed in without protest. She seemed almost content, the way she snuggled into the seat and buckled her seatbelt. She gave Mayo another one of those inexplicable pleading looks. It wasn't a "please protect me" look. It was "do you love me?"

It was a chilly September morning, and Mayo thought wistfully of the late afternoon hike she had planned that morning at breakfast. As she headed back into the store for the evidence bag full of Heather's clothes, a bearded man in a rusted pickup truck pulled up next to the gas pumps and rolled down his window, squinting with irritation.

"Is there a problem here, miss?" He couldn't quite bring himself to call her "marshal," she gathered, despite her marshal's uniform, including the marshal's hat they'd given her, with its neat little tassel. The concept of female law enforcement was still pretty raw in Sugarloaf; she'd been warned to give these crabby old timers plenty of "leeway."

"Zippy's is closed at the moment," she said. "You'll have to come back later." He spit some black goo out the window of his truck. She'd seen this guy around somewhere but hadn't shaken his hand yet, as was the custom in Sugarloaf.

"How the hell can I come back if I'm outa gas?"

But he didn't stay around to argue about it, instead gunning his engine and squealing off.

As she went back into Zippy's, she tried again to figure out what was bugging her about the scene. Inside, McKern was standing at the counter, eating one of the burritos from the warmer. He swallowed and nodded at the counter. "Don't worry, I put a couple bucks down."

Mayo gazed at him as he crammed another bite into his mouth. She could kick herself — her brain had gone lame after all these months of coasting. "Dulce's breakfast burritos," she said.

"Hmm?" McKern screwed up his face — dumb-looking but handsome, even with bulging cheeks.

She held out her hand. "Let me have a bite of that."

McKern handed it over with a peeved expression, and she could imagine the future anecdote formulating in his mind about this indignity. She peeled away some foil and took a bite. The soft flour tortilla was stuffed with scrambled eggs, sausage, fried potatoes, refried beans, cheese and Dulce's homemade salsa. It was hot and fresh.

She handed it back to McKern.

"What's wrong with it?" He sniffed it before taking another oversized bite.

"Just making sure Dulce cooked it up this morning," she said, a sense of clarity and resolve rising from somewhere deep inside. She hadn't experienced this brand of satisfaction in a while, and it felt kind of sweet as a matter of fact.

"Tastes fresh to me," McKern said through the food in his mouth.

Mayo climbed back into the SUV, happy to play it cool. Heather sat quietly in the front seat, bundled up in her blanket, picking at the label on her water bottle.

"Do you have some family or friends you want to call to meet us down at the hospital?"

Heather nodded eagerly. "My sister, Jody."

Mayo pulled out her phone. "What's her number?"

She pecked out the numbers as Heather recited them, and a young-sounding woman answered on the second ring. Heather listened carefully, nodding while Mayo explained. She did not ask to speak to her sister.

"You doing okay?" Mayo asked Heather once they were on the canyon road that led to Boulder. The ride would take 35 minutes — plenty of time for some quizzing.

"I guess so." Heather succeeded in getting the label off her water and dropped it on the floor.

"Just to clarify a couple things," Mayo said evenly. "You said the guy came in through the back door behind you as you were opening up the store?"

Heather curled on her side in the seat and closed her eyes, a clear indication that she was not interested in further conversation. "Hmm," she murmured.

"You said you unlocked the front door and turned around and there he was?"

Heather tugged the blanket up closer around her chin and sighed. "Yes, ma'am. Thank you so much for coming to help me. God sent you, I know, the good lord made you come for me."

*

Mayo lingered at the wind-blasted picket fence, watching Dulce Salazar hang sheets on a sagging clothesline. The linens flapped pleasantly in the breeze, and the sound of it conjured memories of Mayo's own humming mother hanging the wash in their cramped back yard in Denver. Back when life was a straightforward parade of fish sticks, weenie roasts, and kickball up and down the street.

When Dulce finally noticed her, Mayo waved, reluctant to break the spell of the scene.

"*Hola, Dulce. Cómo estás?*"

Dulce, who probably had a perfectly operable dryer in her house, left the clothes basket and joined Mayo at the fence. She was a thickset, attractive woman with black silver-streaked hair down to her waist. They shook hands—a custom among Sugarloaf residents that had become strangely important to Mayo.

"*Buenas tardes*, Marshal," said Dulce. "Ma said there was something going on earlier at Zippy's." Dulce's elderly mother waved at Mayo from a rickety lawn chair next to their back door. The Salazar bungalow was a few hundred feet beyond the parking lot behind Zippy's. Old Mrs. Salazar began to get up but Mayo gestured her back into her seat.

"No time for tea today, *Abuelita*," Mayo called.

Mrs. Salazar waved again and settled back into her seat. She routinely invited Mayo and anyone else who happened by into the house for a cup of strong black tea. Everyone in town called her "Abuelita," which meant "Little Grandmother."

After the long morning with Heather down at the hospital, the tea would have been a welcome break, but Mayo still had work to do.

"Did you deliver your burritos to Zippy's this morning?" Mayo asked Dulce.

"*Por supuesto.*" Of course.

Mayo leaned on the fence. "Did you see Heather Holloway inside? The new girl?"

Dulce thought for a moment. "No, but somebody was using the bathroom when I went in. I heard the toilet flushing. Their plumbing makes a terrible racket. I think they may have some roots in the pipes."

"What time was that, do you remember?"

Dulce shrugged. "My usual time, seven o'clock. Zippy's is my first stop."

"Exactly at seven?"

Dulce gave her a look. "About as exactly as I ever am, which doesn't mean exactly exactly."

Mayo smiled. She liked that about Dulce. "Do you use the front or back door?"

"I don't like that back door—it's too heavy to pull open with my arms full—so I always walk around the front, even though it's a big pain in the rear to walk all the way around."

"You left the burritos there and didn't wait to talk to her?"

"I take the burritos in and turn on the warmer and then I leave. That new girl don't talk much even when she's there. What happened? Is she dead?" Dulce didn't look overly dismayed at the prospect.

"She's alive and well," Mayo said. During the couple of hours she had just spent with Heather, the latter had lurched from needy child to petulance to catatonia, and back around again. Mayo had been glad to let Heather's sister take her home.

"Are you going to tell me what happened?" Dulce said.

"She said a man came in and assaulted her. You didn't see—"

"Assaulted?"

"—you didn't see anyone? Or hear anything?"

Dulce clutched a fence post. "No one!" she said. "It didn't happen right there in Zippy's, did it?" She looked anxiously back at her mother.

"Take it easy, Dulce. I don't think you have anything to worry about."

The back door of Zippy's swung open with a metallic groan and McKern came out. He jerked a hand up in a military salute, a pompous gesture that Mayo guessed was for Dulce's benefit. He had changed out of his paint-spattered pants.

"Thanks, Dulce." Mayo headed over to where McKern waited for her. She felt Dulce's eyes on them as she and McKern met in the lot. He made a big show of removing his protective gloves. "Nothing stolen, nothing left behind. I ran the white Jetta," McKern nodded at a car parked behind the store. "It's Heather's."

Mayo led McKern to the back door, out of Dulce's hearing range. The door was now smeared with black fingerprint dust. "I don't see any crime scene tape, McKern. Did you leave the scene unattended while you went to get changed?"

He paused. "It only took a couple of minutes."

10

"Don't ever leave a crime scene unattended until we're finished."

"Sorry, boss." McKern pulled on the thumb of a latex glove and snapped it. "Patty's here. She asked if she could open up again."

Mayo sighed. "Did she notice anything missing from the cash register?"

"She said no."

"Is there a safe?"

"Yeah, it's okay. There's about sixteen trillion fingerprints all over everything and nothin' from the blue light."

They walked inside where Zippy's owner, Patty Fields, was trying to scrub fingerprint powder off the counter. A large friendly blonde, Patty rushed over and engulfed Mayo in a hug.

"How's Heather doing? Is she okay?" Her breath smelled like cigarettes.

Mayo wriggled gently out of Patty's arms. She liked the hand-shaking a whole lot better. "She's fine. Her sister took her home."

"I wonder if I should call her." Patty glanced doubtfully at the phone. "I don't know what to say. Do you think I should call?"

"Only if you miss her," Mayo said.

Patty looked so startled, Mayo regretted her words. Patty had an affable, benevolent nature that made cretins out of everyone around her by comparison. And Heather was still officially a victim.

"How long has she lived in town, do you know?" Mayo asked.

"Just a few weeks." Patty headed back to the counter, picked up a black-stained rag and started scrubbing the fingerprint powder again. "Is this stuff ever going to come off?"

"Lots of soap and water," Mayo said.

"So was it her ex?" Patty asked.

"What ex?"

Patty stopped scrubbing. "Didn't Heather tell you she was being stalked by her ex-boyfriend?"

"She didn't mention that." Interesting detail to leave out, she thought. "Did she report it?"

Patty shrugged. "I don't know."

"You know about any complaint, McKern?"

"Nope."

"Double-check that, please."

After McKern left, she turned back to Patty. "What do you know about it?"

Patty tossed the rag down and wiped her hands on her jeans. "That stuff is terrible! What is it?"

Mayo gathered some patience from somewhere. "What about this ex?"

Patty was still frowning at the grey smear on her white countertop. "She said that's why she moved here, to get away from this ex-boyfriend who'd been pestering her."

Mayo drummed her fingers on her holster. "What time does the store open?"

"Six-thirty."

"Is she a good employee?"

Patty wiped her hands on her jeans again, then inspected her French tip nails. "She shows up at work when she's supposed to. She can count change okay."

Patty was one of those queer types who actually seemed to think everyone she met was wonderful. At Christmastime, she handed out shiny but useless trinkets to everyone who came into the store. Zippy's had once been robbed and Mayo had heard that Patty argued for leniency with the judge because the robber was only 18 and had junkies for parents. She hugged everyone, loved everyone. She should have been gushing about how terrific Heather was.

"C'mon, Patty, help me out here," Mayo said. "It's a gorgeous fall day and I was going to take Monte's dogs up the Orange Blossom trail but no, I'm stuck trying to get some basic gossip out of the one woman in town who supposedly knows everything."

"Can we go outside and talk? I need a cig."

The two women went out the back door, which was propped open with a small boulder. Mayo waited while Patty lit up.

"So what's the story with you and Monte?" Patty asked.

"What?"

Patty blew smoke out the side of her mouth. "You said I'm the one who knows everything. But you and Monte are a big mystery around here."

"Do you generally leave this door open during the day?" Mayo asked.

"C'mon. It's a small town. No secrets allowed."

"Monte is my brother-in-law, or was my brother-in-law when my husband was alive. Now he's my housemate. There is no big mystery."

Patty's face went from amusement to confusion to embarrassment. "I'm sorry. I didn't know. I mean, I heard about your husband being dead and all. I was really super sorry to hear about it. So he was Monte's brother?"

"Do you generally leave this door open during the day?" Mayo asked again.

Patty looked glumly at the heavy door. "Yeah. It's a pain to come out and smoke and have to keep opening and closing the thing. It sticks. Maybe I should stop doing that, eh? Look, I'm really sorry I—"

"Tell me about Heather."

Patty puffed on her cigarette. "Okay, all right. I feel bad for the kid, you know? She just got raped, didn't she?"

Mayo caught an uneasy look on Patty's face, and she wondered if McKern had been blabbing to her that there was some doubt about Heather's story. But McKern didn't seem to have caught on during the burrito discussion.

"We're still trying to sort it out," she said. "And I get the feeling you have something you need to tell me."

Patty flicked ashes onto the pavement and watched McKern climb out of the police unit. "She's just kinda weird, that's all."

"Like how?"

"Tell her about this famous book," McKern said as he approached.

"What book?" Mayo asked.

Patty had another look at her nails, inhaled some more smoke. "Oh, she's always going on about some book she's supposably writing. Something about Indians being massacred in the wild west and her grandfather knowing the true facts."

"Indians, eh?" Mayo said. "Like American Indians?"

"Yeah, but I don't remember the story exactly. I got the feeling she just wanted to make sure I knew she was better than all this."

McKern huffed through his nose. "She wants everyone to know how stupendous she is."

Mayo lifted her face to the sky. A chinook wind was coming down from the western peaks and she sniffed the air for the scent of possible rain. She took a deep breath of the cool delicious mountain air. A few clouds were gathering behind the Divide, but they didn't look heavy. A late afternoon hike would have been just the thing, but she wouldn't get upset. Even if this did turn out to be a promotional stunt for a frigging book.

"Did you find a report about Heather being stalked?" she asked McKern.

"No record of a report."

"Okay." Mayo skimmed over the notes she'd taken throughout the day, then snapped her notepad shut.

"Can we open her up?" McKern said. "Patty's already lost half a day's income." He and Patty exchanged glances.

Mayo caught a whiff of something between the two of them — they were standing quite close together and she sensed a warm familiarity, probably even a buzz of sexual tension. She remembered his anxious question when they first entered the store that morning: *Is she okay? Is it Patty?*

Mayo didn't know much about McKern's personal life, except that he lived in an oversized log house on Hummingbird Lane with his Uncle Davy — the same wily geezer who had hoodwinked her into taking the marshal job. Davy Brown, a peppy old timer with a Mark Twain-style blast of white hair, was the former marshal and current mayor of Sugarloaf. Mayo's affection for him would make it more difficult to get on McKern's case, even though McKern was undeniably dumb enough to get tangled up with Patty Field. At least fifteen years older than McKern, Patty was married to Corey Field, a gravel-voiced firearms aficionado and regular pie-eyed troublemaker at the Peregrine Pub. None of which was good.

"I think we're finished here," she said.

"So what's the deal?" McKern asked. "Do we know what happened?"

Patty shot him a glance that looked like a reprimand.

Mayo felt a sudden cramp inside. She and her husband, Glen, used to do that, she remembered. They'd had their own vocabulary of signals and gestures, a way of communicating with each other without words. She pushed away a sudden urge to tell Patty all about it. She and Monte never talked about Glen. She wasn't sure if that was because of Monte or because of her.

"We'll find out more tomorrow," she told McKern. "When I talk to Heather again."

A meeting that will be Come-to-Jesus time for the young lady.

She looked at her watch. It was after five o'clock and she wanted to go home and forget about the case. She wanted to drink a glass or two of wine and soak in the hot tub.

She wondered how upset Davy would be if she wriggled out of the job after less than a week. Surely he would understand that she'd made a dreadful mistake, that she wasn't ready. She still felt like a wreck. After all, she had clung to her husband while he died in a snowy ditch. She still had that movie running in her head. Maybe Davy and Monte thought a year was long enough to get over it, but she didn't.

Two

"Same again, Marshal? I just love saying that to a woman."

"Sure, Candy. Same again." Mayo stood at the counter fishing out money while Candy made her usual double latte. Mayo couldn't handle the stuff spit out by the office coffee maker.

"Heard about the thing at Zippy's yesterday," Candy said as the espresso machine began to gurgle. "You figure that stuck-up girl's a fake?"

Frigging Deputy McKern, Mayo thought. Quickly blabbing his way out of a job, uncle or no uncle. "Your brother tell you that?"

Candy made a zipping gesture across her mouth. "Mum's the word, I promise! Don't be mad at Roger." She had extremely thick reddish hair and dimples, a female version of her brother. Good-looking and dumb as a prairie dog.

"I'd appreciate you keeping whatever he said to yourself," Mayo said. "Case is still open and he should know better."

"I instantly didn't like her," Candy went on heedlessly. "Very unprofessional when you go in to pay for gas. Doesn't know diddly about customer service." As though to demonstrate how it's done properly, Candy dowsed Mayo with an effervescent smile as she put her latte on the counter.

Mayo took a small table in the sun of the front window, savoring the warmth and the rich coffee. She had another fifteen minutes or so before Heather was due in the office to make her statement, and she was in no hurry. It wasn't going to be a pleasant interview.

Outside, the main road through town was unusually quiet for a Friday morning. Not for the first time, she marveled at how deeply she had become attached to the place. With a population of a thousand or so, Sugarloaf was a former mining camp that had somehow survived the end of mining in the region. The Old Town comprised half a dozen streets cluttered with modest houses in various states of repair—or not. Sugarloaf Road, the main drag, had been spruced up into a series of winsome storefronts—Dumpling Cottage, Bartleby's Grocery, Daffodils

Café, the Peregrine Pub. Outside of town, tucked among the trees along winding mountain lanes were mansions and log cabins used by weekenders from Denver and Boulder.

Dangling in the window was the Daffodils sign, created by Monte. Made of brass, it was decorated on both sides with an engraved village nestled among mountain peaks with clusters of daffodils along the bottom and the name "Daffodils" in a rainbow arc at the top. It was all adorable, Mayo liked to say, and the thing she loved best was the habitual contentment of Sugarloaf's permanent residents. She didn't believe it particularly, but she enjoyed watching them act it out. On occasion, she even tried pulling it off herself.

When she first accepted Monte's invitation to come and "regroup" after Glen's death, Mayo had worried she'd feel over-exposed in tiny Sugarloaf, but she came to enjoy being greeted by neighbors and strangers. To her surprise, she even liked living with Monte. In years past, Mayo and her husband had privately joked about his brother's oddball life style. There were his incomprehensible art projects, plus his wildly eccentric eating habits, which, during his long distance running phase had consisted mostly of Grape Nuts and bananas, which made good material for jokes. These days, Mayo no longer cared about the Grape Nuts and bananas or whatever else the man did; Monte had gathered her up out of a heap of grief and dragged her back to life.

She checked her watch, then brought out her pad from the day before and skimmed her notes. Today, she intended to get Heather to explain why she lied about how the thing happened, if anything happened at all. She expected that Heather would break down and admit she'd invented the whole episode. There was no "one-eyed Indian," and there probably was no ex-boyfriend stalking her. The nurse examiner at the hospital had told Mayo that Heather's arms showed she'd been a cutter for years. For Mayo, this meant that all bets were off with Heather. It was like dealing with an alcoholic.

A false report like this wasn't common but certainly not unheard of. Heather could be doing it to promote her supposed book. But after spending some time with them, Mayo now suspected that the real motivation behind the drama had to do with Heather's sister, Jody.

When Jody showed up at the hospital the day before, Heather had collapsed into a cantankerous mess. Until that moment, she had been cooperative and dry-eyed. Jody hovered over her sister as they waited for the nurse. She made calming coo noises and played with Heather's hair, running her fingers through it and tucking it behind her ears. Jody was short and thick, the less attractive of the two, with a pair of heavy black eyebrows that gave her otherwise intelligent face a rustic look. It was a touching scene, and Mayo had even felt a momentary pang of envy at the show of affection. Later, while Heather was in with the nurse, Jody mentioned to Mayo that Heather had been trying to get her to come live with her in Sugarloaf.

The "attack," Mayo decided, could be Heather's way of making that happen.

After watching from her sunny table as Heather and Jody arrived across the street, Mayo waited for another five minutes before heading into the office.

While McKern made small talk with Jody, Mayo escorted Heather into the interview room. Three hard chairs were set up in a semi-circle around a side table with a tape recorder on it. Heather took a seat, clutching a denim bag in her lap. McKern still hadn't finished with his painting project and one wall remained decorated with inexplicable crayon marks and coffee spatters from decades of neglect under former Marshal Davy Brown. The room was pungent with the smell of paint but Mayo closed the door anyway.

"What's that?" Heather said, pointing at the tape recorder. Her knee jumped up and down and she kept scratching at her forearms through her sweater. It was hard to be in the tiny room with her.

"It's just so we don't miss anything." Mayo got the recorder going, recited her name and case information into the microphone. She levelled a humorless gaze at the young woman—a dose of authority. Though McKern's half-baked paint job didn't help much, she wanted to impress Heather with the idea that she was now in official surroundings, on the record. No more vague explanations or curling up for a nap to avoid Mayo's questions.

"Heather," Mayo began, "please start from the beginning and describe for me what happened yesterday."

Heather did an odd little dance with her fingers, then dropped her hands in a show of hopelessness. "I was just getting everything all opened up and this man suddenly showed up behind me. He must have come in through the back door."

"What time was that?"

"I think it was around six-forty-five. I was a little late."

"Did the guy have a weapon?"

"You already asked all this."

Mayo had been around a lot of women during the hours and days after a sexual assault and she had seen many different reactions — anger, fear, denial, shock, numbness, shame. Heather displayed none of these this morning. She simply looked irritated. The law-and-order atmosphere of the marshal's office was clearly having no impact.

"You need to give a formal statement," Mayo said evenly. "It's procedure."

Heather crossed a leg over the other and began swinging her foot. She wore a pair of silky-looking black slacks and a grey cashmere sweater, and the elegant get-up did not match her air of rebellious boredom. She seemed out-of-balance, highly complex. Unpredictable.

"Heather?" Mayo repeated. "Tell me about the weapon."

Heather's foot abruptly stopped moving. Her shoes were not exactly appropriate for mountain living — soft black leather with buckled straps, the toe section embroidered with yellow, brown and pale pink flowers. Mayo was no shoe aficionado, but she guessed this pair had cost at least a couple hundred dollars. A lot of money for someone working part-time at Zippy's.

"Like I said before," Heather said stiffly, "he had a gun."

"What kind of gun was it?" Mayo asked, her voice calm and pleasant. "Did it have a magazine or a cylinder?"

"I don't know."

"Did it have a round thing on it that holds the bullets?"

"I don't know."

"What color was it?"

"Silver."

"Did the man say anything to you?"

Heather took a quick breath. "I don't really—I think he said something about it being my turn now. I think he said, 'Your turn now, bitch.'"

This statement sounded so ludicrous that Mayo had to force herself not to snort. Heather was screwing with her, she was absolutely certain of it. She felt an urge to get up and walk out of the station and get into her car and drive into the high country, maybe up to Yankee Doodle Lake, where she would park and hike up past timberline to Rollinsville Pass, up to the Divide and beyond, all the way to the Middle Park basin and then ...

She returned to the airless, paint-stinking room and the muddled drama of Heather Holloway, who was still officially a traumatized victim and not yet officially a crazy jerk wasting police time.

"What do you think he meant by that?" she asked.

A look of cunning crept across Heather's face. She had obviously given this part of the story a good deal of thought. "I never did anything to anybody. I think it all has to do with my great grandfather Alonzo Holloway. I am working on a book about him and my search to find his grave."

Now Mayo could not prevent herself from scowling. "A book. Okay, go on."

Heather brushed a hand down her silky slacks, glancing only briefly at Mayo. If she noticed the scowl, she gave no sign. "Alonzo Holloway fought at the battle of Sand Creek and was horribly injured by a Cheyenne chief. He wrote a diary about it. There are a lot of people who don't like what he wrote."

Mayo let her gaze rest on Heather for a good number of seconds. She pictured newspapers getting involved, perhaps a TV station in Denver—all rushing in to interview poor Heather about the attack and its connection to her book.

"I see," she said. "When is this book coming out?"

Heather's eyes narrowed. "Next year maybe. I haven't finished it."

"And do you have a publisher?"

Heather's chin moved out. "Not yet. I've been talking to some people though."

"Patty said you mentioned an ex-boyfriend stalking you."

Heather's hand rose to her throat, her eyes wary. "No," she said. "I mean, no, it wasn't my ex."

"I was surprised to hear it from Patty, " Mayo went on. "I wondered why you didn't mention it to me yesterday."

Heather moved her shoulders—more like a twitch than a shrug.

"Heather?" Mayo pressed.

"No!" Heather snapped. "This has nothing to do with him."

Mayo made some notes in her notepad. She took her time before finally looking up.

Heather was staring down at her beautiful shoes.

"Did you tell Patty you were being stalked?" Mayo asked again.

Heather sighed. "Yes, but this has nothing to do with him. I shouldn't have even mentioned anything to Patty. It was nothing."

Mayo could make no sense of this angle, and suspected that the ex-boyfriend himself was an invention.

"Okay," Mayo said after a brief silence. "Now, Heather. I'd like to back up a little bit, please. Tell me everything that happened between the time you got out of your car yesterday morning and when the guy showed up behind you."

Heather's hand dropped back into her lap. "I unlocked the back door and pushed the rock to keep it open, which is what Patty told me to do. I went in, put my purse down behind the counter, unlocked the front door and turned around and there he was."

Once again, this time on tape, Heather had walked right into a corner. "Are you absolutely sure that's everything you did before he showed up?"

Heather narrowed her eyes. "Yeah."

"You unlocked the front door, turned around, and there he was."

"That's what I said, isn't it?"

Mayo cocked her head at Heather, amazed at how deeply annoyed she felt at this moment — at Heather's impatient tone, her smug little face, the fancy clothing. Had she always felt this hostile about being lied to? She couldn't remember. That was all a different life.

"When did Dulce come in with the burritos?" Mayo asked.

Heather blinked. She adjusted her feet. Her lips moved as she seemed to silently repeat the question to herself.

"Fresh burritos on the counter," Mayo said when Heather didn't answer. "I even tasted one of them. Hot and delicious. I love Dulce's burritos, don't you? You ever tried one?"

"No." Heather took refuge again in staring at her shoes.

"I asked Dulce about it and she says she delivered them sometime around seven o'clock that morning, maybe a bit before then. So the part I don't get is how she got her burritos safely delivered and laid out all pretty and yummy under the heat lamps if you were attacked by this guy right as you were opening up the front door."

Heather didn't answer.

"Do you see where my confusion is, Heather?"

"I don't remember seeing her."

"In fact, Dulce says she heard someone in the bathroom when she came in."

Heather looked defiant now. "Well, I must have gone to the bathroom — she just comes in and drops them off. I don't really pay attention."

"But Heather," Mayo said. "How many times have you told me now that you unlocked the front door and turned around and there he was?"

"What difference does it make? I mean, you're acting like I'm the criminal here."

Mayo indulged in a pause, during which she gazed steadily at Heather. Heather stared back for a few moments, then looked away.

Mayo no longer felt angry or even irritated. She had caught the wind in her sails and was skittering across the waves with a sense of jubilation she had not felt in a long time. Nothing could stop her now.

"Then what happened?" she asked.

"What do you mean?" Heather snapped. "He raped me."

Mayo continued quickly in a sharp, efficient tone. "Did he penetrate you vaginally?"

Heather looked away. "Yes."

"With his hand or his penis or both?"

Now Heather looked up and grimaced at her. "What?"

"I'm sorry, Heather, but these are the kinds of questions I have to ask after a sexual assault." Mayo narrowed her eyes at the woman. "Did he use his hands or his penis?"

Heather's jaw came out, but she answered. "Penis."

"Did he ejaculate?"

"Oh, God," said Heather.

"Did he?"

Heather's hand moved up to her throat. "He made some noises but I don't know."

"Did he penetrate you anally?"

"No!"

"Did he do anything else? Oral?"

"Oh my God! No!"

"Where was the gun while he was assaulting you?"

Heather's chest rose and fell and she checked the beautiful shoes again. "He put it on the floor, I guess."

"How long did the assault last?"

"I don't remember. A couple minutes."

"Did he say anything to you during the assault?"

"Yes." Heather lifted her eyes. They were dry and empty. "He said I was paying for the sins of my ancestors. I told you, this has to do with my great grandfather's diary about the battle of Sand Creek. I wrote papers about it in school and I'm writing a book about him. There are some descendants who don't like what he wrote in his diary about it."

Mayo sighed. "Descendants of whom?"

"Indians—Native Americans. Arapaho and Cheyenne. Plus the descendants of some other white people who said it was a massacre."

Mayo was unwilling to hear more about this theory. "What happened next? When he finished?"

Heather crossed her arms over her stomach. "He left."

"Did he ever ask you to open the register?"

"No."

"Or open the safe?"

Heather gazed at Mayo with loathing. "It wasn't about money."

There was a sharp rap at the conference room door. Exasperated, Mayo stopped the tape and opened the door.

Glancing into the room, McKern beckoned her out. Mayo closed the conference room door and followed McKern to the rear of the office.

"This better be important," she hissed.

He held a finger to his lips, dipping his head toward the reception area, where Jody Holloway waited.

"I just hit the motherlode," he whispered. "Ran that background check on her."

After hearing what he had to say, Mayo went back into the interview room.

Heather was now standing, clutching the denim purse across her abdomen. "I'm done," she said. "I want to go home now."

"Sit down, Heather," Mayo said sharply.

Heather glared at her in surprise, but returned to her seat. Mayo started the tape again.

"The thing is, Heather," Mayo began. "We've got a little problem with your story. You told me that a guy followed you into the store and raped you. You've repeatedly said he was right behind you when you unlocked the front door, but this doesn't allow time for Dulce to deliver her burritos. When I pointed that out, you changed your story."

Heather sat very still in her seat, her face as empty as a broken TV. "It's all a blur now. I do not remember exactly who did what and when."

Mayo went on: "I'm willing to bet that when the lab gets back to me with results from the rape kit, they're going to tell me there's no sign of sexual assault."

Now Heather stood up again, her eyes narrowed at Mayo. She began to speak but Mayo interrupted her.

"You know what I think happened?" Mayo said. "I think you are trying to get some sort of attention — maybe for this book you keep bringing up. Maybe to get your sister to move in with you.

"I did not!"

"I think you went into work yesterday morning, planning to stage this assault. You unlocked the front door then used the bathroom, which is when Dulce brought the burritos in. You came out, were too focused to notice that fresh pile of tasty burritos on the counter. Or maybe it didn't occur to you that it would be an inconsistency in your story. You threw a few snuff tins and cigarette packs over the floor, smacked yourself in the lip, yanked off your own clothes, then called 911, got the razor out and went to work on your arm to steady your nerves."

"You're crazy," Heather said a low growl. "You're a psycho cop. I'm going to complain about you."

"It's the only explanation that fits all the facts," Mayo said. "Your story certainly doesn't."

Heather clutched her bag over her stomach. The muscles around her mouth were twitching and her eyes looked shiny. "I am going to sue you to kingdom come for the way you're treating me. You can rest assured I will do it." She headed for the door.

"Do you remember Detective Gonzales from the Denver P.D.?" Mayo asked.

Heather stopped, her hand on the doorknob, but did not turn around.

Mayo continued: "My deputy just had a little chat with him. Detective Gonzales says you made rape accusations against your boss at the Colorado Frontier Museum, a Felix Arkenstone. You also made rape accusations against a professor at Colorado Western University and against your own father. What do you have to say to that?"

"I have nothing to say about it," Heather said turning to face her. "You won't believe me anyway so why should I try?"

"One thing I do believe is that there's a pattern here, Heather, and it's not a pretty one."

Heather pulled a tissue from her purse. She unfolded the tissue, then re-folded it precisely into thirds and blew her nose. Mayo wondered how such an apparently orderly mind could come up with such a weak story. Heather hadn't remembered about Dulce's burrito delivery, hadn't noticed the hot burritos on the counter when she came out of the bathroom, and she had incorrectly assumed they would not check into her past.

Mayo almost felt sorry for her.

"Why don't you get all this junk off your chest?" she suggested. "We can start this conversation over right now and try to make some sense out of what's going on. You've obviously been under some stress. Sometimes we just lose track of what we're doing and we act out."

"I didn't make it up," Heather said dully.

"You realize," Mayo went on, "I could charge you with wasting police time."

Abruptly, Heather stepped close and angled her small face up at Mayo's. She was very pale, her eyes wet and bloodshot. "I don't care if things don't make sense to you or if you don't believe me," she snapped. "Someone's trying to get me and if they do, it'll be your goddamn fault."

She opened the door and went out. Jody jumped up as she marched through the office area. Mayo gestured for McKern to stay back. Heather rushed out the front door, her frightened sister scurrying along behind her.

"I guess that's that," McKern said. He headed up to the front area of the office, watching out the window.

Mayo moved up beside him just in time to see Heather and Jody disappear on foot around a corner.

"Did she admit she made it up?" McKern asked.

Mayo paused. It would have been much better if Heather had spilled about her lie, but she was a tough girl. Crazy as all hell, but tough.

"She'll never admit it," Mayo said. "But she made it up."

"Can't we charge her with false reporting or wasting police time?"

"You feel like schlepping her down to Boulder County Jail?"

"No thanks," McKern said with a big grin. He headed back toward his desk. "Wowzer. That is one crazy lady."

"Good work," Mayo said, going back into the interview room to stop the tape recorder. She felt her heartbeat returning to normal, the adrenaline settling. She pulled the tape out and labelled it. For the first time since the car accident that had killed Glen, she felt fantastic.

Three

Mayo didn't close the Holloway case yet, but gave it a temporary status of "probable false report." She'd wait for the final results on the rape kit to get rid of the "probable."

The brief detour into a real case had turned out to be simple and unexpectedly satisfying, but now she was pleased to drift back into the quiet routine of life in Sugarloaf. On Saturday, her first weekend on the job, she strolled through a cold early morning mist to Bartleby's Market. A small autumn snowstorm had moved through during the night and the landscape had a fine dusting of white. She was an early riser but others were about. Patty waved as she rolled over the speedbumps on Sugarloaf Road, on her way to open Zippy's. Mayo relished the silence of the town, the aroma of fresh bread and German pastries wafting from the ovens at Dumpling Cottage. It had taken some work, but she had trained herself to notice these little details in Sugarloaf life. They helped.

She crossed Sugarloaf Road and ambled along the covered wooden walkway that fronted the stores. She got a big kick out of the walkway—it was the sort built in the frontier west, complete with hitching posts for horses. Local legend had it that Davy Brown had designed and paid for the thing himself back in the 1980s when he began orchestrating the town's facelift. Monte said that most of the chirpy downtown facade was a product of Davy Brown's family fortune.

She entered Bartleby's—a small store with a creaking wooden floor and jars of old fashioned candy sticks on the counter. As was his custom every morning, Davy Brown was there, leaning against the front counter talking to Pete Nippers, the ancient proprietor. Davy's thick white hair stuck out in several directions and a long moustache curled over his lip. He was a perfect complement to Nippers, who always wore a dusty-looking French beret and a stiff blue bow-tie. Monte warned that the two had been actors somewhere, and not to believe anything they said.

After picking out a few oranges from a crate by the door and a loaf of bread, she headed for the counter, where she shook hands with Davy and Nippers.

"You lied," she told Davy. "You said nothing ever happens around here."

"Some folks find it stimulating." Davy showed her the Saturday edition of the *Front Range Bulletin*.

Mayo groaned at the gigantic headline: *Town Stunned Over Rape: Quiet village of Sugarloaf scene of violent attack*. Story by Brin Beedle.

Davy smoothed out his moustache. "Our intrepid Miss Beedle is going to keep her knives sharp over this one. It's not often she gets some red meat to hack away at."

"Too bad the case is already closed," said Mayo.

Davy cleared his throat and read from the newspaper story: "'A recently-arrived Sugarloaf resident was brutally attacked and sexually assaulted early Thursday morning, according to a Sugarloaf Marshal's office spokesman. The victim says her attacker was a Native American male missing an eye ... '

"No comment." Mayo headed over to the refrigerator for the milk and snagged a carton of eggs on her way to the counter. She and Monte had agreed that she would have her own two shelves of the fridge for her "animal and GMO stuff."

"We need to get out a posse?" Nippers asked, showing tobacco-stained teeth.

Mayo put money on the counter. "I don't believe a posse will be necessary, thank-you. I'll take a copy of that paper too."

"You saying there's no story here?" Davy rattled the paper.

"There's no story here."

"It's been all over town," said Nippers. "Caused a minor panic. Sold out the last three locks in stock yesterday, plus two baseball bats, three rifles and every last box of ammunition."

"So you're not this 'Marshal's office spokesman,' eh?" Davy winked. "I hope it wasn't my nephew."

"Oh, you mean Deputy Blabbermouth?"

"Ouch. That's my kin you're talking about."

"Your kin knows it was a sham, so why would he spin all this b.s. for Busy Brin Beedle?"

"So it's not only no story but it's a sham?"

"Don't quote me on that. I'm not 100% there, just 99.9% there."

"Maybe Deputy Roger Blabbermouth, as you call him, is innocent of all charges. Maybe this girl—Heather Holloway—called the paper."

"Okay," Mayo agreed. "Fifty-fifty chance. She's definitely the type."

"Kookie stuff," said Nippers. "You can always count on kookie stuff from the flats."

"Yeah," Mayo said. "She's from Denver so she must be nuts—just like me."

Davy draped his arm across her shoulders. "You were nuts when you came but you're okay now."

"So you think I should try to get control of this wayward story?" she asked. "I actually don't particularly give a damn but you laid-back Sugarloaf types might have some preference. I'll do it your way."

Davy stroked his moustache. "I don't mind having a bit of drama and scandal to liven things up once in a while. Even if it's a sham. How about we just let natural forces make a fool of our Busy Brin."

"Meanwhile," Nippers put in, "it's good for business."

Monte's house was situated on Geese Lane, three blocks back from the sporadic traffic of the main road. The house was compact and compatible with the Sugarloaf motif of stress-free charm. Once a decrepit miner's bungalow, Monte had painted it serpentine red with pale grey shutters. He landscaped the front yard into a garden of moss rocks, wild roses, bluebells, and columbine. He had gutted the interior to a degree that would have been entirely unrecognizable to its former inhabitant, a grizzled old hard rock miner known as Dynamite Dale. Mr. Dale had passed away years back and his grandson quickly sold the place to Monte Mayo, who had recently been divorced. Since then, Monte had expanded and upgraded the bathroom with slate tiles and moss rock, and they splashed pure Rocky Mountain spring water across their faces at heavy vessel sinks.

The kitchen, filled now with tofu, wheat berries and spinach salad instead of Dynamite Dale's famous venison steaks, gleamed with polished granite and stainless steel.

As Mayo returned from her walk to Bartleby's, the front door was open and the sound of Monte's trumpet filtered into the lane. Playing the trumpet was Monte's latest "new adventure," as he called it. So far, he hadn't shown any talent for it.

His two greyhounds leapt from their dog beds and banged against her legs as she came in, even though she had only been gone twenty minutes. In the kitchen, Monte formed a silhouette against the light of the sliding glass door at the back — he had his foot propped on pillows on an easy chair. He nodded at Mayo and kept honking on the trumpet, his cheeks puffing at the mouthpiece.

Their eyes met as she entered, and he followed her with his gaze as she went into the kitchen and put her groceries on the counter. He did this a lot — watching her, and she hadn't figured out why. Sometimes she wondered if he blamed her for Glen's death; she was sure some people back at the Denver P.D. had. She had seen their looks at his funeral. Lately, she thought she detected that same probing expression on Monte's face. He could be inspecting her for signs of guilt, of moral impairment, lethality or treachery. He was looking for *something* anyway.

A kitchen timer went off and Monte rose, hobbling over to the oven. He had twisted his ankle on a hike a few days earlier and it didn't seem to be getting better.

"You want an oat-pumpkin muffin?" He pulled his latest concoction out of the oven and dumped the muffins onto a cooling rack.

Mayo lingered near the coffee machine, inspecting the muffins with a skeptical eye. "I'm having toast."

Monte shrugged. Like his brother, he had been blessed with good looks. His thick blond hair stuck straight up more often than not. His eyes were sometimes blue and sometimes grey, far too much like Glen's eyes for Mayo's comfort. Both brothers had boyish faces, which led people to trust them. But the similarities ended there. While Glen, the cop, possessed all the brawn and testosterone, the more cerebral Monte had made a lot of money doing something in computers. A few months after Glen's death, he had sold his company for a "pile," as he put it, and officially retired. Still in his 40s, he told Mayo that he hadn't decided yet what to do next. Meanwhile, he kept himself busy blow-torching sculptures out in his workshop or tinkering with bewildering technical projects on his computer. Or watching Mayo.

He pulled a used cardboard egg carton out of a cupboard and went to work nestling the small muffins into each egg compartment, reserving one for himself. "Hmm," he said, eating half of it in a single bite. "It's good stuff, I promise."

She dropped two slices of bread into the toaster and shoved down the lever. Picking up Monte's trumpet, she blew a single sour note and put it back down. She felt his eyes on her.

He handed her a muffin. "Come on, try one. It won't hurt you."

Mayo avoided his gaze—it felt aggressive. But she took the muffin. It felt strangely heavy but she bit into it.

"It's not exactly those fabulous feathery pastries they serve over at the Dumpling Cottage," he said. "But this won't give you high cholesterol either."

"Yum," she lied. "It's good." It tasted even heavier than it felt. He used some kind of dark syrupy stuff instead of sugar.

"You should trust me more," he said, probing each muffin one by one with his finger. She poured herself a coffee, added milk and sugar. Stirred. Sipped. Finally, he seemed satisfied with the muffin inspection. He secured the lid of the egg carton and stashed it into one of the "Monte shelves" in the fridge. It struck her that he was a feminine soul trapped in a frat boy's body. She wondered how he and Glen could have come from the same family.

"How's the new sculpture coming along?" she asked. "Any progress?" Aside from Monte's stained glass signs, which were beautiful, Mayo did not understand any of his creative work.

"I'm having a blast," he said. "That was a double-entendre in case you didn't catch it. Hey, what's this all about?" He picked up the *Front Range Bulletin* Mayo had brought in. "You didn't say anything about an assault at Zippy's. Was it Patty?"

Mayo finished chewing and swallowed. "It wasn't Patty, but I can't really talk about it — except to say we're still investigating."

"Yeah, but this is *me*," he complained, scanning Brin Beedle's article. "Besides, if it happened at Zippy's, that means Patty knows about it, which means everyone in town knows — except me apparently. What the hell?" He rattled the paper, frowning. "I just realized — it wasn't Heather, that anxious little thing? Early twenties? Just moved to town."

Mayo sipped from her coffee mug. Monte's tone made her uneasy. "You know her?"

"I met her a few weeks ago at Daffodils," he said. "And I see her at Zippy's. Are you kidding? Little Heather got raped?"

Mayo sat down with her coffee. Her toast popped up in the toaster but she ignored it. "She reported a rape, yes."

"Hmm, she was right, then," he went on. "I couldn't tell if she was just being paranoid or what."

"Paranoid about what?"

"The SUV."

"What SUV?"

"The one that was hanging around outside Zippy's. The other day I stopped by to get a paper. Heather was in the doorway, peeping out. She looked like a little mouse. She said there was someone sitting in an SUV outside and watching her. She was babbling about the war with the Cheyenne, you know, the Indian wars. Someone was coming for her. It didn't make any sense. I looked and there was a car sitting there but it took off — "

A knock rattled their screen door in front, followed by a man's voice. "Anybody home?"

"Come in!" Monte hollered.

The door opened and their visitor entered. It was Deputy Rick Gumble with a grim look on his face. Mayo had met him before but he'd been on vacation since she started her job as his new boss.

Mayo put down her coffee mug. She didn't like his expression.

"I'm overjoyed they finally hoodwinked someone into taking the job, Marshal," Gumble said. "Congratulations! And we got a dead body up at Wolftongue."

Wolftongue was an abandoned mining camp located in a high windswept meadow a couple miles north of Old Town Sugarloaf. Still within the expansive town limits, the road leading there wound through a mixture of forest, aspen grove, open meadow, and a smattering of oversized homes. There wasn't much left of Wolftongue itself — several broken down stone structures, the remnants of a log house, and dozens of tungsten mine pits filled in with rocks and debris.

On the way, Gumble contacted McKern and Nutt, who were on call.

Mayo's watch read 9:42 a.m. when they arrived. Faint patches of snow remained here and there from the night before. On a ridge above the ruins was a flat parking area flanked on one side by a bank of lodgepole pine and underbrush. Parked near the trees were two cars. One was an open black Jeep with two teenage boys inside. Mayo recognized the other — a white Volkswagen Jetta.

They positioned the SUV cross-wise in the road below the parking area so no one could pass in or out. She didn't want McKern and the rest to contaminate any possible tracks.

She and Gumble got out and walked up the road.

There *were* tracks — plenty of them. Both tire tracks and footprints, jumbled up in the rocks, dust, pine mulch and fallen pinecones. An investigative nightmare.

Sitting in the Jeep, the boys puffed on cigarettes, looking pale and sweaty despite a chilly breeze. As Mayo and Gumble approached, she caught the word "marshmallow."

As they arrived, the boys jumped out of the Jeep.

"Fellas, get back in, please."

One boy pointed down the hill at the log ruins. "There's a dead lady in that cabin."

"Back into the Jeep, please. Gumble, check out the Jetta."

Mayo followed the path down the hillside. The southern wall of the cabin was still mostly intact; the northern wall was gone. The east-west walls were partially collapsed, and crumbled bits of roof lay strewn across the interior space.

As she approached, the legs came into view first.

Mayo stepped in through a small doorway. Inside, the woman lay on her stomach, the face turned. Her eye was open. Both hands lay at her sides, the palms facing the sky, and the left hand gripped a clump of heavy alpine sedge. The recent cuts still showed as angry red stripes on her bare forearms. The only other injury Mayo could see was a shallow wound the size of a fifty cent piece at the top of her scalp, as though her head had been grazed with a sharp weapon. It wasn't an injury that looked fatal, but Heather Holloway was definitely dead.

Four

Mayo looked around. The floor of the cabin consisted of sedge and low shrubbery. A couple patches of old snow had managed to survive the summer in the shadows of the cabin walls, but the dusting from the night before had melted. There were no footprints.

She knelt in front of Heather's body, her breath shallow and unsatisfying. She paused, took a deep, deliberate breath, and another. Better. She could do this. It was just a job. Her job. She had training, experience. She wasn't a marshmallow.

She touched Heather's neck at the jugular vein. Cold.

She rose at the sound of someone racing up the road with a siren screaming.

"Turn off that siren, McKern," she barked into her radio. "Call the coroner and CBI for a forensics team—"

"Already called," Gumble put in.

"Good. Suit up and tape off the parking area and cabin. Gumble, bring a camera down here, and Tyvek."

Mayo focused. Heather was dressed in a jogging outfit—a grey zip-up hoodie with the sleeves pulled up to her elbows, lightweight running pants, expensive-looking running shoes. Her clothes and hair were dry, which meant she wasn't lying here when it snowed, which started around midnight and stopped sometime before Mayo got up at 6:30 a.m. Her face seemed to be tightening up into a grimace, her one exposed eye receding slightly. She was going into rigor mortis, which meant she'd probably been here at least two hours. Mayo checked her watch: 10:13. Keeping it very broad, Heather had been killed sometime between midnight and 8:30—probably between 5 a.m. and 7 a.m.

She became aware of McKern and Gumble behind her.

"Holy crap," McKern said. "It's her. Jesus H.C. Holy mother of —"

"—McKern," Mayo interrupted, "I asked you to tape the perimeter."

"Holy crap," McKern said again. "She's dead, man."

She slipped into a Tyvek suit and grabbed one of the two cameras Gumble was holding. "We'll need shots of the tire tracks in the parking area," she told him. "Do two shots of everything, with and without a scale. Use a flashlight to help with side lighting if you need it."

"Found this on the floor of the car." Gumble handed over Heather's denim purse. Grateful for the deputy's calm, she unzipped the purse. Inside was a wallet containing three credit cards, a single twenty dollar bill and some loose change, a driver's license. At the bottom of the bag lay a jumbled collection of make-up.

"No phone." Mayo mused. She thought back, couldn't remember Heather using one. Mayo had called the sister, Jody, on her own phone.

Jody Holloway. Shy, polite, a quiet intelligence. Devoted to her sister. Mayo wondered how she would take the news, which would be delivered by a victim advocate and a uniformed officer who knew nothing about the case, who wouldn't be able to tell her anything except that Heather was dead and that someone would be contacting her. Mayo remembered how Jody stood behind Heather at the hospital, playing with her sister's hair.

"Jesus, boss." McKern was still standing around gaping at the body. "We're up the creek."

Mayo kept her voice low. "We're not up any creek, McKern. Go take care of the tape, please."

He gestured in Heather's direction. "Don't you think we should cover her with a sheet or something?"

"No sheet," she said. "We don't want anything transferred."

"Our little friends up there are anxious to leave," Gumble said. "They've already been on the phone. I told them to knock it off but—"

"Can't we just take their phones?" McKern demanded. "That punk Sigi—"

"No, we can't take their phones," Mayo said. "Now, go on, McKern. Let's keep the intrusion in this area to a minimum."

"How'd she die?" Gumble said after McKern left. "That head wound doesn't look fatal. Bizarre, but not a killer."

"I'm guessing we'll find another injury when we roll her over. We'll wait for the coroner."

"Too bad we didn't get here a little bit earlier," Gumble noted, looking around. "We would have had footprints and tire tracks all over the snow."

"Our bad guy is very lucky," Mayo agreed.

After Gumble left, she began shooting photographs. After she'd finished doing her job here, then she'd take some time to figure out whether or not this was her fault.

Except for the body and a few vague marks in the doorway dirt, the place seemed untouched by humans. Heather might have come here to run and simply encountered the wrong person or persons. Possible, but doubtful. The cabin wasn't on any sort of path where a runner would go, Heather showed no signs of sweat, and her running shoes looked clean. The fact that she'd left her keys and purse in the car and didn't lock it could indicate she hadn't meant to stray far.

The position of her body was odd. She was lying on her stomach, but she had a clump of grass in her hand, which rested palm up, the bits of grass showing through her clenched fingers.

Her hair looked well-brushed and shiny. Mayo imagined her that morning, perhaps humming as she worked on it. Mayo looked closer at the exposed eye—no make-up. Her fingernails were impeccably groomed and polished, none broken. Even her running pants looked fresh and clean, no stray bits of grass or dirt.

Aside from the raw circle on her scalp, Heather looked in perfect order. She looked like she got up that morning, put on her running clothes, drove up to Wolftongue, hiked down into the cabin, and got herself killed—all with no fuss.

Perhaps someone had lured her here—but how?

Mayo finished taking pictures and headed up to the parking lot. Gumble was setting up evidence cones around a jumble of tire tracks beneath the lodgepole pines.

"These look pretty recent," he said, pointing to one set of tracks.

"We're going to have to do a spiral search and we better hurry," Mayo said, glancing at the darkening sky. "I think it's going to snow again, or maybe rain, probably within the hour."

"You doing all right, boss?" Gumble said, his eyes focused on the tire tracks.

She paused. Gumble didn't come off as the sort to ask personal questions unless it was absolutely necessary. "Do I look like I'm not doing all right? And I'm not asking rhetorically."

"Just checking," he said, glancing at her. "Welcome to the new job, I guess."

"I'm fine." Her apprehension must have shown in her face — she'd have to get a better grip. "Take some samples from the parking area," she went on. "Dirt and mulch. Maybe we'll get lucky and find a suspect with junk stuck in their tread or tire wells."

"I'm on it," he said.

"And Gumble." She tapped his arm and their eyes met. "I'm a little rusty and a bit surprised, but everything's cool."

He flashed a smile, his eyes bright and sympathetic behind his glasses. "I gotcha covered."

The boys looked cold and uneasy. Davy had already warned Mayo about Sigi Zimmerman, whose criminal career had begun at age ten when he was arrested for siphoning gasoline from cars parked in the lot behind the Dumpling Cottage, his grandmother's restaurant. He then used the gas to shred pristine meadows on his motocross bike. Bobby Watson, on the other hand, was a well-mannered, good-looking boy with oversized eyes. He had never been in trouble that she knew of.

She shook hands with them and wrote their names in her notebook. "Sorry you fellas had to see this," she said. "Just want to ask you a few quick questions and then you can go."

They nodded.

"What were you doing up here?"

"We were gonna go hiking," said Sigi.

Mayo refrained from rolling her eyes. More likely they were up there to blast the car stereo and smoke dope. Both had a red glaze to their eyes.

"Where's your hiking gear?" she asked. "Backpacks? Water bottles?"

Bobby glanced at Sigi, who shrugged.

"We weren't mountain climbing or nothing," Sigi said in a petulant tone. "We were just bumming around, minding our own business and we saw the dead body. We called the cops, didn't we? Look at the thanks we get."

Mayo sighed, remembering other gossip she'd heard about him. When he was very young, his parents had divorced and dumped their son on his grandmother, the narcissistic chef, Analiese Zimmerman, proprietor of Dumpling Cottage. By all accounts, Sigi had not coped well with these difficulties.

"Listen," she said. "I'm guessing that you two were up here to get high and you probably have some nice buds in your pockets. But I'm not interested in that—unless you make me interested. We're here to talk about the young lady who's lying dead down there. Okay?"

The boys nodded. Even Sigi seemed suddenly hesitant, and he looked carefully around as though searching for a killer lurking about.

"This is really messed up," Bobby said. "I mean, she's really dead and everything."

"I want you to try and clear your heads and remember if you saw anything at all that might help us find out who did this."

"What about that black SUV?" said Sigi.

"What black SUV?"

"A Ford," Bobby said. "We saw it when we headed up the Wolftongue Road. You know where the spring water comes out of the pipe?"

Mayo nodded. Most locals, including Monte and herself, regularly filled jugs there with cold artesian water.

"Did you see the driver?" she asked.

"No."

"Was it parked or driving?"

"Parked, right there at the spring."

"You didn't see someone filling jugs?"

"No, and when we got here, there was that white car just sitting there," Sigi said. "We thought—I mean, the keys were in it and there was a purse sitting there too. We figured that was pretty weird."

"Did you two touch anything down there or in her car?" Mayo examined their faces, thought she detected a little something. "We're going to be fingerprinting everything," she went on, "so you might as well let me know up front."

They exchanged glances.

"I might have opened the car door," Sigi said.

Mayo moved in closer to Sigi, right into his space. He tossed his head and his bangs flopped over his eyes.

"We're pretty good at getting fingerprints off things like purses and wallets, Sigi," she said, indulging in a slight exaggeration.

He glanced at Bobby, then shrugged. "People shouldn't leave their purses lying around in unlocked cars," he said. "You're just asking for it."

"I told you to leave it alone!" Bobby hissed to his friend.

"It was only 20 bucks," Sigi said. "I put it back after we saw the stiff. And I never touched the credit cards."

Mayo sighed, suddenly wondering why she hadn't thought to bring coffee with her. Down the road, she spotted the forensics van on its way, with Deputy Nutt's car right behind.

She called out to McKern, who had just finished taping up the area.

"Search the boys and the Jeep." She nodded at Sigi. "Mr. Zimmerman here has apparently been into the victim's car and purse."

"Charming." McKern gave the boys a churlish look.

Mayo left the boys in McKern's care and walked down the road to meet the two crime scene people from Colorado Bureau of Investigation. They were already out of the van and suiting up. The driver was a slow-moving man with a drooping face. He was breathing heavily—probably from being at ten thousand feet of altitude.

"Troy," he said, giving a nod instead of shaking hands.

"Thanks for getting here so fast," Mayo said, introducing herself.

The second, younger man, shook her hand with enthusiasm, introduced himself as Harry McGlothlen. He had a round face and a large nose, which he rubbed as he scanned the meadow, where the grass and brush moved under a rising wind. "Bummer," he said as he got his equipment ready. "The evidence is blowing away."

Mayo described the mish-mash of tire and footprints in the parking area.

"Those two kids involved somehow?" Troy pointed placidly at the Jeep.

"They found the body."

"I'll get shots of their shoes and tires." He headed around to the back of his van.

"Where's the deceased?" Harry McGlothlen fiddled with a GPS device.

"Down there in those ruins." Mayo pointed. "I'll be right there."

As the two men got to work, Mayo intercepted Deputy Nutt hiking up the road. He was a small 24-year-old with black hair and strangely pink skin.

"Sorry I took so long boss," he said. "I was down in—"

"—Deputy Nutt," she said. "We need to organize a couple checkpoints—on 119 and the canyon. Call the sheriff's department for help. Check driver's license, take down license plate numbers, find out if anyone saw anything unusual in the area this morning between midnight and now. We're looking for cars, trucks, bicycles, ATVs, weird noises. Anything at all. In particular, we want a dark-colored Ford SUV. It was spotted earlier down by the spring."

Nutt saluted. "Yes, ma'am." He spun around and trotted down the hill back to his car.

When Mayo returned, the two boys were sitting in the Jeep with McKern standing next to them, his arms folded, his feet planted wide apart. A baggie of marijuana rested on the Jeep's hood.

"What you want me to do with them?" McKern said. "Got about half an ounce of illegal contraband here."

"Let 'em go with a warning," Mayo said. "Move the SUV out of the road if they can't get around it."

McKern stepped close and lowered his voice. "Boss, don't you want—"

"Let 'em go," she said.

The two boys exchanged grins.

"I want something in return," she told them. "I want you to keep your mouths shut. You can tell people you found a body but don't say anything else. No details whatsoever. And what I mean by that is you say absolutely nothing. You do not answer a single question. You're gonna play the lads with a big secret that you won't give up. Do you understand?"

They nodded and started the Jeep. McKern snatched the baggie off the Jeep and stood back sullenly.

"And boys," Mayo added. "If any details get out, I'll know it came from you."

She was pretty sure the details would be out within the hour, but there was no harm in trying.

"Get a tow truck up here for Heather's car," she told McKern when the boys had gone.

"How come you didn't let me bust 'em?" McKern said. "They're breakin' the law."

"We've got bigger fish to fry right now." Mayo checked on Gumble, who was shoveling pinecones, dirt, and mulch from the parking area into a couple of evidence bags.

She felt raindrops as she hiked back down to the cabin, where McGlothlen was measuring Heather's body and sketching the scene. He had fastened paper bags over her hands.

"It's starting to rain," he said. "We'll have to cover the body if the coroner doesn't get here soon."

She appraised the situation. Outdoor crime scenes were bad in general, and this one was about the worst—heavy grass, wind, melted snow, storm on the way. She had a mess of tire tracks, a purse in the car, possible dark Ford SUV, two stoned kids. Not much. Maybe they'd get some prints from the car, learn something from Heather's autopsy, at least figure out what killed her. She thought of the sketch of Heather's supposed rapist—the

American Indian with the wandering eye. She had assumed Heather invented him, but now she couldn't take that for granted.

She moved slowly up the hillside toward the parking area, scanning back and forth across the grass.

McKern appeared behind her. "Tow truck is on the way," he said. "What do you want me to do now?"

"You and Gumble start a spiral search," she said. "Use the cabin as ground zero. Look for anything—cigarette butts, soda cans, weapons—anything that looks like it hasn't been here long."

He pointed. "Here comes the coroner's van."

Mayo headed over to meet the coroner, McKern tagging along beside her.

"The girl's family is gonna sue our socks off, aren't they?" he said, licking his lips. "She says she was raped and all that crap, and we ignore her, and then she's murdered. There are a million scumbag lawyers ready to jump on this one."

Mayo halted. McKern was a good foot taller but he blinked as she scowled up at him. "Listen carefully, McKern. Heather wasn't raped. She made up the whole damn thing. Her story had a gaping hole in it, not to mention her history, which *you* dug up, remember? Don't lose track of what you already know."

She started walking again.

"But I don't know what I know," McKern protested as he hurried to catch up.

The coroner's van pulled over a short distance down the road and parked.

Mayo stopped again and faced her deputy. She wiped moisture from her face. It was sprinkling again and a sudden gust of wind hit them hard enough that they both took a step. McKern was a good kid, she thought, basically decent. She felt a little guilty that she was almost always irritated with him, and she wondered if it was at least partly her own fault. She knew that Davy wanted her to teach his nephew how to be a good officer. She had a soft spot for Davy but wasn't the least bit interested in trying to forge a cop out of his impatient nephew.

"Get going on that spiral search," she said.

Down the road, a young woman climbed out of the white coroner's van. Mayo had worked with Deputy Coroner Laura

Chase once already when one of Sugarloaf's old timers had died at home the previous Monday—Mayo's first day on the job. Chase was a thin woman with a high, round forehead and silky blonde hair, which she wore in a cheerful ponytail

Chase shook Mayo's hand with a knuckle-crunching grip. "Geez, that's a long drive," Chase said, looking around at the meadow and ruins. "Twice in one week! Maybe you brought bad ju-ju with you from Denver, eh?"

Mayo waited glumly while Chase suited up, then escorted her across the grassy hillside, back to the cabin.

Surveying the body, Chase gave Mayo and McGlothlen a disapproving look, as though they had come up with the vile business themselves. A few raindrops hit her face and she touched it with a fingertip. "Uh-oh."

"We better get her moved before the storm gets going," Mayo said. "It's been threatening for a while."

"Can you have someone bring a bag from the van?" Chase said, peering at the body.

Mayo called Gumble.

"There's a small bit of blood in the grass there," McGlothlen gestured at an evidence marker he had placed a foot or so away from the body. "I'm just about to bag it."

While McGlothlen scooped a chunk of grass and dirt into a bag, Chase put on a pair of gloves, knelt in front of Heather and rolled her over. Heather's young face seemed slightly misshapen from being pressed against the grass, and Mayo looked away from it. A smear of blood showed on the girl's abdomen, with a matching wet spot in the grass below. Chase worked the material of the hoodie away from the injury.

Mayo gazed up at the sky, felt more raindrops. She hadn't been up close to death since Glen, and that had been so close she could still taste it at the back of her throat a year later. She shut her eyes, thought about what it must be like up at Arapaho Pass. She really ought to just get the hell out of this place, this damn job, grab the dogs and head on up. The last time she was at the pass—a few weeks earlier—it was storming madly, with lightning and thunder banging in her ears, and vicious sheets of rain, topped off by a muddy rock slide that wiped out part of the trail. And through the mayhem, a powerful scent of rainwater, pure, and fresh from the clouds. Going up there was a good way of finding out what was real and what wasn't.

"Our girl was moved," Chase said.

"I agree. That hand clutching the grass isn't in the right position."

"Yes, and look at the blood flow." Chase pointed out a smeared line of blood, visible on Heather's running pants. The line flowed down from the abdominal wound, then hit the groin where it spread in both directions. Chase glanced at McGlothlen. "She was in a sitting position for a short period, already injured in the abdomen, which is when she must have yanked out the grass. She was sitting there long enough to bleed into the ground. Then our baddie pushed her over onto her stomach." Chase poked her fingers around the wound on Heather's head. "Probably so they could do this."

"What the hell is that about?" Mayo said.

Chase shrugged. "Who the hell knows? But there's not much blood, especially for a head wound. She was already dead when this happened."

She dug into Heather's pockets, which produced nothing.

"What kind of weapon?" Mayo asked. "Or weapons?"

"No signs of gunshot residue or stippling, so I'm guessing she was stabbed," Chase said in her perky voice. "Something with a slender blade. Can't tell much more right now."

"How long do you think she's been dead?"

Chase twisted her mouth. "Couple hours at least. Probably longer. What's the temperature been like this morning?"

"It snowed around midnight and was warming up by nine a.m.," Mayo said. "Probably got up to around 55 before this new storm started coming in. How soon can you guys do an autopsy?"

"Got to check the M.E.'s schedule," said Chase. "Maybe today, maybe not until Monday. He's off tomorrow. Give us a call early afternoon."

Gumble arrived with a white body bag. The rain increased as the four of them lifted Heather's tiny body into the bag and got her zipped up. They carried her across the meadow and loaded her into the coroner's van, which would take her for the last time down the mountain.

After Chase left, Mayo walked back up to the parking area where Troy was bent over in the dirt preparing material for a tire track impression. Feeling as though she'd been on scene for days, she watched him work for a few moments. The raindrops apparently didn't disturb him. There was something hypnotic and comforting about his sloth-like movements as he poured water into a plastic bag of dental stone and kneaded the mixture.

Gumble appeared at her side and handed her a slip of paper. "Got a call back from the sister," he said. "She wants to know when someone is coming to talk to the family." He nodded at the paper. "That's the mother's address in Boulder. There's a victim advocate with them now."

"I'll head down in a minute," Mayo said. "Where are you at with the spiral—"

"I've got some good sequencing here," Troy interrupted, making a satisfied huffing noise. "Which makes us very happy."

"Still got a ways to go," Gumble said and headed off again.

Troy knelt down and poured the mixture into a tire track, his upper teeth gripping his lower lip as though it took great effort. One of his front teeth was unusually long and crooked.

"These," he said, nodding toward the track, "are from a vehicle that was parked next to the victim's car before the Jeep came in." Mayo followed as he pointed along the tracks.

"Here," he went on, "they're partially obscured by the Jeep's tracks, but over there, you see where the tracks crossed over tracks from the vic's car?"

"Uh-huh," Mayo said.

He grinned, revealing another view of the crooked tooth. "So we know this vehicle came in before the Jeep and after the vic."

"Excellent," Mayo murmured. She wondered if she ought to stay on scene instead of driving down to talk to the family.

"They look pretty common though," Troy said, "so don't get your hopes too high."

Mayo sighed, pulling her car keys from a pocket. "I never do."

Five

Jody Holloway slumped against the wall, her hand over her mouth.

Mayo touched her shoulder. "I'm very sorry."

A woman with long dark braids appeared from down the hall. "I'm Sally, victim advocate with the Boulder P.D."

Mayo nodded.

On either side of Jody, they escorted her into the living room and got her settled on the sofa, Sally next to her with a box of tissues.

Mayo became aware of another person in the room—a tiny, wrinkled woman watching the scene from an oversized armchair. She had blank brown eyes, wore a cheap-looking brown wig and a yellow velour jogging suit. The armchair upholstery matched the yellow suit, rendering her nearly invisible. Next to her on a side table was a half-empty martini glass. Behind her on the wall was an oil painting of a toga-clad Jesus walking across a sea of wild waves. Mayo guessed this was the owner of the white Saturn parked in the driveway whose bumper sticker read, "Every Knee Shall Bow."

Heather and Jody's mother.

She approached and held out a hand, which the old woman shook briefly.

"I'm Marshal Mayo. I'm very sorry for your loss."

"Please sit somewhere," Mrs. Holloway said. "You're looming."

Mayo sat in an armchair. "I'm here to fill you in on what we know and try to answer your questions."

Jody stopped sniffling and gazed at Mayo, who waited with a sense of resignation for the accusations to come.

They did not.

"What happened?" Jody said. "Nobody seems to know anything."

Mayo took a deep breath. On the drive down, she'd been rehearsing how to phrase things, but there weren't many good ways to tell a story like this one.

"Heather was found this morning by a couple of local boys in a place called Wolftongue," she said, "It's a ghost town near Sugarloaf. Her car was parked there, she was dressed in running clothes, and she'd been killed sometime after midnight, probably by a knife. At this point, we really don't know much more than that."

"That other cop didn't tell me nothin'," Mrs. Holloway said impassively. "Came in, said my girl was dead, then took off again. " She gestured at Sally. "Left this stranger here. My girl is dead and we got a house full of strangers."

It occurred to Mayo that Mrs. Holloway was either drunk or drugged, or both.

Unlike her mother, Jody wore an expression that Mayo had seen before. Her face still looked like Jody Holloway, but Jody herself had been shattered into bits then hastily reassembled into something else by some mysterious automated process. She was functioning but was not present in her body. As of this morning, she was no longer the same Jody and never would be again, and later on, she would remember very little about this meeting.

"Heather was stabbed?" she asked.

"I'm very sorry for your loss." Mayo searched her memory for the things she had said in the past to friends and family of people who had been killed. *Sorry for your loss. Condolences. I know it's difficult.* None of it fixed anything but the acknowledgement was important.

It was odd that neither Jody nor Delia was blowing up at Mayo, who had disregarded Heather's story about the attack at Zippy's. Now Heather was dead. Jody and her mother had every reason to be angry with her, assuming they knew.

"When's the last time either of you saw or spoke to Heather?" she asked.

"We had dinner together last night," Jody said. "She drove down to meet me here in Boulder. She was upset about the ... you know. We stopped by the grocery store and then we split up around eight o'clock. And now I won't see her any more..." She covered her mouth again.

Mayo turned to Mrs. Holloway. "How about you?"

The old woman shrugged. "Haven't talked to her in months."

Mayo decided to leave that one alone for the moment. "Do either of you know why Heather might go up to Wolftongue early in the morning? Do you know where Wolftongue is?"

"I know it," Jody said. "She ran every morning but used the trail at the end of her street."

Mayo plunged into the heart of the matter. "Jody, are you aware that we had some problems with her story about what happened at Zippy's?"

Jody stared down at the hands in her lap. "I know."

"What do you think happened there?"

The girl glanced at her mother, who was looking at her daughter but may or may not have been listening. Her expression still looked entirely vacant.

"I believe what my sister said," Jody said.

She's lying, Mayo thought. If she believed Heather's Zippy's story, she'd be all over Mayo right now for dropping the ball.

"Okay," Mayo said gently. "Heather told her boss at Zippy's that she moved to Sugarloaf to get away from an ex-boyfriend who was bothering her. What can you tell me about that?"

Jody opened her mouth, then closed it. She appeared to be thinking this over. Again, her reaction did not make much sense.

Abruptly, Jody got up from the sofa. "Where is she now? I want to see her."

Interesting change of subject, Mayo thought. "Was there an ex-boyfriend?" she pressed.

Jody pursed her lips, looked around the room as though searching for an escape route, then sat back down with an air of resignation.

"Jody?"

The girl took a deep breath. "She moved there because our grandfather left us the house and she didn't have to pay rent."

"No ex-boyfriend stalking her?" Mayo pressed.

Jody shook her head.

"Why would she tell her boss that?"

"I don't know," Jody said. "Maybe she was embarrassed about being broke."

A reasonable explanation, Mayo thought, though almost certainly another lie. Jody was hiding something.

"Why should she be broke?" Mrs. Holloway barked. "She already spend all that money the old man left you girls?"

Jody did not look at her mother. "I don't know why, she just was."

Mayo paused, watching mother and daughter. The two barely looked at each other.

"Can we go see her now?" Jody said.

"You'll be getting a call from Laura Chase, the deputy coroner," Mayo said. "You'll have to discuss that with her. But it may not be such a good idea, Jody."

"All the cops these days seem to be women," Mrs. Holloway put in. "Why you women want to be cops?" She leaned over the side table, picked up a pen and began to draw on a spiral bound notepad. She drew something that looked like two elongated ovals, then put the pen down. Mayo wondered if the ovals represented two female cops.

"They're not going to cut her up, are they?" Jody asked.

"It's a homicide," Mayo said, "which means there will be an autopsy."

Mrs. Holloway picked up the pen again and pointed it at Mayo. "She was always in trouble, ya know." She drew a box next to the ovals and went to work shading it in. "My Heather was always gettin' into it, some way or another. She was a problem. I don't want to go see her, Jody. You go ahead, I'll wait here." On the pad, she drew an arrow pointing into the box.

"I wish you'd just shut up for once, Mother." Jody got up and went into the kitchen.

Sally rose from the sofa and followed Jody.

Mayo edged closer to Mrs. Holloway, who now seemed engrossed in her drawing. She wasn't convinced the old woman was as stoned as she seemed.

"Mrs. Holloway, when exactly is the last time you saw Heather?"

She shrugged. "I don't know. We don't generally see each other. And don't call me Mrs. Holloway. People just call me Delia."

"You weren't on good terms?"

Delia gave her a look of bald hostility. "She made a formal announcement a couple years ago that she had *disowned* me. Can you imagine? Disownin' your own mother? Well, fine. There's a word for people like her—*pathological liar*. I read about it. But you already knew that, considerin' you're the cop who didn't believe her when she hollered rape, aren't you? Jody said so."

Delia Holloway was not to be underestimated, Mayo decided. "Do you believe her story about the Zippy's attack?" she asked.

Delia closed her eyes and pinched the bridge of her nose, the first sign she'd shown of feeling anything besides irritation. "No more'n anyone with half a lick of sense would," Delia said. "She was makin' up stories like that when she was nine years old. Told the most foul lies anyone could imagine comin' up with. Disgusting stories. You couldn't even believe they'd be comin' out of a child." She leaned toward Mayo, and Mayo smelled the booze on her breathe.

"Just figure out who she's been lyin' about lately," Delia whispered, "and you'll catch the guy who did her in."

Mayo edged back. "What kind of lies, exactly?"

"Oh, you know." Delia narrowed her eyes at her. "Half the men on the planet tryin' to get at her. She made up stories like that in high school too; did I mention that?"

"Can you think of anyone specifically?"

Mrs. Holloway flashed the sort of smile that seemed staged, but at the same time, Mayo caught a hint of uncertainty. "I can't remember names of them damn high school kids," Delia said. "Heather'd accuse a squirrel if it ran by at the wrong time."

Mayo suddenly remembered something McKern had told her about his conversation with Detective Gonzales in Denver, who said Heather also claimed she'd been molested by her father. "Is your husband here? Heather's father?"

"Dead over 10 years," Delia said, now speaking in a faraway, robotic voice. "Never would have let this happen. Never, never, never."

Mayo proceeded carefully. "I understand there were some accusations against him as well."

This roused her. Mrs. Holloway drained her drink and plunked it back on the end table with a sharp crack. "That is one big load of crap. Where the hell did you hear that? From her? You heard it from the little traitor herself?"

Mayo sat back, considering the possibility that Delia Holloway had killed her own daughter. The old woman was hostile enough, and certainly capable from a psychological perspective. She calculated Mrs. Holloway's physical strength. She couldn't be much more than five-feet-two or so, and probably weighed about 100 pounds. She was even smaller than Heather. Still, she didn't seem exactly feeble.

"That your Saturn out in the driveway, Mrs. Holloway?"

The old woman fixed her faded eyes on Mayo, fluttering her bony hands as though to swat Mayo out of her presence. "Yes, it's my damn Saturn. What, you think I raced up to whatever-you-call it ghost town joint and killed my own daughter? That's a real good one, lady cop. My God, I can't believe people any more. I just can't believe 'em." She picked up her empty glass and banged it down on the table again. "I got a dead daughter gettin' stiff on a table somewheres and you want to know if I got a car. That's just dandy, lady cop. Just spunky dorie or whatever they call it. So do I need to hire a goddamned lawyer or what?"

Not an entirely unpredictable response, Mayo decided, though it was hard to imagine any normal mother describing her own daughter the way Delia Holloway had just described Heather.

"That's up to you, Mrs. Holloway," she said.

"I think I will, as a matter of fact." Delia Holloway smiled, showing a row of stained teeth. "I'm not so sure I like the way you handled my daughter's rape case."

The rape case that the old woman was sneering at a few moments earlier, thought Mayo.

"Once again," she said, "that's entirely your right. Meanwhile, I'll be needing your permission to search Heather's house."

One corner of Delia's wrinkled lip went up into a sneer. "Ask Jody. She's the owner now." She reached once again for her martini glass but abandoned the effort when she saw again that it was empty.

"Jody owns the house in Sugarloaf?" Mayo prodded.

"My husband's old man left the rotten rubble heap to the girls," Delia said, "even though they were still practically babies when he kicked the bucket. He didn't care much for me or my husband so we got skipped over. Not that it's worth a damn. Nothin' but a termites nest..."

Delia looked up as Jody and Sally appeared in the kitchen doorway, Sally holding Jody's elbow.

Sally nodded at Mayo. "Jody's got something to tell you." She guided Jody back to the sofa and they sat down again. Jody was wearing a different expression now — her mouth looked tight and her gaze was more direct than before. She looked as though she had made a resolution or figured something out.

"Go ahead, Jody," Mayo said.

Jody blew her nose and cleared her throat. "I was just telling Sally that I remembered something that happened yesterday at the supermarket, just before Heather left to drive back up to Sugarloaf. We went into the supermarket to get some groceries and I think maybe someone was watching us when we came out."

"Go on," Mayo said.

"When we came out of the store," Jody continued, "there was a man sitting in a truck in the parking lot."

This caught Mayo's attention. "A truck — not an SUV?"

"It was a truck."

"What kind?"

"I don't know. It was dark-colored — maybe black. And big."

Mayo considered the story. It seemed odd that Jody just "remembered" the truck.

"What makes you think he was watching you?" she asked.

"Because he was!" Jody blurted. "He was sitting there alone in his truck, and when we walked by behind him, he turned in his seat to keep watching. He had to twist around, which is why I thought it was weird. And I'm pretty sure he winked at me."

"Winked, huh?" Mayo said. "That's odd. Was he just some guy maybe flirting with you?"

Jody shook her head emphatically. "No. I can't explain — it wasn't like flirting. It was like 'ha ha, I'm watching you and I want you to worry.'"

Mayo pondered this. Jody didn't seem entirely forthcoming, but she still struck Mayo as reasonably intelligent and honest. Jody was nothing like her sister, possessed none of the agitation or ego or craftiness that Heather displayed. Jody Holloway seemed like a decent kid trapped in a poisonous family.

"But you don't think this is the ex-boyfriend Heather mentioned?" Mayo asked.

Something flashed across Jody's face again that Mayo couldn't quite interpret. Even if she were telling the truth about the truck, the girl was definitely hiding something. Something important.

Jody shook her head. "She never said anything to me about a boyfriend. I don't know — maybe there was one. She didn't seem to notice the guy in the truck so I didn't say anything."

Mayo tried a different angle. "Do you know if Heather's been bothered before by anyone else?"

Jody picked at the neckline of her blouse. The gesture looked defensive.

"Anything come to mind?" Mayo prompted. "A professor at college? Her boss at the museum?"

Jody frowned. "No. I don't know what you're talking about." Her tone was bland, unconvincing, and she hid her throat behind her hand. *Deceptive*, thought Mayo.

Mayo decided to take a risk and press her. "Did you really believe your sister's story about the man at Zippy's?" She ignored the disapproving glare she was getting from Sally, the victim advocate.

Jody narrowed her eyes. "Of course I did."

Mayo didn't believe her, but she didn't see any point in pushing further at this stage. She reached into her pocket, pulled out the folded police artist's sketch of Heather's Zippy's assailant and handed it to Jody.

"Is that the guy in the truck?"

Jody puzzled over the picture. "No. Is that who attacked her at Zippy's?"

"That's the guy she described."

Jody handed it back. "The man in the truck was a white guy. It was hard to see his whole face because he was wearing a hat, but he had a big moustache."

"What kind of a hat?"

"Like in that movie, 'Indiana Jones.'"

"Can you remember anything else about him? Clothes? Anything strange about the truck? License number?"

Jody shook her head.

Mayo sighed. Too many disparate details were accumulating and the mish-mash led nowhere. "Did you see him again?"

"No. Heather got into her car and I got into mine and we left."

"So it's possible he might have pulled out after you and followed Heather?"

Jody looked uneasy, and glanced at Sally before answering. "He could have."

Mayo showed the picture to Mrs. Holloway. "Have you ever seen this man?"

She lifted her lip in distaste. "Something wrong with his eye."

Mayo was getting frustrated with Delia Holloway. "Have you ever seen him?"

The woman glowered. "No, I haven't."

Jody suddenly bent over her knees and covered her face with her hands. "I should have done something. I should have. I just can't believe this."

Mayo got up and squatted in front of Jody. "There's nothing you could have done. Honestly, none of us has enough power to control what happens to other people." She glanced at Sally. "Have you got hold of any of Jody's friends that could come and help out?"

Sally tilted her head to indicate "No."

Mayo rested a hand on Jody's arm. "We're going to need your permission to go through the house in Sugarloaf." She got up and retrieved a consent to search form, which Jody signed.

"I didn't find any house keys in Heather's purse," Mayo said.

"She leaves them under the mat on the front step."

THE TROUBLE WITH HEATHER HOLLOWAY

Sally brought her a glass of water and Jody took several small sips, then sat holding the glass, staring down at her sneakers. Sally removed the water glass from her hand and put it on the end table.

Mayo could not shake the feeling that Jody's distress sprang from more than the pure grief of a loving sister. She also looked confused.

Mayo moved back to her spot in the armchair. "Did Heather have a cell phone, Jody?"

Jody blew her nose. "She got rid of her phone. Said she hated it."

"How did you communicate with her?"

"Email."

"Did she go running every morning?"

Jody nodded. "She always gets up at 6 a.m. and goes for a run first thing. There's a hiking trail off Bobcat Terrace, at the end of the street. The Orange Blossom Trail."

"Yes, I know it. Did she wear specific clothes or use a water bottle or an iPod?"

Jody showed signs of annoyance, but answered. "She has some running outfits and used one of those water packs with the tube you drink from. No iPod."

Mayo stood and handed each of the Holloway women her card. "I think that's all I have right now. Do either of you have any questions for me?"

Neither answered.

During the drive home, Mayo could not get Jody's attitude out of her mind. Jody had barely mentioned the Zippy's incident. Her statement that she believed Heather's story about it showed no trace of confidence.

Mayo surmised that Jody did know about the past events described in the police report from Denver, and probably others—maybe the high school incidents mentioned by Delia Holloway. It made sense that Jody would protect her beloved sister by denying these past episodes. Jody's devotion to Heather seemed extreme. Mayo had seen symbiotic relationships like this one before—the caretaker who couldn't stand it when things were not all right, and the drama queen who couldn't stand it when they were. Mayo speculated that the two sisters had a long history of Heather making messes and Jody cleaning them up.

What Mayo could not understand is why Jody would consider it more important to mask Heather's lies than to find out who killed her. Especially when the existence of phony accusations was already known. There had to be another angle to the story.

Meanwhile, Mayo calculated how she would try to manage the flow of information back in Sugarloaf. Despite her deal with the boys, she assumed that Sigi and Bobby had not kept their mouths shut, but there was one important detail she hoped they hadn't mentioned to everyone else in town: the wound on Heather Holloway's head.

And then there was the other issue — the brand new town marshal had dismissed a young woman's claim of rape, and the woman was killed two days later. Mayo hadn't been around long enough to have any real enemies in town, aside from those who had general objections to a female marshal. Still, if anyone wanted to come after her, now was a good time. Despite her lecture to McKern, she wasn't one hundred percent sure she hadn't committed a monumental — and deadly — screw up.

She felt fatalistic about the possibility. If they wanted to hang this on her, fine. She'd resign under a cloud — she'd done it once before — and leave the mess for Mayor Davy to clean up. It wouldn't take much effort to pack up her scant collection of personal things and move on to some other new town where no one knew her, where maybe her past wouldn't continue to hang over her. She could sell her Victorian in Denver, live off the proceeds until she figured out what her next move should be. The idea sounded incredibly appealing.

She turned off the state highway and headed into Sugarloaf proper, slowing down for the speed bumps. The town looked placid, welcoming. The problem was, she did not want to leave. She was fond of Monte — more than fond — and she didn't want to dump a mess for Davy to clean up. Maybe this time she should stick around and face things.

As she pulled up in front of the station, her cell phone rang. It was McKern.

"Hey, boss!" he said through a rush of static. "You gotta get back up here. It looks like we got our murder weapon."

Up at Wolftongue, the rain had stopped, the CSI van was gone, and the police tape flapped mournfully in the wind. McKern met her out on the road, spattered with rainwater and mud. He was exhilarated.

"You're not gonna believe this, boss!" he blurted. "You gotta see for yourself."

She followed as he led the way upslope toward a bank of aspen trees beyond the parking area. It was late afternoon and the sky was clearing. The sun hovered over the mountaintops in the west, peeking through clouds to cast an eerie light against the delicate white trunks of the aspen.

They scrambled up the damp hillside and through a rain soaked aspen grove. In a small clearing stood a gnarled piñon pine. The deputies had attached a plastic awning to the tree and secured it in place to protect an area beneath it. Gumble was hunched over, taking pictures.

Beneath the awning was a salad of pinecones, leaves, mulch, and a clump of wild roses. In the center of this, a patch of disturbed soil surrounded a rectangular hole about two feet long and half a foot wide.

"We got all kinds of goodies in here," Gumble said as they approached. "I waited for you before touching anything."

"Any footprints?" Mayo asked.

"Nothing," he said. "Some disturbed mulch but nothing good."

Mayo knelt next to him and peered into the hole. It was about a foot deep, several feet long, peppered with rocks.

"Must have been a huge pain to dig that," Mayo observed.

"Agreed," Gumble said. "Not something you could do in a rush."

She focused on the biggest thing lying in the hole—a long blade with a handle. It was a bayonet.

"You got enough pictures?" she asked.

"Uh-huh."

Mayo pulled on some gloves and lifted it out of the hole. The blade was flat and crusted with something dark — probably blood. Stamped near the gold-colored handle was a manufacturer's name and logo of a tiny crown. It said: VR Enfield 1848.

"Real antique or fake?" Mayo said.

"My money's on a fake," Gumble said.

McKern produced a bag and Mayo dropped it in.

"There's a Bowie knife too." Gumble pointed.

Mayo extracted the knife. This one also had stains on it and she slipped it into a second evidence bag.

Gumble leaned into the hole. "Holy mother — what's that now?" He took a quick series of pictures.

Lying in the dirt, beneath where the weapons had been, was a clump of tangled hair. Human. Dyed red.

Mayo pulled at it, disengaged it from the dirt. The hair was straight, thick, about six inches long. At one end was a curled chunk of flesh. Mayo guessed that it had come from Heather's head.

She dropped the thing into another bag. "I do believe," she said, "they used to call this taking a scalp."

Six

By the look on Monte's face, Mayo knew instantly he'd already heard.

But he was quiet as Mayo unloaded her gear and knelt down to greet the dogs. She spent a few moments stroking their bony backs while they pushed at her face with long noses. They felt like a cleansing wash after a day immersed in the murder of Heather Holloway.

Mayo finally stood up. The TV was muted, tuned to a cable news program with three arguing heads and two moving text strings. She nodded at Monte, who was stretched out on the sofa.

"Stepped wrong on my bad ankle," he said. "And I'm a *bit* cranky."

"I thought we agreed we couldn't both be cranky at the same time."

Before he could grill her, she headed down the hall. It had been a very long, miserable day and she was exhausted. Back in her other life, she used to chip away at a case all night long, then go with her buddies for a giant greasy breakfast on Colfax. Now she just wanted hot soup and bed.

In the bathroom, she stood over Monte's beautiful vessel sink and splashed cold water on her face. Then she did it again, and once more. The water felt cool and refreshing. She rolled up her sleeves, soaped a washcloth and scrubbed. Leaning into the mirror, she spotted a rogue hair on her chin. Swearing softly, she grabbed tweezers from the medicine cabinet and yanked. Her blue eyes looked crazy-bright, her lips pale. Just for the hell of it, she put on some eyeliner and lipstick.

She'd worked dozens of homicides back in Denver. She'd had a year to get herself together since the *event*. Yes, she had ignored Monte's long-ago suggestion that she talk to a professional, and sure, it was possible some therapy might have helped. But that was all irrelevant now. She had stepped into a new job that she was perhaps not quite prepared for, and within a week, events had turned on her.

Still, unless she got canned for dropping the Zippy's business, she was in this thing and there was no backing out, no scurrying off to some shrink to whine about her situation. Besides, she hadn't been wrong about Heather being attacked. She wouldn't forget what she already knew. She remembered what to do, how to proceed. She could handle this, one step at a time.

No problem.

Back in the living room, Monte watched her as she passed through into the kitchen. In the fridge, she found a pitcher of iced tea. On the stove was a pot of vegetable soup, but it didn't smell appealing.

She poured tea and drank it at the sliding door.

"Eat some soup!" Monte called. "You liked this recipe last time I made it."

Outside, the subdued colors of twilight made the yard look soft and beautiful. Monte's confusing metal sculptures dotted the landscape—supposedly a greyhound, a farmer bending over a plow, and a small girl jumping rope. This is what Monte told her anyway; she couldn't see any of it.

Mayo was grateful to Monte and felt comfortable around him—much more now than she ever did when Glen was alive, back in those easier days when she and Glen had joked about him. During their earliest months in the house together, right after Glen's death, she and Monte had been locked into a sort of grieving slow-dance, poking each other occasionally to pay attention to the day, eat something, maybe even smile. And then, Monte had started getting better—a lot more quickly than she was.

Now, she noted a quiet but ever-present pressure from him to feel better, achieve "recovery." Lately, he jumped on it when Mayo did something promising: *Beth, I'm proud of you for taking that job. I figured you and Davy would hit it off. I think you love greyhounds as much as I do. That hiking does you good. You're looking content this morning.*

She wanted to tell him she'd get better in her own damn time.

Situated in the far corner of the yard, flanked by aspen trees, was Monte's hot tub, and Mayo often headed out during quiet evenings with a candle and a glass of wine. She should have some soup, then a long, forgetful soak. But she was too edgy to be able to sit still and relax. She had to clear her mind and focus on the case. She did not want to screw this up.

In the living room, Monte was talking to his hounds. Mayo strained to hear, but couldn't.

She wandered over to the pot, then ladled some into a bowl and tried a mouthful. To her surprise, it tasted delicious. She carried the bowl out to the living room, stood in the middle of the room and ate ravenously.

"Didn't realize I was hungry," she mumbled.

Monte changed his position on the sofa.

"Does it hurt?" Mayo asked.

He punched his pillow to reshape it. "Probably, but I'm on drugs."

The room was silent for a time. Monte unmuted the TV, but muted it right away again.

"Sit down," he suggested. "Nobody should eat standing up."

She spooned a warm chunk of celery out of the bowl and stuck it in her mouth, thinking of Delia Holloway: *You're looming.*

She checked her watch. Gumble was taking the stuff from the hole down to the lab in Boulder. They had talked about heading back out to search Heather's house, but he had some kids and a wife to get home to. She was too fried to go out again.

Heather's house could wait until morning.

"I heard about Heather," Monte said.

Mayo finished chewing before she answered. "What exactly did you hear?"

"Only that she was killed. Is it true?"

"Yes."

"What happened?"

"She was stabbed."

"What the hell."

Mayo swallowed. "I'm sorry, Monte," she said in a softer voice. "Allow me to apologize in advance right now for all the blunt and probably tasteless things I'm inevitably going to say and do in the coming days. I'm a cop again and I've got a murder on my hands."

She finally sat down on the sofa, sharing the end with Monte's feet. "Don't give me that look," she said. "You urged me to take this damn job and here I am."

"Don't be mad," Monte said.

"I'm not mad. Just feeling maybe unprepared."

"Glen always said you were a brave and methodical cop," he said. "You'll do fine." He nudged her with his foot.

"You were going to tell me something about Heather and the SUV this morning," she said. "What was it?"

"The SUV," he said. "Heather said it was hanging out near the pumps and asked me would I look and see if there was anyone inside it. But the windows were tinted so I couldn't see."

"What color was it?"

"It was dark. I didn't notice the model. It was smallish. I wasn't paying a whole lot of attention."

"How well did you know Heather?" Mayo asked.

"Not well," he said. "I chatted with her when I went in. She was unfriendly at first, but then warmed up."

"What did you talk about?"

He tilted his head. "I probably did most of the talking. I felt sorry for her. She seemed like a little injured sparrow to me."

"I thought you said she was a mouse."

Monte adjusted himself, nudging his foot against her thigh again.

Mayo had arranged to meet Gumble at Heather's house early Sunday morning and she arrived after a sleepless night. In the morning shadows, the place looked old and dilapidated, its rust-colored paint peeling off in thin dry strips. The front yard was an ugly spread of gravel and weeds shriveling from an obvious dousing of weed-killer. A loose piece of flagstone grated when Mayo stepped on the front step. Someone had recently installed a peephole in the front door—bits of sawdust still showed amongst the black fibers of a worn mat on the front step.

Gumble was there ahead of her, sitting on the sofa with two plastic tubs in front of him on a burl table.

"Morning, Gumby," she said, using his nickname. Everyone called him "Gumby" after the cartoon character because of his extreme height and a slender build that somehow seemed bent sideways. "You found the key, I see."

"Yup. Under the mat like you said."

"You been here awhile?"

"Couldn't sleep," he said.

"Ditto that." She put her briefcase down and had a quick look around. The place had a bone-chilling cheerlessness about it. Three milk crate-sized windows in the living room were covered with heavy maroon curtains and the walls were paneled in dark knotty planks. A wood burning stove in the far corner was rusted and missing the stovepipe.

She took a deep breath, turning away from Gumble in case there was any uncertainty in her face. She'd spent a long night of thrashing around in bed, trying to beat back her anxiety about Heather. She had disliked the girl, was irritated by her attitude. She didn't like the whole "blame an Indian guy" thing. Had all this made her jump to the wrong conclusion?

"Welcome back, by the way," she told Gumble in an overly cheerful voice. She toned it down a bit. "Didn't get a chance to say so yesterday. How was Mesa Verde?"

Gumble grinned and shook her outstretched hand. "A week in a tent with a type-A wife and three squabbling kids. Pure joy." He had watchful blue eyes and wore thick black-framed glasses.

Pulling on her gloves, she zeroed in on a hydration pack lying on the floor near the front door.

"Did you move that backpack?" she asked Gumble.

"Nope. Thought you'd want to have a look. Seems out of place."

She took a picture of it, then picked it up—it was full of water. She dug through its pockets, found a tissue packet and a tube of Chapstick. "Looks like she was heading out for her morning run but ended up leaving this behind for some reason. Looks like she was in a hurry and just tossed it on the floor."

"I think you'll find that 'something' in the kitchen," Gumble said.

On the kitchen table, already bagged, was a double-folded piece of white copy paper. Mayo removed it from the plastic evidence bag and unfolded it. On it, someone had printed in block capitals: "Alonzo Holloway is buried at Wolftongue."

"It was on the table when I came in," Gumble said.

"I don't remember seeing a cemetery at Wolftongue."

"That's 'cause there isn't one." He picked up a gadget that looked like pliers connected to a pair of straw-sized tubes, each with a plastic bell at the end. "I'm going to need an after-school baby-sitter for a while, aren't I?"

"I'd give that a likely 'yes.' What *is* that thing?"

"Something naughty, I suspect." He put it back in the tub, rummaged around and came up with a small black strap-like assembly held together with a cloth strawberry. "You think my wife would like a strawberry G-string for Christmas?"

Mayo allowed him a quick smile. "Where'd you find those bins?"

"Tucked under the bed," Gumble said. "So, are we getting sued? McKern's already squawking about lawyers and feminist demonstrators and prison time."

"McKern's hysterical."

She examined the note. On the outside of the fold, she detected faint specs of reddish brown. She re-bagged it, then pulled a piece of paper from her notepad.

"Heather's sister probably does not have me on her Christmas list," she said, folding the paper from her notepad. "Though her mother didn't seem too crushed. Are you sure you don't want to be marshal?"

"Sorry, boss. I'm happiest at a distance."

"You're happiest taking lots of time off."

"That too."

Mayo sighed. "Someday I'm gonna learn to say 'No' to Davy Brown."

"Best way to do that is when you see him coming, just run the other way."

She headed out the front door and closed it. She stuck the folded paper into the crack between the door and doorframe. The gap was just right, and the paper stayed put. She pulled it out, then carried it back into the house and held it under a lamp. The test paper showed similar traces of reddish brown paint.

"Looks like someone stuck the note in the doorway." She made a quick cruise through the tiny bungalow. "No regular phone," she said. "And no cell phone."

"Who's Alonzo Holloway?" Gumble asked. "I remember old man Holloway lived here when I was a kid, but his name was Charlie. He used to chase us off with a rifle if we rode our bikes across his crummy lawn."

"Which of course you did at every opportunity."

"Of course. Anyway, old man Holloway died a good twenty or twenty five years ago, must have been about two hundred years old."

"I'm guessing Alonzo was Charlie's father or grandfather." Mayo recounted Heather's story about her ancestor's diary.

"You don't suppose that's what this is all about, do you?" Gumble said. "Some byproduct from the wild west? Revenge for the massacre? I mean, we've got scalping, stabbing with a bayonet from 1848 and a one-eyed American Indian."

"God, I hope not." Mayo rubbed her eyes. "It could be someone just wants us to think so. You haven't seen an antique diary lying around, have you?"

"Nope."

"So, someone stuck the note in Heather's door, maybe during the night. Heather finds it on her way out to run, forgets the run and drives up to Wolftongue. It had to be someone who knew she would do that. But how is this connected to the thing at Zippy's?"

"I'm only going to ask this once," Gumble said. "Are you absolutely one hundred percent positive she wasn't attacked at Zippy's?"

"Look, Gumby," Mayo said. "I'm not one hundred percent positive you and I and everyone else are not experiments squirming around in some cosmic Petri dish."

He smiled.

"Listen to the interview tape and look over my notes and the police reports that McKern got," Mayo went on. "And then we'll restart that conversation."

She found nothing of interest in the bathroom medicine cabinet. In the bedroom, she pawed through the closet. Heather organized her clothes according to color, and she had very expensive taste.

"Money, money, money," Mayo chanted. "Where'd she get it?"

Not by working at places like Zippy's.

On the floor of the closet, she found something that stopped her cold: a small, blue-tinted granite tombstone. It was about two feet high and a foot wide with an inscription: *Alonzo Holloway 1845 - 1920.*

Mayo carried it into the living room and showed it to Gumble, who was setting up the fingerprinting kit.

He responded with a signature whistle.

"It looks brand new," Mayo said. "She must have had it made."

"Why would you have a tombstone made unless you had a place to put it?" asked Gumble. "Which would imply she knew where the grave was before she got the note."

"And if she knew where the grave was," Mayo said, "why would she believe the note?"

"And if she *hadn't* seen the grave," Gumble went on, "how would she know it didn't already have a tombstone?"

"Maybe she thought she'd found it but it turned out to be wrong." Mayo turned it over, looking for a manufacturer's stamp, but there was nothing.

The tombstone only muddled the story more. So many odd little things, none of which added up to any sort of narrative.

Mayo took several pictures of the tombstone, then went back into the bedroom. She opened drawers, felt through panties, bras, socks, all precisely folded, stacked, and rolled.

In the desk drawer she found car insurance papers and a diploma from Colorado Western University — a B.A. in History. She found no sign of bills, credit card statements or bank statements. Under the bed she found a portable paper shredder.

She made a thorough tour of the house, checking hopefully in the trash cans, but all had been emptied. Trash pickup for Sugarloaf was the day before, an unfortunate fact she confirmed by going out front and checking the empty bin in Heather's yard. Heather had left behind no paper trail.

Back in the bedroom, Mayo pressed the alarm button on the clock — set for 5:30 a.m.

She moved back to the desk and turned on the laptop computer.

It did not prompt for a password, and she scanned through the desktop icons — a poker game and an internet browser. She opened the browser and searched through Heather's favorites. Several banks were bookmarked, but all wanted an ID and password.

After half an hour of digging around in Windows Explorer, she found a file called pswd.txt. *Bingo*. The file contained a list of Heather's login IDs and passwords — everything needed to access all her online accounts. Mayo had found three credit cards in Heather's purse, and they were all set up to be paid online from an account dubbed "Heathers Bank," but it didn't give the bank's name.

Based on her credit card records, Heather spent a lot of money. The statements showed debits from clothing stores, restaurants, hair salons, day spas, a massage chain. Most of the merchants were in Boulder, along with numerous charges from casinos and restaurants in Black Hawk, a gambling town about a forty minute drive south of Sugarloaf. She had also made several purchases from a web site called Discreet Fantasies. The sex toys.

Except for periodic payoffs amounting to thousands of dollars, Heather paid the minimum amount every month. It had been awhile since a payoff, though, and the most recent statements were overdue. At the time of her death, Heather was carrying a credit card debt of over twenty thousand dollars — money the credit card companies would probably never see.

Heather's email Inbox held three weeks' worth of emails, mostly marked as read. Her Trash and Sent Mail folders had recently been emptied, so there were only a few emails in each. There were half a dozen or so unread spam emails, mostly for Viagra, "XXX young babes," and an "Urgent Help Trusted Friend" plea from someone in Nigeria. Mayo stopped at an email from Jody, which arrived at 6:12 a.m. the morning of Heather's death.

"Just checking up on you. You doing okay? Please think about what I said."

The fact that the email was marked as "read" meant that Heather had been at home as late as 6:12 a.m., which put the time of death no earlier than 6:30 or so, since it took about 15 minutes to drive to Wolftongue.

Unless someone other than Heather opened the email.

She checked the Sent Mail folder to see if Heather had answered it. She hadn't. The most recent outgoing message was sent Friday evening, the day Mayo confronted Heather about her story. The email was to a userid "fivecardstud" and read, "I got attacked at my new job at Zippy's They threatened to arrest me when I told them I'd been raped. They said I was lying. Don't want to play this weekend. H."

Mayo wasn't surprised at Heather's twisted version of events but the rest of the email was puzzling. *Don't want to play this weekend.* Could mean any number of things. Play, as in play with the G-string. Play, as in music, as in Black Jack, tennis, electronic games.

Judging from the name "fivecardstud," and the numerous credit card charges in Black Hawk, gambling seemed the most likely answer. It could also explain the irregular flow of money.

Fivecardstud had answered within a minute: "I want to help," but Heather had not responded.

There were older emails from Jody, sent before the Zippy's incident:

"Want to have lunch this Saturday? My treat."

"What's going on? Haven't heard from you. Are you okay? I'm worried!"

"Are you avoiding me? Why don't you answer my emails? When are you gonna get a phone? Heather, it's not that I don't believe you, but I just don't see how. Please, talk to me!"

Mayo was right that Jody had been hiding something. Heather had told her something that she wanted to believe out of loyalty, but couldn't for some reason. The email was sent before the Zippy's incident, so it wasn't about that. So, what didn't she believe? The previous cries of rape?

The Inbox also contained two emails from a user called "MudPuppie," sent on the previous Tuesday and Wednesday.

"Yo Heather, Say your mothers name 100 times and You will get kissed by next Saturday by the Love of your Life. This really works! Sincerely, an admirer."

"Dear Heather, Say your name 5 times. Say your True Love's name 10 times. Do it three times every day and your true love will come to your door within one week. If you don't then something awesomely bad will happen to you. Sincerely you know who (or you dont)."

Heather had not responded to these.

The Sent Mail folder offered a long email to Jody, written the previous weekend, at the end of Heather's second day on the job at Zippy's:

"I'm not avoiding you. I'm just so darn tired all the time now. I can't sleep and you know why. I'm not making it up. I thought I could get away up here but it hasn't stopped. I saw him again yesterday, I'm sure of it. He was watching me. And this job is driving me crazy already. The boss is a complete idiot. My first day, she disappeared in the middle of a rush. There must have been half a dozen pissed off drunken mountain morons lined up trying to get chips and junk food and cigarettes. I finally got a second to go look for her and there she was standing outside the back door smoking a cigarette and smooching it up with her stupid cop boyfriend. The guy hangs around here all the time — and she's married too! Our tax dollars at work, right? Please, please, please move up here with me. I'm scared, Jody. I don't understand what's going on. I know it sounds crazy. Maybe you could switch classes to Tuesdays and Thursdays only. I'm so nervous. Heather."

Mayo re-read the email. *I saw him again yesterday.* If someone had been following her, why didn't she tell Mayo about it? And why didn't Jody mention it?

The more Mayo learned, the less she understood.

She turned on a small desktop printer and printed each of the emails, then, brooding over the comment about the "stupid cop boyfriend," a likely reference to McKern, she shut down the computer and got it ready for a trip to the computer forensics lab down in Boulder.

"Anything good?" Gumble said when she returned to the living room. He was lifting prints from the front door knob.

"Heather was here as late as 6:12 this morning," Mayo said, "and she's got big spending habits and a very uneven source of income." Resisting the urge to dump on Gumble about McKern's shenanigans with Patty, she dropped onto the sofa. She felt another rush of pessimism. She didn't like the case, didn't like being in Heather's dismal house. She wanted to go back to coasting through her days and licking her wounds. She wasn't finished with that, didn't feel like getting on the ball again.

She leaned forward and looked over the two tubs on the table. She opened a folder from on top of the pile in the first tub. Written in heavy magic marker on the front was the title: "The Search for Alonzo Holloway's Grave, a book by Heather Holloway."

The folder contained scribbled notes — "Search for AH grave: We lost without ancestor." "Search for AH — thoughts about him lying in unmarked hole in ground... present at important historical events — can't let him stay like that." "Search for AH grave — Maybe was in Aspen for a period."

Aside from these few odd notes, there was no sign of an actual manuscript or even an outline for a book. There'd been nothing on the laptop either.

If there was no book to promote, Mayo pondered, that probably wasn't the reason Heather came up with the Zippy's drama.

Assuming of course that it really was just a drama. Mayo needed to review the case file again — for her own satisfaction. And hunt down Heather's prior "assaults."

She picked up a photo album and paged through numerous shots of busy street scenes.

"Looks like she wandered around the 16th Street Mall in Denver taking pictures of people," she said.

"Hmm," Gumble responded, still busy dusting the door. "Doesn't sound entirely normal."

"Not entirely," Mayo murmured. "And not entirely surprising." One particular man in a dark vest and a winter cap appeared in several of the pictures. In the street scene, he was looking sideways, nose-to-nose with a woman in sunglasses and a hoodie. She had her hands laced together on his shoulder, her chin resting on her hands. She wore a lot of large bracelets and rings. It didn't look like Heather but it was hard to tell. There were other pictures of him in other locations — several in what looked like a university setting with lawns and brick buildings behind him. In all the pictures, he seemed unaware that he was being photographed.

"See any one-eyed Indians?" Gumble asked.

"Nope." She closed the album. She'd go over it again later.

"So what about this mysterious source of income?" Gumble asked. "Drug dealing? Theft? Blackmail?"

"A couple things point at gambling. If it's theft, she probably would have cleaned out the cash register and safe and Zippy's and blamed her attacker."

"She in the business maybe? She's got some interesting equipment there."

"Maybe, but she didn't strike me as the type. She's a regular at Black Hawk and writes emails to someone called 'fivecardstud.' Talks about 'playing.'"

"Sounds like gambling," Gumble said. "Oh, well."

Mayo pawed through the tub. It held dozens of unopened packages of mascara, eye-liner, lipstick, and other types of make-up. Along with the sex toys.

"That stuff makes me feel very innocent and pure," Gumble said, glancing at a lumpy purple dildo Mayo was holding up.

"You *are* innocent and pure. Why do I get the feeling that Heather didn't actually use this stuff?" She found a re-charging pedestal that fit the purple dildo.

"You're going to get some disease," Gumble murmured.

"Nah. Looks awfully fresh and clean."

Gumble stopped working and watched while Mayo sniffed the thing.

"Oh, man," he said, "you *smelled* it."

"It's never been used."

Mayo pictured Heather's sorry little expeditions through the Discreet Fantasies website, typing in her credit card number and her address, later opening the neatly disguised boxes when they arrived, examining the secret treasures. Then dropping them into the plastic tub.

"Maybe she put them in the dishwasher or something," Gumble suggested.

Mayo put the sex toys into an evidence bag and went on to the second tub. A smaller photo album, pink and decorated with red butterflies, contained several pictures of Heather a bit younger — perhaps college or high school. She wore an expensive-looking bobbed haircut, dyed a very dark black, which gave her a goth look. Another picture showed her with a group of people out in a field, apparently searching for something. Squinting into the camera, Heather looked hot and uncomfortable. Another showed Heather and Jody sitting together in a Japanese restaurant, saluting the camera with small cups of sake.

Mayo flipped through the remaining blank pages. "Not too many personal shots."

She put the photo album aside, still fighting a growing sense of gloom. The Heather Holloway story felt like something worse than a simple homicide case. Heather came off like an unstable, mistreated dog — possessing enough intelligence to bite those around her but not enough to save herself. Even the collection of snapshots that recorded happier days seemed scanty and pitiable. Her smile in the pictures looked phony, joyless.

Mayo had dealt with enough killings in her Denver days — particularly during a two-year stint in a newly-formed hate crimes unit. Once upon a time, she knew how to co-exist with murder and its aftermath, to keep herself separate from it. But now she couldn't shake the urge to drop this junk back into the tub and scramble out of the toxic little house and forget about the whole thing.

She got up and went into the kitchen. Pouring herself a glass of water, she drank it at the sink. She focused on the refreshing mountain water, felt its cool journey down her throat. She was fine, absolutely fine.

After a few minutes, she returned to the sofa and continued digging through the bins. Underneath the photo album was a padded 11 x 14 envelope labelled "BA Thesis," which contained a velo-bound document of about 100 pages, written by Heather Holloway, entitled "Sand Creek: Who Was Really to Blame?"

She opened the document, read Heather's brief introduction:

"The Sand Creek Massacre occurred in 1864 southeastern Colorado. Today, many historians take a black and white view of that event, putting all the blame on the white man. They say the white man attacked, scalped, and mutilated the peaceful Cheyenne and Arapaho who were camped at Sand Creek. However, Alonzo Holloway's eye witness account reveals that the Indians at Sand Creek were not as innocent as they claimed. This is the story of my great grandfather, Alonzo Holloway, a cavalry soldier in the Colorado Third—one of the 'hundred days men.' He fought under the heroic commander John Chivington at Sand Creek and was horribly wounded by the notorious Chief Lone Bear of the Cheyenne. He left behind a diary that tells the true, untold story of that battle."

"What do you know about the Sand Creek Massacre?" Mayo asked Gumble. He was putting away his fingerprint kit.

"Ah, not a whole lot. Women and children were slaughtered by the U.S. cavalry after they surrendered. The leader, a man named Chivington, was looking for easy glory—wanted to be senator or something like that. Not the most commendable moment in Colorado history. What you got there?"

"Heather's college thesis, along the lines of 'Bad Savage Indians, Good White Man' at the Sand Creek Massacre."

"That should piss some people off." He snapped his fingerprint case closed and joined Mayo on the sofa. "Can't imagine someone getting murdered over a college thesis though. What's that?"

Mayo held up a sealed letter-sized envelope in front of the lamp. Through the paper showed the outline of a key.

Seven

After attending Heather's early-morning autopsy, Mayo arrived at the station a few minutes late for a meeting with Gumble and McKern. The department's part-time volunteer receptionist, Emlyn, put her knitting needles down to shake Mayo's hand.

"Good morning Marshal. I thought I better come in today, considering everything."

Mayo still felt queasy after watching the closed-circuit television screens while the ME opened up Heather's chest, chanting streams of medical jargon in a low, bland voice.

"Thanks, Emlyn," she said. "We appreciate it."

"I hope you're going to catch this guy!" Emlyn went on, lapsing into an anxious whisper. She fingered her necklace, a hand-made construction of painted mother-of-pearl discs. "It's hard to believe this happened in Sugarloaf!"

"Don't fret," Mayo said in a confident tone that she knew would appease her. "We'll find out who did it."

Emlyn played the role of mother-hen in the office—both to Mayo and the others, bringing in snacks and fussing over "my officers." A retired gymnastics coach, she was a slim woman with short hennaed hair and delicately pale skin that revealed blood vessels at her temples. She created a somewhat unprofessional atmosphere in the station, with balls of yarn rolling across the floor, and her cookies and cakes and chatter, but Mayo liked having her around. Plus, she answered the phone.

"I made fresh scones," Emlyn said, picking up her knitting. "And I can come in every day if you need me, for the time being." As she spoke, the phone began ringing. Emlyn rolled her eyes. "Absolutely everyone in town is calling this morning," she said, reaching for the phone. "People want to know what's going on."

"Tell them it's still an ongoing investigation," Mayo said, heading past her into the office area. "Don't say any more than that."

Emlyn picked up a pen and jotted "ongoing investigation" on her notepad. The department had no money for a paid receptionist, and Emlyn insisted her reward was "being useful," but Mayo made a note to herself to at least take her out to dinner.

The three deputies were in front of their computers, sipping coffee and munching Emlyn's scones. The office felt crowded with everyone there at once. Gumble pulled off a pair of headphones—the plastic cassette container for the Holloway interview sat on the desk in front of him.

Mayo shook their hands. "Deputy Nutt," she said. "You're going to be mostly holding down the fort while the rest of us are working this case. Think you can handle that?"

He nodded sharply, with his fresh-out-of-the-academy enthusiasm. "Yes, ma'am. Here are my notes from the traffic stop." He handed over a folder neatly labelled, "Wolftongue Homicide Traffic Stop." "There's a list of license plates, make and model, and names."

"Good work," Mayo said, scanning the list. Nothing jumped out at her. No black SUVs.

"Just let me know how I can help," Nutt said.

Mayo gave him an approving nod. He provided a refreshing contrast to McKern's bumbling, second-guessing, and endless fussing. She wondered if she ought to bring Nutt in on the case and let McKern tread water in the office. A possibility to keep open anyway.

She beckoned McKern and Gumble into the conference room and closed the door. At the whiteboard, she picked up a marker. "I hope you realize we're all going to be working long hours."

She turned to the whiteboard and began to jot notes as she spoke.

"Just came from the autopsy," she said. "Heather died from internal bleeding caused by a puncture wound to her abdomen that nearly went out the back side. It nicked the spinal cord."

She glanced at her deputies. McKern looked pale but Gumble seemed calm and attentive.

"Have either of you worked a homicide before?" she asked.

McKern shook his head, but Gumble put up his hand. "A few."

"Good to know," Mayo said. "Okay. The killer was facing her, probably standing fairly close and was at least a few inches taller. Someone strong, but not necessarily male."

"How about the bayonet from our dirt hole?" Gumble asked.

"ME says it was probably the murder weapon," Mayo said.

"I'll ask around and see if any locals own antique bayonets," Gumble said. "And I can check memorabilia sellers. Just about everyone I know has a Bowie knife though."

Mayo tapped her marker on the board thoughtfully. "Our bad guy might have come up beforehand to dig that hole. It's been a dry summer—the dirt was like concrete. I'm guessing it took a lot of effort to dig, not something you'd want to do in a hurry while there's a body lying around."

Gumble spread out the pictures he had taken on the table and looked them over. "Why would they bury it there anyway? Seems stupid."

Mayo scrutinized the pictures. "Maybe they didn't want to risk getting blood or other trace evidence in their vehicle. Or, maybe they wanted us to find it. It could fit in with an attempt to point blame at an American Indian killer."

"Or maybe it *was* an Indian guy and he buried the stuff in some kind of old-time ceremony," McKern said.

"The wound to Heather's scalp was post-mortem," she went on. "The ME confirmed that the bit of scalp was from Heather's head." She checked her notes. "Based on rigor and livor mortis, time of death was probably between 6:30 and 8:00 a.m. No sign of sexual assault. No defensive injuries and nothing under her fingernails."

"So there's a decent chance she knew her killer," Gumble said.

Mayo nodded. "I'd say so. Whoever wrote the note knew about her interest in finding Alonzo Holloway's grave." She handed a copy of the note to McKern. "I left the original at the lab, but I'm not holding my breath that we'll get anything useful from it. Fingerprints are hard to get off paper and the printing was very plain."

She pulled the police artist's sketch of Heather's Zippy's assailant from a folder and handed it to Gumble. "Okay, we need to post this around town since the paper won't come out again 'til next week. Front Range Bulletin doesn't have a website, do they?"

"Nope," said McKern. "Brin keeps saying she's going to build one but they never do."

"Anyway," Mayo said, "the sketch is bound to create an ugly smell and I have doubts that this guy is involved or if he even exists, but we still have to follow up."

McKern gaped at her. "I just don't get how you can write this off! It's our best clue!"

"I hope we're not going to have this discussion again, McKern," Mayo said. "Did you listen to the interview? You're the one who dug up her crazy history, remember?"

"What about the lab results?" Gumble asked quietly. "The rape kit?"

"That could take weeks," Mayo said.

"You're makin' it too complicated," McKern said. "We've got a dang picture of the killer!"

Mayo turned back to the white board and wrote "Notices — SUV."

"We need to put notices around town asking if anyone has seen an unfamiliar black SUV around lately. And we've got tire tracks."

"Pictures here." Gumble pawed through his stack of photographs and pulled out shots of the tracks that Troy had identified. "Troy said he'd call when he figures out what kind of tire they were."

"Let's each get a clear printout of these," Mayo said. "Check tires around town for a match but don't be obvious about it."

She skimmed over her latest notes, which she had jotted down when she woke up at 3:15 a.m. and couldn't get back to sleep. "With luck, they might find foreign fibers on Heather's clothing." She jotted a few more notes on the board.

"What about the diary?" Gumble put in.

"Yeah," said McKern. "Isn't that all about some big Indian battle? More Indian stuff."

Mayo wrote "Diary as motive?" on the board, but left out any note about an "Indian stuff," mostly just to piss off McKern. She would bet money there was no crazed one-eyed Indian wandering the county. Heather Holloway might be a murder victim, but that didn't mean she wasn't a damn liar.

"No sign of the diary at Heather's house," she said. "If we're really lucky, the key we found opens a safe deposit box somewhere. McKern, you need to run Heather's computer down to the computer forensics guy in Boulder. Do you need the address?"

"I know where it is," McKern said.

She sighed, looking over the board. "We've also got a photo album with shots of street scenes and one particular guy that shows up several times. We need to find out who he is." She wrote "guy in photo album" on the board.

She tapped her toe on the floor, thinking. "We've got a couple reports of Heather supposedly being followed, and some stories that she was being stalked by an ex-boyfriend, which her sister denies. We have a witness who saw a dark SUV in front of Zippy's, which may or may not be the one the boys saw at the spring. The sister reported a truck at the supermarket in Boulder. The truck had a white guy to go with it—Indiana Jones hat. Plus we've got Deputy Nutt's list of license plates from the checkpoints."

"Too many little things," Gumble observed.

"We get to figure out which bits are just noise and which aren't. So who else in town knew Heather?" she asked. "We need to talk to her neighbors."

"Patty says she's only lived here for a few weeks," McKern said. "And she told Patty she didn't like any of her neighbors."

Sounds about right, Mayo thought. She wrote "Neighbors" and "Heather's history" on the board.

"I'm thinking our best bet is to hunt down the folks from Heather's two prior assault accusations in Denver," she said. "Have a friendly chat, try to find out if they were in the area, sneak a look at their tires."

"That's what I was thinking," Gumble said.

"I'm guessing this was brewing long before Heather came to our little town," she went on. "She accused her previous boss at the museum of sex assault and there was another incident in college. Both cases dropped.

"We got a good tip this morning," Gumble said. "Detective Gonzales from Denver called—"

"Hey, that's my tip," McKern objected. "I'm the one who talked to him in the first place."

"Sure, McKern," Gumble went on. "Anyhow, Gonzales read in the paper about what happened and he remembered something. It turns out someone was keeping track of our girl. They sent an unsigned letter to Gonzales when he was investigating the museum incident telling him to check into the college thing. Gonzales is sending over a copy."

"Good stuff," Mayo said. "It would make me very happy if we could find out who wrote that letter."

"We should also check the Charlie Holloway angle," Gumble said. "Everybody in town hated him. Maybe someone hated him more than usual."

Mayo wrote "local grudges" on the board.

"We've also got two email IDs to identify." Mayo wrote, "FiveCardStud" and "MudPuppie" on the board. "Either of you recognize those names?"

The deputies shook their heads.

"Okay," she said. "Let's divvie up the chores."

They went through the list again and Mayo assigned tasks. "Make sure you both listen to the entire interview tape with Heather," she said. "When you're done, if you still think she was really attacked at Zippy's, let's talk about it."

Gumble and McKern nodded.

"Today if you can," she said.

As the others headed out, Mayo went back to her desk and dialed the Colorado Frontier Museum, where Heather had made accusations against a Dr. Felix Arkenstone, the museum curator. As the phone rang at the other end of the line, the front door of the office opened and an elderly woman struggled to get in, her walker clanking against the glass door. Emlyn jumped up to hold the door for Mrs. Poe, a pale, wizened busy-body with curly grey hair and a perpetually sour face.

"What on earth is going on?" Mrs. Poe demanded. "I want to talk to the marshal!"

Mayo scooted back in her chair so she was hidden from Mrs. Poe's view. On the phone, a woman answered.

"May I speak to Felix Arkenstone?" Mayo said.

"Dr. Arkenstone and his assistant are out of town," the woman said. "Can I help you?"

Mayo explained who she was and asked when Arkenstone would be returning. Up front, Mrs. Poe was haranguing poor Emlyn. "They're saying they killed that young woman from Zippy's!"

"They'll be back tomorrow," the woman on the phone said.

"Who are these crazy people?" Mrs. Poe wailed. "Has the marshal caught them?"

"When did they leave?" Mayo asked, keeping her voice low.

"Saturday morning," the woman answered. The morning of Heather's death.

As Mayo hung up, Mrs. Poe clattered her way past Emlyn and thumped toward Mayo's desk. Emlyn fluttered behind her, mouthing apologies at Mayo.

"There you are, marshal." Mrs. Poe stationed herself in front of Mayo's desk. A wayward bobby pin dangled from one of her curls. Her humorless, rheumy eyes were clamped on Mayo. "I'm very concerned and no one seems to know what's going on."

Mayo got up and walked around her desk. Mrs. Poe was about a foot shorter than she.

Mayo touched her arm reassuringly. "We're working on the case, Mrs. Poe. As soon as we can, we'll release more details about it."

She'd heard about a run-in Davy Brown had with the old woman when he was marshal. Mrs. Poe's next door neighbors reported that she had hobbled up to their front window and peered into their living room. She knocked on the glass, insisting they come outside and listen to her complaints about the weeds in their lawn. The neighbors had called because she wouldn't leave, so Davy arrived and escorted her home, during which he received a lengthy lecture about deadly toxins the government secretly stored in weeds.

"It's probably gangs from Denver." Mrs. Poe shifted her walker so it rubbed against Mayo's leg. "Are we all going to have to just stay home from now on?"

Mayo nodded at Deputy Nutt who jumped up from his desk and began escorting Mrs. Poe toward the front.

"If you're really worried," Mayo said, "that might be a good idea — staying home — for the next few days."

The old woman seemed to be formulating another question, but stopped when the front door opened again. Mayo looked up to see what had succeeded in interrupting Mrs. Poe's remarks. It was Brin Beedle, barging up to the front counter.

"Good bye, Mrs. Poe!" Mayo said cheerfully.

"Hello, Marshal!" Brin waved at Mayo, ignoring Emlyn. Brin and Emlyn were somehow related and did not get along.

"You can't go back there!" Emlyn barked. According to Davy, Emlyn had long been a pro at keeping the young reporter out of the marshal's hair. In fact, he had suggested that the pleasure of doing so was Emlyn's real reason for volunteering.

"It's all right," Mayo called to Emlyn. "C'mon back, Brin."

Emlyn lifted her hands in an "Are you crazy?" motion at Mayo.

Brin made an unfriendly hand gesture in Emlyn's direction as she moved stiffly past the reception counter and into the back area.

Mayo winked at Emlyn and mouthed, "Thank you."

"Why do you let that old witch run your office like that?" Brin demanded. "It's bad for public relations."

Deputy Nutt returned to his desk after seeing Mrs. Poe to the door. He watched with interest for a moment, then turned back to his computer and looked absorbed in his reading.

"Have a seat, Brin," Mayo said. "I've been wanting to talk to you." Brin did not live in Sugarloaf so Mayo didn't feel obliged to shake her hand.

"I'll bet you have." Brin sat down across the desk from Mayo and pulled out a notepad and a pen. She was loud, skinny and long-armed and her eyes were too big. She reminded Mayo of a spider monkey. "So..." Brin flashed a malignant smile. "We've got us a little murder, haven't we?"

"No need to shout," Mayo said pleasantly. She hadn't had any contact with her since she'd become marshal, and their prior social encounters had been brief. Davy liked to say that Brin Beedle was probably the only person in the area who actually had enemies. In particular, Sigi Zimmerman's gas-siphoning incident had earned Brin the ire of Analiese Zimmerman, when Brin ignored laws about publishing the names of juvenile offenders in the paper.

"Who's shouting?" Brin looked up at Deputy Nutt with an innocent expression. "Was I shouting? So, tell me, marshal. Was she really bayonetted and scalped?"

Mayo sensed a reaction from Emlyn. "Where'd you hear that?"

"It's a small town. You can't keep a lid on something like this. I mean, first you ignore her story about being attacked and raped and then she's apparently killed by the same guy."

Mayo smiled. She enjoyed tangling with people like Brin. It was liberating to toss away any concern about wounding the other's feelings. "You know, Brin, people sometimes injure themselves when they jump so far to a conclusion."

"Oh, gosh, I'm such a jerk." Brin smiled broadly. "Excuse me while I just vanish from the universe."

"Fact is, Brin, I do want to talk to you about this."

"Well, good. So explain this: A lot of people are wondering why the Sugarloaf Marshal's Office dropped a rape case and then let the victim get murdered."

"Why don't you just shut up, Brin?" Emlyn said from across the office. "You have always been such a little—"

Mayo lifted up a hand, gesturing at Emlyn to back off. "It's all right, Emlyn. Brin is just doing her job." She felt a small glow of appreciation for Emlyn's protectiveness.

She waited for Emlyn to turn away. "Put your fangs away, Brin," she said. "I want to work with you on this one." She pushed a copy of the police sketch across the desk at Brin, who stared at it with obvious relish.

"So this is the attacker?" Brin said. "He looks Native American."

"Your next issue doesn't come out 'til next Saturday, does it?"

"No—"

Mayo kept her voice pleasant. "Too bad. You're probably not going to be of much help then. Still, hopefully you'll be able to print the latest details this time. We need to do one of those 'Has anyone seen this man' deals. We're also asking if anyone saw a black SUV or other vehicle on the Wolftongue Road or saw anything strange Saturday morning before 10 o'clock. I hope you're going to be a help on this case, Brin. We really need you. You sure you can't put out an in-between issue?" Mayo gave her a luscious smile.

Brin returned the smile with something a little less fetching. "I'd still like to hear your explanation about dropping the case."

"The investigation revealed there was nothing to pursue."

"Did you actually do an investigation?"

"Listen, Brin. The case is complicated and will make great copy when it's all sorted out. If you play your cards right, you could get a byline in the Boulder and Denver papers. There's enough good stuff beneath the surface of this, you could even end up with a series...or hell, even a book. In light of this, I would not advise you to fire off some half-baked story and then have to retract it later. I'm telling you this as a huge favor."

Mayo and Brin locked gazes and Mayo prayed to the cosmos that Brin would be blinded by the glittering possibilities, at least for the moment.

"I catch your drift," Brin said finally. "I just don't particularly believe it."

Mayo flattened her hands on the desk. "Look—the obvious conclusion at this point is to say that the Marshal's Office simply screwed up and poor Heather was attacked a second time by the same man and that's all there is to it. I'll resign and go back to my life of hiking with no complaint. But I'm telling you, that's not what happened. There is a lot more to this story. A helluva lot more."

Mayo saw signs of softening on Brin's face. The reporter tapped on the police sketch with a fiery red fingernail. "So if you don't think it's this guy, then why do you want to publish his picture?"

"Because we have to follow up every lead. He's not a suspect at this time but he may be a person of interest."

Brin picked up the picture. "The racist morons are gonna come out of the woodwork on this you know."

Mayo sat back in her chair. She had won—at least for now. "Brin, your sensitive side is showing."

Brin twisted her mouth. "I'm not sensitive, but I'm not blind either."

It was another beautiful autumn day—the sky a pastel blue dotted with a few bright cumulus clouds, the sun blazing at high noon. Walking across Sugarloaf Road to Zippy's, Mayo thought wistfully of the greyhounds back at the house. A late afternoon hike through fall colors would be divine.

Around back, Patty's Subaru was parked near the Dumpster, and alongside it was a dented Toyota Tacoma truck whose bottom half looked as though it had been dipped in mud.

In her briefcase, Mayo had Gumble's pictures of the tire tracks from the scene. She knelt at Patty's Subaru. The picture showed a diagonal tread—parallel slashes with a slight curve. Patty's tires had acutely curved lines—not even close. The Tacoma sported oversized off-roading tires with a zig-zag tread, and she ruled it out as well.

Inside Zippy's, a teenaged boy in a Rockies cap stood behind the counter. He was tall, with a friendly face and a smattering of whiskers.

"Oh my God!" Patty lurched out of nowhere and Mayo found herself in a bear hug. Under the fluorescent lights, Patty's eye makeup looked ghoulishly heavy and smudged. She pulled out a tissue and smeared it some more. "It's really true, isn't it?"

"Sorry I couldn't let you know personally," Mayo said. "It's been hectic. You all right?"

Sniffling loudly, Patty nodded. "I'm just in shock, that's all."

Mayo turned to the boy and held out a hand. "Hello. I'm Marshal Mayo. I've seen you around but we've never properly met."

"That's Danny," Patty said.

He shook Mayo's hand, made brief eye contact, then leaned back against the counter and folded his arms. He seemed more uncomfortable than he should be.

Patty blew her nose. "We really can't believe she's actually dead, can we, Danny? Roger—Deputy McKern—came by last night and told us the real story. There were some terrible rumors going around, that she got her head blown off, or it was chopped off."

"What did Officer McKern tell you?" Mayo asked, wrestling with yet another wave of ire toward her deputy. She'd have to drill some procedures into his head. If he couldn't cope, she'd throw him out. But firing someone in the middle of a murder investigation was a stupid idea. For now, she was stuck with the guy.

"He said she was stabbed." Patty groped behind the counter for another tissue. "I still—I mean, I've never known anyone who got murdered before, much less someone working for me. It must have been the same guy who attacked her here in the store! I never really understood why you dropped that whole thing. What happened anyway? What the hell is going on?"

Mayo paused while Patty blew her nose again. "Take it easy, Patty," she said presently. "It's too early to say anything yet. I was wondering, did Heather come back to work after the incident the other day?"

Patty's eyes grew large. "No. She said she was too upset."

"I guess you two had to fill in for her, then? Who opened up Saturday?"

"Me," said Patty. "Danny came in around nine."

Mayo switched her gaze over to the boy. He was clutching his stomach with thick arms. She kept her voice light and friendly. "That your Tacoma outside, Danny?"

He jerked his head yes, unfolded and refolded his arms.

She smiled. "Big off-roading fan, eh?"

His face brightened and he seemed to relax a bit. "Uh-huh."

"Your truck looks like you've been doing some mud-bogging. I never tried that but I heard it's a blast."

He smiled. "Yeah. There's some awesome spots up by Hessie."

Patty nudged him, her round face still anxious and tear-streaked. "Danny and Heather worked together a couple days the past week. You guys got along all right, didn't you?"

He made an unpleasant face. "She was okay."

"You don't sound too thrilled," Mayo said. "Any problems with her?"

He shrugged. "No."

"You all use email?" Mayo asked.

Patty looked puzzled "Email? Sure. Everyone does. Why?"

Mayo switched her gaze between the two. "Either of you ever send Heather any emails?"

Patty shrugged. "Never had any reason to."

Mayo leveled a gaze at Danny. "How about you?"

He reorganized his arms again. He had the round, hard biceps of someone who lifted weights. "I don't think so."

Mayo cocked her head, keeping her voice chatty. "Emails about saying your mother's name or your true love's name? Just playful stuff like that?"

Danny glanced uneasily at Patty then looked down at his sneakers.

"That sounds pretty weird," Patty said. "What kind of email is that?"

"Just messing around kind of thing." Mayo pulled out her notebook. "What's your email address, Danny?"

He grabbed the back of his neck and kneaded.

"What is it, Danny?" Patty said. "You better tell the marshal if you know something."

He let go of his neck and banged the counter with his fist, jostling the heat lamp and Dulce's burritos. "She was comin' on to me pretty much from the second she walked in here. That first day she went home for lunch and brought back some kinky stuff. I never asked to see it, she just showed up with it. And then when I wanted to kiss her she pushed me away and got all upset. She's a complete nutjob! Plus I saw her steal some make-up."

Patty stared at her young employee. "What do you mean you saw her steal some make-up?"

Danny shrugged. "It looked like it to me anyway."

Mayo kept her voice low and pleasant. Her prodding had produced more than she expected. "Is your email ID 'MudPuppie,' Danny?"

He hung his head. "Yeah, but I send those out all the time, like jokes and stuff. I didn't mean anything by it. I didn't do anything wrong. Didn't kill her, for sure!"

"Take it easy," Mayo said. "Nobody thinks you killed anyone. I didn't read much into the emails. I just wanted to know who sent them."

"I was just kidding around," he said, glancing anxiously at Patty. "She was comin' on to me."

Mayo felt a fresh stir of dislike for the late Heather Holloway. "How old are you, Danny?"

"Sixteen."

"All right. So Heather was flirting with you?"

"Yeah. She's crazy. She came up out of nowhere and kissed me. I don't even know how old she is. She had this stuff ... sexy stuff."

Mayo pictured Heather showing Danny the purple dildo, the strawberry g-string.

"Sounds like Heather may have been messing with you a bit, Danny, " she said. "Not such a good thing for her to do."

"Geez," Patty said. "What the hell?"

Danny's eyes looked wet and shiny. "You're not gonna tell people, are you?"

Mayo turned to go. "Tell people what?"

Eight

Mayo rarely went back down to Denver, and she felt unsettled as she wound her way through downtown and headed southeast toward Colorado Western University. She and Glen had lived in the Cheesman Park neighborhood in the home she inherited from her grandmother—a cool, airy Victorian with creaking wooden floors. They had spent many weekends updating the old place, painting walls, renovating the bathroom and kitchen, refinishing the floors. Monte had often come down to help out, and had convinced them they also needed vessel sinks like his. They hadn't gotten around to it yet.

Since abandoning the house, Mayo had received offers from several eager buyers, but she could not bring herself to sell it. For now, she hurried through the area, driving quickly past their street without a glance.

She headed to Colorado Western University, where it took her another fifteen minutes to park and find the right building, the right hallway and the right room.

Carl Mason, Dean of Arts and Sciences, answered her knock. Standing in the doorway, Mayo held up her badge and introduced herself. In his mid-fifties with watery, red-rimmed eyes and pocked bloat of a steady drinker, he shook her hand with a crushing grip.

She hadn't warned him she was coming but had called the administrative offices first to get his schedule. Judging from his lack of surprise, the secretary must have told him that someone from law enforcement had contacted them.

"Have a seat, ma'am." He pointed to a wooden chair. "Is that the wrong thing to call you? You like 'marshal' better?"

The question was too annoying to answer, so she made a production out of observing his office while she sat. The room was large but its clutter and the man's bulk made it feel cramped. A single window overlooked a patch of lawn outside.

"What can I do for you?" Mason's chair groaned as he sat back and made a steeple out of his fingers, stationing it over his mouth.

"I'm here to ask about a former student in your history department, Heather Holloway."

Mason's eyes narrowed. "What about her?"

Mayo watched him carefully. "She's been killed."

Slowly, without disturbing the steeple too much, he massaged his lower lip with a thumb. "Is that so," he said finally. "What happened?"

"She was murdered."

The steeple fell apart and his palms went down to the desk. He began to rise, but stopped himself.

"What is this?" he said.

"What is what, Mr. Mason?"

"Is this some kind of—I don't know. Some kind of petty crap? Another manipulative little scam? Who are you really? Did she send you here?"

"Hmm, now why would she do that?"

"Let me see that badge again."

Mayo was not wearing a uniform, but she had her badge clipped to her belt. She unclipped it and slapped it onto the desk.

He glared at it, checking the other side, then tossed it back onto the desk and stood. "Is this real? How the hell am I supposed to know? It looks like something you could buy online." He marched around the desk and loomed over her. "Who the hell are you? Who the hell calls herself a marshal?"

"Relax." Mayo gave him a sideways glance. "Call my office. Sugarloaf Marshal's Office. Don't take my word for it."

"I am going to call. My assistant will call."

He left the office. While she waited, Mayo rubbed the marshal's badge on her sleeve and clipped it to her belt again. He returned presently and sat down again at his desk. He positioned the steeple over his mouth again.

"Can't be too careful," he said. "She was a student here, of course. Are you sure it was Heather Holloway, from our school?"

"I gather you knew Heather. Rather well, I'm guessing."

Mason twisted his mouth, gazing at her with tight eyebrows. "You gathered wrong. I've heard stories, that's all. Bad stories."

"What bad stories?"

"Nothing specific. General warnings to keep a distance. Fake accusations sort of baloney. Can't even blink at a woman these days without some sort of ensuing drama. What does any of this have to do with me? Rounding up the usual male suspects?"

"What did you mean by 'another manipulative little scam?'"

"I didn't say that."

"You did say it, and it made me think right away that maybe Heather had worked on you personally with a 'manipulative little scam.'"

"You thought wrong. I'd been warned—I don't know how many goddamn times—'Watch out for that little manipulator.' It was all over campus. I just figured maybe it was my turn."

"Dr. Mason, for a short period last summer, Heather worked as an intern at Colorado Frontier Museum. She accused her boss of assaulting her—"

"See? What'd I tell you?"

"Someone sent this note to the investigating officer." She pulled out a copy of the note Detective Gonzales of the Denver P.D. had sent over and put it in front of him on the desk.

He rubbed his nose sullenly, then put on a pair of glasses and picked up the paper.

In plain type, it read: *Heather Holloway is a liar. Don't believe anything she tells you. Check into her college career of lying and ruining an innocent man. Colorado Western University. History dept., last spring.*

"There, you see? Bad news. That's what people said about her."

"Did you send this note?"

"No, I did not send a note. I know about rumors, that's it. You haven't answered my question. Why are you talking to me about it?"

"You sure you didn't send the note?"

"Why do I always have to say things twice around here? No, I did not send the note. I am not surprised that someone did, given the rumors. It was probably Dr. Hull."

"Who is Dr. Hull?"

He smiled. "Oh, you don't know about him. I see. The thing is, I'm not sure if I can discuss it with you. There are privacy laws—"

"I'm a police officer investigating a homicide, Dr. Mason."

He stood abruptly, picking up a large coffee mug from the desk. "I need coffee if this is going to take all day to explain. If you want some, you can come along."

Mayo followed him down the hallway into a coffee room lined with vending machines. She assumed he was buying time to dream up his story. He clearly had a lot more involvement with Heather than just "rumors."

Turning his back to her, he filled his mug and a Styrofoam cup from a pot of murky-looking coffee.

"Creams are in there." He pointed. "Sugar, fake sugar."

Mayo added two creams and two sugars to the coffee he handed her but still found it undrinkable. As they left the break room, a short, husky blonde woman appeared in the hall.

"Dr. Mason," she said. "There you are. Do you have a minute?"

Mason's lip twitched. "I'm in the middle of something. Can it wait?"

The woman stepped in his path as he tried to walk away. "We've got to go over those Cherokee Trail project numbers—"

"I can't right now, Kate."

Kate switched her gaze to Mayo and gave her a frank inspection, her eyes coming to rest on Mayo's badge.

Mayo stepped past Mason and shook the woman's hand. "Hello. I'm Marshal Mayo. I'm here looking for information about a former student here, Heather Holloway."

She was facing away from Mason, but sensed movement behind her. She turned in time to see the tail end of his gesture. He was telling Kate to vanish.

Kate was young, maybe in her late twenties, with light-colored frizzy hair, pale skin and small blue eyes, which were still fixed on Mayo.

"Dr. Kate Russell," she said. "Why are you asking about Heather Holloway?"

"I'm afraid Heather has been killed," Mason said impatiently. "Shall we head back to the office, Marshal?"

"Seriously?" Dr. Russell said. "What happened?" She didn't sound upset.

Mason checked his watch. "I've got to leave in a few minutes so we'll need to hurry up." He pointed back down the hall toward his office.

Mayo pulled a card from her pocket and handed it to Kate Russell with a pen. "I'd like to talk to you. Can you write down your number?"

"That woman is chummy with Dr. Hull," Mason said when they were back in his office. He checked the hallway before closing the door. "Just so you know, she's not going to be a very reliable source, if you catch my drift."

Mayo brought out a notepad and jotted some notes. "Which drift is that?"

"Kate and some of the other faculty were upset when Toby Hull left. She started up a petition to keep him, roused the rabble, that sort of thing."

"Toby Hull is the professor that Heather accused?"

"Yes."

"Where is he now?"

Dr. Mason gazed at her as though trying to gauge something. "He was not invited back this semester and I don't know why it would be my job to keep track of his whereabouts. Apparently he wandered off without notifying his family, which doesn't surprise me. A while back his father showed up here looking for him and slinging accusations."

"What accusations?"

"Again, as though I'm responsible for monitoring Hull's movements. The fellow insisted I knew something. I practically had to call security to escort the screeching ape out of here."

Mayo's interest grew. "I see. Have you heard anything since?"

Dr. Mason slurped at his coffee mug. "Not a word. Why would we? We fired him. Once again, why the hell would we keep track of the man?"

"So let's see if I have this straight. You fired the guy even though his accuser had a reputation for scamming?"

He glowered. "It was beyond my control. Like I said, you can't even blink around a woman these days. These college girls know how to operate."

"All right. Let's back up a little bit, please. Tell me about Heather."

He narrowed his eyes at her. "All right." He swung to his computer, tapped in some information, then squinted over his glasses at the screen. "Uneven student. Attendance issues, and the rumors of course, but she squeaked out A's and B's. Fact is, she produced some very good work on her great grandfather. Caused a stir. Got some of the political types worked up. She had discovered an important document—the great grandfather's diary." He glanced up. "Historically significant. Alonzo Holloway, I believe was the diarist. Heather was a clever girl, leveraged it to her advantage, wrote a paper—I said that already. It won her the internship at the museum."

"And what exactly happened with Hull?"

He swiveled away from his computer screen and grinned. "As I said, I don't know that I'm at liberty to say. There are privacy concerns. The matter was personnel."

To her surprise, he yanked open a desk drawer, pulled out an old-fashioned silver flask and enhanced his coffee with something that smelled like whiskey.

She waited while he drank.

"You all right?" she asked.

He drank some more and added another dash from the flask.

"Sometimes you reach a point," he said.

"What point would that be?"

He gestured at his flask then tucked it back into the drawer. "Medicine. Doctor's orders even. Believe it or not, as you wish."

"I don't believe or disbelieve anything at this point."

"I haven't done anything. You can believe that."

"I'm just here gathering information, Dr. Mason. I have the impression you aren't being entirely up front with me. Frankly, I'm still stuck way back there at 'manipulative little scam.'"

He pulled the flask from the drawer and drank directly from it this time. He held it out to her and she shook her head.

"What happened between Heather and Dr. Hull?"

"As I said, I can't—"

"Give me a break," she said. "I'm getting cranky here. I've got a dead girl in the morgue and you're dinking me around with your flask and your 'manipulative scams' and your 'I've only got 15 minutes.' Just tell me what happened."

"All right. Here is the entire sordid tale—sordid enough to destroy my department's reputation so I'd appreciate not reading about this in the *Denver Post* again. Heather came crashing in here one day, crying and wailing. Had to talk to someone, she said. Hull had taken her out for dinner somewhere. Can't remember which place. She was flattered, it was upscale, so on. She liked the attention, admired him a great deal, et cetera ad nauseum." He waved his hand dismissively. "Hull was one of those—a number one pet with the co-eds. Anyway, during this meal, she began to feel sick and then doesn't remember what happened afterward, except that she woke up in his bed."

Mayo scribbled on her notepad.

"No clothes, by the way. She said she got dressed, and apparently found him in the kitchen making coffee. Nasty business. She asked him what happened and he pretended to be surprised, as in, 'What do you mean, what happened?'"

"Did she go to the police?"

"Oh, yes. That's what I told her at the time, we needed to notify the campus police."

"I'd like to get a copy of that police report," she said. "What was the determination?"

Mason consulted a sheet of phone numbers, then scribbled something on a sticky note and handed it to her. "Here's the number for the campus police. She refused to go at first. It took me several days to convince her."

"And the findings?" she asked.

"No actual physical evidence. She had delayed too long. I think I said that, didn't I? But I believed her story anyway. Why would she lie about something like that? But then the rumors started and then the business at the museum and now this—it's horrible. Just horrible." He frowned deeply.

"Just to clarify, did the rumors start before or after these specific accusations?"

"Oh, hell, I don't know. After."

Mayo flashed a brief smile. "After, of course. What did Hull have to say about it?"

"He denied everything of course, but there was tremendous pressure not to renew his contract. Fortunately, his was a non-tenure-track position—I mean it seemed fortunate at the time. The story was already all over the campus, though I'm not sure how the word got out. I certainly didn't call in the press, but they got hold of the story and in no time it was 'Rapist in the History Department' and so on. What a nightmare."

"What was Hull's side of the story?"

He scanned the ceiling for a few moments. "He said Heather was annoyed at his comments about the diary and also claimed she had a personal interest in him—a crush, if you will—and became upset when he rebuffed her. He said she had cooked this up to get revenge, which in retrospect—. But at the time, she was more believable than Hull."

"Why is that?"

"Because I know him. Hull is an arrogant S.O.B. At the time, none of it came as a surprise to me."

"Go on."

Mason's eyed narrowed. "Rumors again. He had the women after him. And he worked on them too—you know the sort. Always trying to wheedle something out of people, always spouting off big ideas, always scheming. It was perfectly believable to me that he would be involved in this unsavory event."

"But the campus police didn't charge him with anything?"

"No. They cited lack of evidence. I still can't imagine—she seemed genuinely distraught, though as I said, I later heard things and I was not at all happy with the way she handled the business in the end."

"Why is that?"

"Well, first of all, it must have been Heather who spread the story around, got the press involved. Who else would have done it? And then, she wouldn't let it go. She wasn't satisfied that I got rid—let him go. Hull had been waiting to hear about a grant studying the Sand Creek Massacre. Heather later told me that she had written to the grant organization and informed them about the rape."

"I see. And the result was ...?"

"I don't know if the two events were related, but I heard later that he did not get the grant. Of course, he probably wouldn't have got it anyway, without the university association."

Mayo studied his face. "Professor Hull couldn't have been too happy about that."

"Would you be? I imagine not."

Mayo guessed that Mason, who didn't mind screwing Hull over on the basis of unproven accusations, probably wouldn't mind accusing him of murder either. She decided to test this theory.

"Do you think he was upset enough with Heather to have done something violent?"

Mason did not hesitate. "I think it's certainly possible, yes." He pulled out a handkerchief from his pocket and patted his mouth. "Hull was—let me find the right word—*dramatic*. There was always drama around him and I had more than a few run-ins with him. Nothing serious about these run-ins, of course, just departmental politics—I'm sure you know the sort. He stormed out of a meeting once. People around here like to say he's creative, but to my mind, he just complicated things. For example, he wanted his students to investigate the Sand Creek Massacre by putting together a full-scale high-tech re-enactment using eye-witness accounts. An incredibly extravagant plan. Who would pay for it?"

"Not a bad idea though," Mayo said.

"I've heard people say he had charisma," Mason went on, "though I couldn't see it myself. Women mostly say it. His student evaluations were gushing, to a degree I found frankly distasteful for an institute of higher learning. He provided *inspiration*." Mason made quote marks with his fingers. "And as I mentioned before, he was also working the women. A ladies' man, to use the nauseating cliché. It was usually the women who raved on his evaluations. I have no doubt his male students were largely ignored."

Mayo gave him a quiet smile. "You sound a little envious, Dr. Mason."

He smashed his palm against the desk, and Mayo wondered what else he smashed when he was mad. "I really must say I resent the suggestion."

Mayo came up with her soothing smile. "I apologize. It's just my way of following each little thread. I'm sure you have to do the same when you study history, don't you? Hunting down all the little facts and clues and subtext?"

"What does that have to do with it?"

Mayo ignored his childish scowl. "Okay, Dr. Mason. I do appreciate all the time you've taken. We're almost finished."

She brought out the artist's sketch and moved it across the desk. "Do you recognize this man?"

He squinted at the sketch. "No. Who is it?"

"Just a person of interest. Would you mind making a copy of this and putting it up in the coffee room? I'll put my contact info on there and who knows, maybe we'll get lucky. And I don't suppose you know where that Holloway diary might be?"

He gave her a blank look. "Oh, the diary. I have no idea. Heather must have it in a safe place. She was inordinately protective of it. She wanted to publish it."

"Have you got an address for Toby Hull?"

"His old address, but like I said, his father came looking for him. Got nasty about it. Don't know where he is now." He turned to his computer again and tapped something out on the keyboard.

"You haven't heard from him at all since he left, then."

"Why would I? Hull blamed me for everything, even more than he blamed Heather. Figure that one out."

Nine

As she crossed the university lawns and headed back to her car, Mayo called Troy, the forensics man who took the tire casts. She was happy to get out of Mason's stuffy office and away from him.

"I was up very late last night," Troy informed her when he picked up. "I just emailed you some pictures. They'll be a lot clearer than the ones your deputy took."

"Thanks. Appreciate your help."

"I've identified the tracks in question as Michelin Energy LX4," he went on. "A very common brand used for cars and light trucks, SUVs. All season."

"Probably on half the cars in Colorado?"

"Yup," said Troy.

As she thanked Troy again and hung up, Mayo arrived back at her car. The meter had just expired so she shoved in a couple more quarters. She got in the car and called Gumble.

He'd been busy.

"Heather's neighbors didn't talk to her except for Honeysuckle who lives next door," he said. "She had several unpleasant comments to make about Heather's hatred for animals."

Honeysuckle was a middle-aged woman who served as the town's unofficial humane society. Mayor Davy had advised Mayo to bring any abandoned animals to her. Somehow, he said, she always managed to find them homes.

"She says she used to see Heather out jogging like clockwork every morning around six or six-thirty," Gumble went on. "She also says she has seen a couple different cars 'lurking around' on the street. People just sitting there in their cars, apparently with nothing to do. She couldn't provide type of vehicle though — claims she doesn't like cars, just big metal lumps to her, quote unquote. No description for the lurkers either.

"More than one car, though?" Mayo asked. "Not just one car?"

"She said a couple of different cars," Gumble repeated. "Okay. McKern went around town and posted the sketch and notice about the SUV the kids saw at the spring and we got a call from Harvey Kellerman. You know him? Good fellow, master carpenter. He figures he's the dark SUV the boys saw that morning—he was filling water jugs at the spring. Said he remembers the Jeep spitting gravel on its way toward Wolftongue but saw nothing else. Said he's got no good reason to be hanging around in front of Zippy's and I'm guessing that's a different dark SUV. Deputy Nutt's been asking around town, says he can't find anyone else who saw an unfamiliar car that morning.

Great, thought Mayo. So no one saw the killer. How the hell did their bad guy pull that off?

"People don't pay that much attention," Gumble said as though reading her thoughts. "A lot of folks from down in the flats come up just for weekends. Locals around town wouldn't necessarily notice a strange car."

"Okay," said Mayo. "What else?"

"Let's see," Gumble went on. "Talked to old Whitey Black who's been here since the dawn of humans—"

"There's actually someone called 'Whitey Black?'"

"You've never met old Whitey, eh? He doesn't get out much anymore, can't walk too good. He remembers Charlie Holloway, confirmed what I already said—the old man was a vicious cuss, just as soon kick your shin as let you pass on the sidewalk. Used to work at the Orange Blossom mill. Got some local girl in trouble and married her way back in the Thirties. Marriage lasted about ten minutes. The girl was bundled away to Denver, where she produced a boy named Doug Holloway. Boy lived with his mother and grandparents in the city but supposedly came up here sometimes during the summer. Different generation from me so I never heard of him, but Whitey says he got into plenty of trouble—drinking and carousing and bothering girls."

Mayo jotted the name in her notebook. "Doug Holloway must be Heather's father. One story says he sexually abused her."

"That wouldn't directly contradict anything Whitey had to say about the guy."

101

"Like what?"

"No specific incidents. Like I said, just your usual unpleasant sort of punk that everyone wishes would get out of town."

Mayo remembered Mrs. Holloway's words about her husband: *Never would have let this happen. Never, never, never.*

She would bet big money there was a world of history behind those words.

"Okay," she said. "What else?"

"Nutt and I both finished listening to the interview tape, by the way. I agree her story was flawed and she comes off like a liar."

"I thought you might conclude that."

"But I wouldn't dismiss it entirely. I'd say there's a sliver of possibility she was telling the truth. Sorry, boss."

"No need to apologize."

"But the fact she made these other accusations does a pretty good job of discrediting her," he went on.

"Agreed," she said.

"Still have to hunt down the Civil War bayonet angle. There are plenty of web sites, plus I've got a re-enactor buddy. Meanwhile, McKern is still on the warpath about the Indian angle."

"Right." She wasn't in the mood to hear about McKern, but she let Gumble go on.

"He wants to scan the felon database for American Indians."

She sighed. "Tell him to go ahead."

"I'll pass that along. You find anything good at the university?"

Mayo described her conversation with Mason.

"People usually have a reason for melting down when they talk to cops," Gumble said. "I'll run a check on him."

"And run a check on a Toby Hull—he lost his job and maybe a grant because of Heather. That might have pissed him off just a little bit."

"Already did. Got his name off the original Gonzales report from Denver P.D. Found a Patrick Hull, Toby's father, who filed a missing person report on Toby last June. Still missing as far as I know."

"Interesting." Mayo read Toby Hull's Boulder address off the printout Mason had given her. "See what else you can find. And there's also an emergency contact for Hull — Joanna Selig." She spelled the name out for him.

"Hang on."

She heard Gumble typing on the keyboard. "One hit. Last known address in Vail."

Mayo felt a rush she hadn't experienced in a long while — the thrill of the hunt. "Excellent. Track her down, find out what she knows about Toby Hull."

"Right away, boss."

"And Gumby."

"Yeah?"

"Did I mention I'm glad you're back?"

It was after five o'clock and Mayo was ravenous. She was enjoying working the case, and that always gave her an appetite.

She pulled out Kate Russell's phone number and dialed.

"I'm glad you called," Dr. Russell said when Mayo identified herself. "I wanted to talk. I can guess what Mason's been saying about Toby, and I can tell you without a doubt that he never touched that crazy woman."

"I'm still on campus and looking for dinner," Mayo said. "Can we meet somewhere?"

They rendezvoused at a teriyaki place near the campus. After ordering at the counter, they found a table on the back patio. Kate wore no make-up and wasn't exactly pretty, but she had an open, friendly face. Mayo liked her. They chatted idly about campus life until the waiter brought bowls of teriyaki chicken with rice and broccoli.

"Good choice, Dr. Russell," was Mayo's only comment while they ate.

"Please, call me Kate."

The food was delicious and the place was lively with students. Mayo felt rejuvenated after the long day, capped off by the tense discussion in Mason's stuffy office. She liked the change of scenery from Sugarloaf and having the noise of Denver around her again. It occurred to her that she might be a little weary of Zippy's and Monte's lingering gazes and McKern's blathering and her sequestered life in the mountains. She had ended up there for a reason, but maybe that reason was beginning to exhaust itself.

And then again, maybe not.

When they finished eating, they settled back in their seats, sipping jasmine tea while Kate Russell spilled out her version of the Heather Holloway-Toby Hull story.

Toby Hull was a fantastic guy, Kate said, and a gifted historian who studied the Alonzo Holloway diary at some length. Heather was enthusiastic at first that he had taken an interest, but he provoked her by concluding that Alonzo Holloway was just an inexperienced, uneducated kid with limited intellect and sycophantic obsession with his military commander, weighted with the visceral fear and hatred of the Cheyenne and Arapaho that was typical of white settlers in frontier Denver. That was where the trouble between Heather and Toby started.

"I don't know why Mason was so keen to believe her story about Toby attacking her," Kate said, "because no one else swallowed it."

"I wondered that myself," Mayo said. "Did you ever talk to Mason about it?"

"Sure, but you can't question his decisions. He just shouts you down — you may have noticed that about him, being a female and all." She winked. "He finds it generally annoying when women talk. But in Heather's case, he said her story had convinced him and that was the end of the conversation."

"Did Toby tell you what happened?"

Kate frowned. "Yes. Nothing at all happened. She made the whole thing up."

"When was the last time you heard from him?"

Kate's face changed and Mayo thought she caught a glint of moisture in her eyes.

"Last June," Kate said. "After he left the university. We were talking about getting together but I never heard back. I was worried about him because of what happened, plus he lost his grant and he had also broken up with his fiancée. He was really going through a rough patch."

Mayo pulled out her notes. "Do you know a Joanna Selig?"

Kate nodded, gazing across the patio area with a dark look in her eye. "His ex-fiancée."

"Do you know where she is now?"

Kate shook her head. "They split up in the spring—he didn't say why. It was all kind of mysterious. I met her at university functions once or twice—got the impression she wasn't quite up to par in the brains department." She smiled. "Sorry, that sounded awfully catty, didn't it?"

"Maybe you kind of liked him?" said Mayo.

"Maybe," Kate said, still smiling. "He drove me crazy though. He was very distant during our last conversation, said he was busy and would be in touch. Really vague and goddamned aggravating. It wasn't like him at all, but then so many things had gone wrong in such a short period—it was understandable. Then his father phoned me a few weeks later, said he got my number from Toby's address book. Asked if I knew where Toby was."

Kate pulled a tissue from her purse and dabbed her eyes, pausing for a minute before continuing. "Sorry. Toby was a good friend and yes, I kind of liked him..."

"Take your time."

After a few moments, Kate continued. "According to his father, Toby went off on a mountain biking trip and never came back." She paused to collect herself again. "The police found his truck in Keystone and they searched the bike trails in the area but there was no sign of him. Several of us went up there—we went to help Toby's dad look for him but we didn't find a thing."

"Where do you think he is?"

Kate took a sip of tea, watching a young couple who were snuggling at the next table. She had a lonely, hungry look.

"Sometimes," Kate said slowly, "when I'm feeling optimistic, I think maybe he just abandoned everything and bolted. It was a big pile of nasty, all hitting him at once. Maybe it was too much for him. Maybe he got the hell out of his life and started over somewhere." She took a deep breath. "But Toby's really not the sort who buckles under pressure. He—the truth is, I think he's probably dead." She stared coldly at Mayo as though Mayo had just stolen something precious from her. "It's the first time I've said it out loud," she said. "I think Toby is dead."

Glen is dead, Mayo thought abruptly. Had she ever said it like that? Out loud? She couldn't remember ever speaking the words.

"Why do you think that?" she asked, refocusing.

"Because he told me that he was going to prove that Heather lied. And I'm sure he could do it too—he was clever. He would figure out a way. But listen, I have to stress, if you think Toby had anything to do with hurting Heather, you're wrong. I can see why you might think that, but you just plain didn't know him. He's completely incapable. Besides, how would killing her help him?"

Mayo decided that this was a good moment to pounce. "What exactly was the nature of your relationship with him? Did he like you back?"

Kate shoved a clump of frizzy hair behind her ears. "No, we were just friends. Look, Toby's got more women after him than he knows what to do with." She flashed another smile. "I tried to make sure I was not one of them."

Mayo smiled. "Took some work, did it?"

Kate rewarded her with a boisterous laugh. "Sometimes it felt like a full-time job. If you met him, you'd understand."

"How about Heather?" Mayo asked. "Did she have a thing for him?"

Kate nodded. "He seemed to think so. He said that was the real reason she had gone after him, because he rejected her."

Mayo refilled their teacups and they drank in companionable silence. She tried to picture Kate running Heather through with a bayonet, then hacking off a chunk of her scalp. It was hard to envision, but she never ruled anyone out because they seemed nice.

Kate abruptly put her teacup down and gathered up her purse and a bulging satchel full of papers. "I need to get back. I've got an evening class."

They paid the bill and walked back toward campus together. The sun was low in the western sky and rush hour was in full swing.

"Can you think of anyone who might have wanted to hurt Heather?" Mayo asked as they waited for the light to change at a busy intersection.

Kate rolled her eyes. "Well, I hesitate to say anything, because I really don't know, but Dr. Mason certainly gets prickly when the subject of Heather or Toby comes up. You saw him gesturing at me in the coffee room, didn't you? He did not want me talking to you."

"Do you know why?"

"No clue. Why should he care? But he does. I'll bet you fifty bucks he comes to see me in the next day or two to find out if we talked."

The light changed and they headed across the street. "What do you know about Mason's relationship with Heather?" Mayo asked.

"I can only speculate. I saw her going into this office more than once. I always considered it questionable that he so readily believed her story, because she was obviously not a stable person."

"Why do you say that?"

"Did you ever meet her?"

"Yes."

"And you noticed nothing odd about her?"

Mayo smiled. "Well, maybe."

"I had her in one class. Her attendance was erratic. She cut herself—did you know that? Her arms were covered with scars and slashes."

"I am aware."

"I survived several high-drama meetings with her, with tears and paranoid accusations on her part—she said I wanted her to fail, I didn't understand her positions because she had a unique perspective, so on, ad nauseum. She was a smart girl, but deeply obsessive about her limited area of interest and completely indifferent to everything else."

"What was that area of interest? The diary?"

"The diary and Sand Creek. The various characters involved in the conflicts of that period. She had plans to write some sort of creative biography of her great grandfather, built around her search for his grave."

"Did she find out where the grave was located?"

Kate shrugged. "Not that I know of."

They reached Mayo's car and Mayo paused to feed a couple more quarters into the meter. "I'll walk you to your class, if you don't mind," she said.

"Sure, but I've got to hurry." Kate glanced at her watch.

"Have you read it?" Mayo asked when started off again. "The diary?"

"No. She wouldn't leave it alone with anyone. I got a quick look at it but she was breathing down my neck the entire time. Toby was willing to put up with her hovering but I remember him saying how weird it was to read the whole thing with her practically sitting in his lap."

"Can you think of any reason why an American Indian might be following her?"

Kate glanced at her. "That's ridiculous."

"I wonder if you know the man in this drawing." Mayo brought out the sketch, explaining briefly about the Zippy's incident.

Kate took the picture and paused to look at it. "Interesting face, but I don't know who it is." She handed it back.

"Were there controversies about the diary, perhaps?" Mayo went on, struggling to put the sketch away as they hurried along the sidewalk. "Some irate classmate who didn't like her theories?"

"She did give a presentation in my class about the diary that got a bit rowdy." Kate pointed. "I'm over this way."

They turned off the sidewalk and headed up a path into the campus.

"What happened?" Mayo asked.

"I expected her to read bits from the diary, which of course does have historical value, with some discussion about the attitudes of the period, but that's not what she did. She painted the old stereotypical picture of brave innocent Christian white boys up against yelping blood-thirsty savages. Like a Hollywood western from the Thirties or Forties. Very bizarre. Her paper about it was actually more academically balanced and rational than her presentation, which was just nutty. It was as though she couldn't resist baiting the class. You know, like an internet troll."

"And how did the class react?"

Kate gestured at a red brick building in front of them and turned up a path toward the door. "Not well. There was a good bit of argument, maybe a few raised voices. Heather fled the room in tears, which was also very strange. Maybe it was an act—hell, I don't know. She did everything she could to get everyone worked up, and then cried like a baby when they did."

Kate held the door open and Mayo entered the building, then hurried to keep up as Kate led the way up the hallway.

"Anyone in particular?" Mayo pressed. "Someone who was more than just generally annoyed perhaps?"

Kate stuck a hand into her satchel, looking for something. "No. Seems to me pretty much the whole class piled on. She asked for it and they gave it to her."

Mayo had a sense that Kate was not just late for class but wanted to get away from Mayo's questioning. She was no longer making eye contact.

A group of students passed by in the cramped hallway, and Mayo lowered her voice. "Any American Indians in that class?" she asked.

Kate's eyes were focused on the contents of her satchel. "Don't remember off-hand."

"Can you check for me and let me know?"

Kate stopped walking and finally looked at her. "You know, I'm not entirely comfortable doing that. Isn't that racial profiling?"

Another clump of students came through and she waited for them to pass before continuing.

"I understand your concern," Mayo said, "but a few days before she was killed, Heather claimed she was attacked by an American Indian. The one in the sketch."

Kate began walking again, with Mayo right behind.

"Let me assure you," Mayo continued, "I am not interested in conducting any sort of witch hunt."

"All right." Kate stopped again, nodding at a heavy wooden door in front of them. "This is my class." She glanced at her watch and stood back while two young women entered the classroom.

"Hi, Dr. Russell!" one of the girls said cheerfully.

"Hello, Penny," Kate said. "Good evening, ladies." She turned back to Mayo. "Look, I'm not trying to be a pain about it, but I'm going to check with the university before we even go there."

"Fair enough." Mayo knew Kate would do everything she could to protect the names. And Mayo would do whatever she could to get them.

"If you could remember anyone who seemed particularly angry—" Mayo waited while half a dozen more students entered the classroom. "—There are other details that point to a possible connection with American Indians."

Kate had started entering the room after the students but this caught her attention and she turned back. This time she glared directly at Mayo. "Like what?"

Mayo kept her voice low. "Look, I can't say at this point. But I would appreciate any help you could give me."

Sighing deeply, Kate stepped back into the hallway. "My class starts in one minute. I've got to go. And no, I can't think of anyone like that."

Mayo gazed at her for a moment. Kate Russell was hiding something.

"Okay," she said finally. "I'm almost out of your hair, I promise. "Did you send a note to the Denver P.D. about Heather?"

Kate waved at someone behind Mayo and smiled, her eyes returning to Mayo. "A note about what?"

"Are you aware of what happened at the Colorado Frontier Museum?"

Kate Russell stepped into the classroom. "I don't think I even want to hear about it," she said before closing the door.

Ten

The following day, Mayo drove back down to Denver, this time bringing Gumble along. Armed with the tire tread pictures from Troy, Gumble disappeared into the parking garage of Colorado Frontier Museum while Mayo headed through the main entrance to talk to Heather's former boss, Felix Arkenstone. Gumble's task was to make a surreptitious tire comparison on Arkenstone's car, then drive over to the university to check Mason's and Russell's cars before meeting Mayo back at the museum. None of the cars had appeared on Nutt's list.

Mayo crossed a spacious lobby pleasantly lighted from skylights and three-story windows. She was feeling sharp and energized, having had a good night's sleep. She felt as though she'd been making progress on the case and now had two good suspects: Mason and the missing Professor Hull.

Behind the counter sat an elderly woman with a set of pale lavender curls arranged in amazingly precise rows around her head. Mayo showed her badge to "Volunteer: Tilly" and asked for Dr. Felix Arkenstone.

"Yes, of course." With a distinct lack of surprise that a police officer had come calling, Tilly picked up the phone and pecked out several numbers. "Dr. Arkenstone? There's a police person here to see you." She hung up the phone and gave Mayo a superior look. "Dr. Arkenstone will be right out."

Mayo pulled the sketch of Heather's assailant out of her briefcase and held it up. "Have you ever seen this man?"

Tilly moved her head back as though to get away from the thing. She pursed her lips irritably. "No, I have not."

"Can I help you?"

Mayo turned as a slender, middle-aged man approached. "I'm Felix Arkenstone. Tilly said you're from the police?"

Mayo took in his features, the most pronounced of which was a shaved head. His blue eyes had an unpleasant severity about them and his mouth was hard and unsmiling. He wore a dark brown suit with highly buffed cowboy boots.

"I'm Marshal Mayo from Sugarloaf." She showed her badge again.

His eyes narrowed. "What's this about?"

"I'm here to talk to you about Heather Holloway," she said.

He glanced at Tilly, who quickly focused on some papers on the counter.

Arkenstone's frown deepened as he led Mayo out of the lobby. "My God," he said when they were out of Tilly's earshot. "Not this again. I thought we'd settled all that bunk. Is that devil of a woman never going to leave me alone?"

"I imagine she will," Mayo said.

She followed him through a "Staff Only" door, down a hall and into a bright, airy office. He gestured her toward an enormous green sofa, which nearly swallowed her when she sat.

Arkenstone pulled up a hard chair and perched at the edge. It occurred to her that his fierce expression seemed overdone—a comfortable academic trying to approximate a drill sergeant. "What's the problem now?" he demanded.

She watched his face. "I'm afraid Ms. Holloway has been killed."

His eyes were steady on Mayo and his lips moved silently. "Seriously?" he said finally.

"Seriously."

His eyes widened briefly but his expression was otherwise unchanged. "I see. Well, I'm—I'm speechless."

"Sorry to bring such tragic news," Mayo said dryly.

"What happened to her?" He now had a tone of solemnity and concern but Mayo wasn't convinced.

"Murdered."

"Jesus. Are you kidding?"

"Afraid not."

"How?"

"Stabbed with a bayonet. Civil war era. Enfield, I believe was the manufacturer." The lab had phoned that morning with the news that the bayonet and Bowie knife had tested positive for Heather's blood, but they found no prints.

"Enfield, eh?" He watched Mayo warily.

Mayo adjusted herself within the folds of the sofa, feeling trapped by the overly soft cushions. "Do you mind?" She rose and pulled up another hard chair next to Arkenstone's and sat. "There. Much better. That's the softest couch I've ever seen!" She smiled lightly.

His wheels were turning, Mayo thought. Still, if she had to bet, she'd say the news about Heather was a surprise to him. Although he was trying not to show anything, he seemed more relieved than defensive.

"Enfield, you said?" he muttered again.

"I don't suppose you're missing anything like that?"

He frowned. "Not that I'm aware of. Look, I'm guessing you know all about what happened when she worked here. Otherwise, you wouldn't be here, right?"

Mayo didn't want to give up what she knew. "I know she worked here."

Arkenstone's blue eyes went very cold. "You must have heard about her accusations."

She calculated. Commiseration and flattery with this one. "I can tell you that I encountered Heather before she was killed," she said conspiratorially, "and found her somewhat less than truthful."

He sat back, relaxing a little. "You've got that right. Am I a suspect?"

"Look, my goal is to waste as little of your time as possible and get you off the potential list."

He flashed an approving smile, flicking a finger absently at his shaved head. "I see. Well, I haven't seen Heather since she left and I don't know where she went."

Mayo leaned forward a bit. "I confess I've heard a few stories about her time here. I'd like to hear your version."

"Of course. We brought her on as an intern last summer." He lapsed into an officious monotone. "We're working on a Sand Creek exhibit and she has possession of a diary written by someone who was there—an ancestor of hers. We wanted to use the diary in the exhibit. There was a bit of flack about it."

"Flack?"

113

His eyes took on the soaring expression of the professional orator. "Her position on the massacre was tainted by some of the old-style racism that dismissed Native Americans as savages. Without going into minute detail, I'll just say that several post-Sand Creek investigations unanimously concluded that it was an unprovoked and heinous attack on a peaceful camp. The Holloway diary depicts a different situation, constantly utilizes the term 'battle,' and implicates several peace-making chiefs along with a select group of cavalry officers who had been involved in negotiations with the tribes."

Mayo pictured Arkenstone giving this same practiced speech to the museum board, which may well have been required of him after the Holloway business. On the other hand, he could be just making noise to deflect her attention.

She decided to test his temper. "Did you hire Heather just to get your hands on the diary?"

He hunched his shoulders and gave her the wolf glare again. "I felt the document would be a significant addition to our upcoming Sand Creek exhibit. If it meant bringing on a somewhat less than ideal student as an intern for a few months, then so be it."

"That makes sense," she said, trying to inject a tone of approval into her voice. "In what way was Heather 'less than ideal?'"

"In what way was she not?" he barked. "When I interviewed her she was agitated. Her comprehension of the relevant events was not entirely serious from an academic perspective. She earned reasonably good marks and came with a good recommendation, but landing an internship at this museum is extremely competitive and her qualifications weren't evident in her interview nor in her subsequent performance. I suppose I was interested in 'getting my hands on the diary,' as you so crudely put it. I won't deny that was the critical point in her favor."

Mayo kept her face blank, hiding the rustle of distaste she felt toward the man. He and Heather were the same sort of opportunistic beast, preying on each other. "Do you have the diary, Dr. Arkenstone?"

"No."

"Any copies?"

Someone knocked on his office door and he went to open it. Volunteer Tilly stood at the door, sagging under the weight of a cardboard box the size of several coffee table books.

"This was just delivered, Dr. Arkenstone," Tilly said breathlessly. She peered past him at Mayo.

"Tilly," he said. "I thought you promised you wouldn't lift things!" Arkenstone relieved her of the box. "Next time, just call and I'll come get it."

Tilly grabbed a final glimpse at Mayo and left.

Arkenstone carried the box to his desk and tore at the packaging. "Posters for our new exhibit," he said.

"Dr. Arkenstone," Mayo said. "Do you have a copy of the diary?"

He glanced at her absently as he fished around in a desk drawer and came up with a box-cutter. "No. She was maniacally fussy about it. She wouldn't let us make a copy and only allowed us to look at it when she was hovering over." He hacked a deep slit in the box and shoved away the flaps. "In fact, her behavior led me to suspect it might be a forgery, but we authenticated it."

He pulled a sheet out of the box and held it high to examine it. Mayo caught the words "Sand Creek Exhibit," in large yellow letters.

"Why do you think she was so concerned about it?" she asked.

He glanced up from the poster and flashed a rueful smile. "It's my opinion she simply enjoyed aggravating people. It's not as though it were the original Emancipation Proclamation or something of that magnitude — damn it, Maggie! Speaking of the diary!"

He held the poster up so Mayo could see. In a lower corner of the poster, a special box promised "The Controversial Holloway Diary."

"Maggie forgot to tell the printer to take the damn diary notice off," he said.

"Maggie?"

He put the poster back in the box. "My assistant."

"So you don't think the diary is worth killing over?" Mayo asked.

He looked startled. "Are you serious? Why the hell would you think that?"

Mayo shook her head. "She believed someone was out to get her."

Arkenstone knuckled his scalp furiously, leaving a pink welt. "Jesus Christ! What do you do with a nutbag like that? Stay far enough away to avoid getting sucked into her crazy universe. She could say whatever she wanted and make ludicrous accusations and even though there's no evidence, nothing to back up her claims, people tend to believe it. We lost more than a couple of our volunteer staff over that episode."

She waited a moment for him to calm down. "How did the accusation against you come about?"

"Try 'out of nowhere.' One Monday morning a Denver police officer arrives, wants to hear about my relationship with Heather. I was completely blind-sided. What relationship with Heather? She works for me as an intern. She's difficult, I put up with it. What else do you want to know? Well, we want to know what happened between the two of you a week ago Friday. What are you talking about? Heather says you've been coming on to her and that you attacked her down in the basement. Her cell phone shows numerous incoming calls from you."

Arkenstone paced around the office. "I used to leave my cell phone lying around — obviously a mistake. The girl got hold of it and called her own number. That's the only explanation." He stopped and pointed at Mayo. "And that's all they had. There was no evidence — the 'poor child' said she'd been too intimidated to report it at first and it was too late for an examination. Thank God some good citizen sent them a letter about Heather doing the same thing at Colorado Western U, a fact my worthy colleague, Dr. Carl Mason, neglected to mention in his glowing letter of recommendation."

"You have any idea who wrote the letter?"

"None. Probably whoever she went after back there."

"How would they know what was going on here? Was it generally known?"

"Not that I'm aware of."

"So Heather failed to show up to work one Monday morning and a policeman came instead?"

"Yes."

"Nothing unusual happened the previous Friday?"

"Not that I recall."

"How long did Heather work here?"

"Not long. Maybe five or six weeks, if that."

"Did you ever notice anyone else in her life? A boyfriend maybe?"

He shook his head. "I never noticed much about her, period. I'm a busy man. I don't have time to get chummy with interns. First she was an intern with the diary, then she was a nightmare. That's all she was to me."

"Maybe she was trying to get your attention."

He smiled, close-mouthed. "Well, she succeeded."

Mayo could easily picture Arkenstone running Heather through with a bayonet, but his story was believable.

She pulled out Heather's assailant sketch and showed it to him. "Have you ever seen this guy?"

He sat down and examined the picture for a long minute, his jaw moving. "He looks familiar, but I couldn't say why. Of course, we get thousands of visitors coming through the museum." He handed the picture back.

"You recently returned from a trip to Sand Creek, didn't you?"

"Just last night."

"Whereabouts is the site?"

"Southeastern Colorado."

"That sounds like a grueling trip," she said, "Two days of driving and only one day there. You must leave at the crack of dawn to get there in a day."

He sighed, glancing at his watch. "It's not that far. We've driven down a number of times and rarely leave the museum before mid-morning. Look, I've got a meeting in two minutes. Are we finished here?"

Good enough for now, she thought.

"May I speak to your assistant?" she asked. "What's her name? Maggie?"

"Of course." He seemed much more relaxed and even gave her a friendly smile as he went to the door.

"Could I remind you to check into that bayonet for me?" she called after him. "Make sure nothing's missing?"

He didn't stop. "It'll take a day or two."

"Thanks," Mayo said to the empty doorway.

Arkenstone was gone less than a minute before another figure appeared. Mayo stood to greet a slender, attractive woman with very dark brown eyes and a playful tangle of hair that was somewhere between white and blonde. Mayo wondered if she'd been lurking outside the door.

They shook hands and the woman gave her a cheerful smile. "Maggie Hurst. What can I do for you?"

"I'm afraid I'm here on some serious business," Mayo said.

Maggie fiddled with an extravagantly silly watch on her wrist, more like a wide silver bracelet with a watch face, surrounded by beads and tiny swirls and inexpensive gemstones. "I heard," she said. "Heather. Felix just told me about it."

She curled up on the sofa with the slow ease of a cat. She wore jeans and a white cotton blouse with tiny pink roses embroidered along a low neckline. The clothes looked luxurious on her.

"Were you close?" Mayo asked, sitting again on the hard chair.

Maggie shrugged. "No, but it is sad, isn't it? Despite what she did. It's kind of like how you feel if you see a dead rattler on the trail. A rattlesnake can't really help being a rattlesnake."

Mayo paused to take this in. Maggie spoke in a soft, friendly tone, but there was a rich pile of hatred behind the metaphor. Had Heather done something to her too, or was she just angry about the accusations against her boss?

"I gather you weren't friendly with her," Mayo said.

Maggie fiddled with her watch again. "You know, I tried to make her feel welcome here and we even ate lunch together in the cafeteria a few times. But she really wasn't the type you could get to know. She was secretive."

"How so?"

"Oh, you know, ask a question, get a minimal answer. She valued her information like a miser values money. Didn't matter if it was important information or not, but it was *hers*."

That fit with what she'd seen, Mayo thought. A closed-up rather than open person. "Did you know Heather before she came to work here?"

"No."

"Did anyone at the museum know her before?"

"Not that I know of."

"Did you ever meet any of her friends?"

"No."

"Did you know about the previous assault allegations at Colorado Western University?"

"No. We found out about it from Detective Gonzales, the officer who handled the case here." Maggie gave herself a small shake, as though trying to rid herself of the whole thing. Like a cat again, thought Mayo.

"Do you know Toby Hull?" Mayo asked.

Maggie looked surprised. "Toby Hull? I think I know who he is — it's a claustrophobic little community, with conferences and so on. Good-looking fellow?"

Mayo smiled. "That's what they say."

"Why? Is he involved somehow?"

Mayo ignored the question. "Did you ever see Heather again after she left?"

"Yes. About a week later."

"When was this?" Mayo asked.

"Oh, about mid-August. She called me and asked me to get her stuff out of the desk and meet her. That included the diary, which she had locked in a drawer. She had the key delivered by bike messenger so she wouldn't have to come in."

"So she hadn't taken her things that Friday — her last day here."

"Apparently not. Maybe she got bored over the weekend and decided she'd been attacked." Maggie smiled.

"Okay. So you met up with her?"

119

"Of course. I packed up her things and met her at a coffee place on 16th Street."

"What exactly did you bring her?"

Maggie scanned the far wall. "A cloth bag full of papers. A very expensive looking leather jacket. A box of chocolate-covered cherries. The diary. I've got to tell you that meeting was very strange. I walked in expecting a grim or at least solemn tone. I guess I even thought she might apologize for all the trouble she'd caused or maybe to try and convince me that he'd really done it. But I was surprised, unpleasantly. There she was, sitting at a window table, happy as a clam, taking great pleasure in a big mug of hot chocolate. And then, the second I sat down, she went weepy. She really laid it on thick, blurting out some gruesome story about her father molesting her, and then a bunch of wacky stuff about her kinky personal life."

Maggie rolled her eyes.

"Can you be more specific?" Mayo asked.

"Let's see," Maggie said, smiling. "Oh my God, I don't even like repeating it. She showed me cuts on her arm, self-inflicted, she said. She couldn't enjoy sex unless she was beaten and she said she had partners to help her along in this little endeavor. I wasn't really surprised. She once had a questionable package delivered to her at work from some place called 'Sex Fantasy' something or other."

Maggie shoved her hair out of her eyes and blinked at Mayo. She had a patrician, refined air about her, but the humor in her eyes said she hadn't really been shocked.

Resisting the urge to commiserate with Maggie about what a nutjob Heather was, Mayo considered the story. It fit in with the tub of sex toys and the behavior that Danny had described. So maybe Heather had some kind of underbelly life going with a series of kinky sex partners. Maybe she pissed off one of them and they put an end to her.

"Did she mention anyone in particular?" Mayo asked without much hope.

Maggie shook her head. "No. She talked about meeting men in hotels—that's 'men,' plural. You can imagine how bizarre this conversation was. She said it was all a punishment for her incestuous relationship with her father, which she claimed she enjoyed."

Mayo raised her eyebrows. "You sure she wasn't trying to shock you?"

"Who knows?" Maggie said. "But she seemed dead serious."

Mayo handed her the sketch of the Zippy's assailant. "Have you ever seen this guy?"

Maggie looked for a long time. "Where did you get this?"

"Before she was killed, Heather said this man assaulted her."

To Mayo's surprise, Maggie touched the picture lightly with a fingertip. "Extraordinary face."

"Ring any bells?" she prompted.

Maggie looked up. "Sorry, no."

"Have you read the Holloway diary?"

"Of course."

"Can you think of anything in it that might make Heather a target?"

Maggie traced one of the swirls on her watch with a fingertip. She thought for a long time. Mayo was about to ask her again when Maggie finally spoke.

"You know, it's hard for us white folks to understand—we aren't terribly connected with history. I mean, some of us are interested in it as an intellectual exercise, but we don't particularly honor our ancestors or identify with them or think about them much. And I'm talking very specifically about Americans of European ancestry. I think it's a very American trait to deliberately sever ourselves from the past. It's considered baggage. We love only the great glorious future, in which anything can happen, most likely something miraculous that will make us deliriously happy and successful. This is what we are raised to expect as American citizens.

"But in cultures such as the American Indian, history is viewed from an entirely different perspective. Something that happened to our ancestors 150 years ago might just as well have happened yesterday to our parents or even today to us. The passage of time and generations is inconsequential. The pain of my ancestors is my pain. In honor of them, I *am* that pain."

Mayo thought about this. "So you're saying it's not a ridiculous notion that someone might want to get back at Heather for her ancestor's participation at Sand Creek?"

"Heather's ancestor hero-worshipped John Chivington, the man who got his troops riled up enough to murder about 150 Cheyenne and Arapaho—mostly women, old people, and children. People who had basically surrendered, who had said they would not fight the white man. They were slaughtered by a bunch of blood-thirsty troops who'd only been soldiers for three months and who would muster out a week or so later. Heather's ancestor was one of those."

Mayo felt as though she and Maggie were stuck in some sort of complicated dance, for which she, Mayo, did not know the right steps.

"Let me rephrase my question," she said. "Do you think Heather could have been a target because of Sand Creek or the diary?"

Maggie picked up the sketch again. "I suppose it's possible this guy is a Sand Creek descendant. There haven't been any real reparations for what the cavalry did. The descendants have hired lobbyists and so forth, but nothing has come of it."

"So I take that as a yes?"

Maggie seemed to sag a little as she met Mayo's gaze. "I hate to think something like that could happen, but I suppose it's possible. After all, Heather was going around bragging about her ancestor's participation. She might have boasted to the wrong person."

Not exactly the same take Kate Russell had, Mayo thought. But Kate wanted to protect her students—maybe more than Mayo realized.

"Why do you want the diary for your exhibit, if you believe it's so far off the mark?" Mayo asked.

Maggie gave her a rueful smile. "Felix and I both agree it's of critical interest. It demonstrates the strange power that Chivington held over some of his men. There were a good number who would have followed him off a cliff, and I think it explains why he was able to whip them into such a frenzy, when they might otherwise have been just a bunch of normal, albeit unemployed pioneers who'd been recruited into the cavalry for a temporary stint. Don't get me wrong—most white folks at that time feared and hated the 'savages' and would just as soon see them removed from the territory. But Sand Creek went way beyond that, beyond even the act of killing them. Sand Creek was the work of those who wanted the tribes exterminated, and to promote this 'final solution' it was necessary to dehumanize them, which is what they achieved with the outrageous mutilations that went on. Anyway, that is how we intended to present it."

Maggie leaned forward and her voice went faintly husky. "As I drove home after my little meeting with Heather, it occurred to me that her fixation with the Sand Creek Massacre kind of fit in with all that kinky sex stuff she was talking about."

Mayo felt the hairs on her arms go up. "How so?"

"There was a lot of scalping and sexual mutilation at Sand Creek. Heather was particularly obsessed with that aspect of it. Not that it isn't a gripping bit of history. I mean, picture a thousand Victorian men, many of them from the sexually-repressed society back east. Now it's 1864, the lawless prairie, no one to enforce the stuffy old rules, and besides, these are just 'savages,' right? It doesn't count! On this day, they are given permission to go on a rampage. Go for it! Chivington tells them. So what do they come up with? They cut off penises and women's private parts; they made tobacco pouches and saddle horn ornaments out of them." Maggie smiled without humor. "Kind of makes the Manson Family look like Boy Scouts, doesn't it?"

"So that's what Heather's ancestor was so proud of?"

"He claims in his diary he didn't see any such thing," Maggie said. "All of the Chivington apologists deny it. But many others who were there and who were properly horrified testified about it in detail. Several talked about a little toddler being shot in the back as he tried to run away. These were the so-called 'civilized' folks, ridding the plains of the 'savages.'"

"Maybe they got the idea from the Old Testament," said Mayo, who had grown up in a fundamentalist household, listening to stories of Biblical rectitude and barbarism. "In First

Samuel, you've got David bringing King Saul the foreskins of two hundred men in exchange for Saul's daughter."

Maggie shook her head. "These are all good reasons why anyone with a lick of sense just leaves history alone." She smiled. "What it teaches is just too appalling to contemplate."

"Too bad it's not just confined to history," Mayo said. "Can you tell me, what was the purpose of taking a scalp?"

"There are different theories, I suppose, but a scalp is clearly a trophy that signifies bravery. Both the whites and the tribes indulged. Of course you'll get a big argument if you try to say who started the practice."

"Did they take the whole head of hair?"

"Not usually. Maybe just enough to make a nice attachment to your headdress or coat. Sometimes multiple people would scalp the same person. And the victims weren't always dead."

Mayo adjusted her seat. "How was it done?"

Maggie's smile was elegant. "You mean, how do you scalp someone?"

"Yes."

"Hmm. Should I demonstrate?"

Mayo hesitated only a second. "Sure."

Maggie stood up, smiling down at Mayo. "You'll have to be the victim then. I promise I won't really scalp you." She pointed. "Lie face down on the floor."

Mayo slipped off the chair and lay down on the carpet, which smelled of glue and dust. She felt a gentle pressure on her back.

"You put your foot between their shoulder blades," Maggie said. "Then grab their hair."

The pressure increased and Mayo's head lifted as Maggie pulled it back by the hair.

Maggie's voice went quiet. "Then you cut a notch..."

Mayo felt a tickling along her forehead as Maggie feigned the cut.

"...and yank!" Maggie said.

Mayo's dropped to the floor as Maggie let go and moved aside.

Mayo sat up, touching her head unconsciously.

"Not for the faint of heart," Maggie smiled.

After leaving a copy of the sketch for the museum's coffee room, Mayo met Gumble in front of the building. She climbed into the SUV and Gumble pulled out into traffic.

"I've just had a lesson in scalping," Mayo said, rubbing the crown of her head. "Remind me to show you how sometime."

"No thanks," Gumble said with a laugh. "I'll stick to harsh language."

"Find anything good?"

"I checked Arkenstone's truck but the tread's completely different. I checked another car parked next to his truck in staff parking. I'm guessing that's the car he drove down south—it's still packed with cardboard boxes and tools and it's covered with dust. Belongs to a Maggie Hurst."

"I just met her. She's the scalping expert."

"She drives a black Subaru Forester, which counts as a dark SUV. No match there either, but I did notice her tires looked new."

"My impression is they left for Sand Creek from the museum parking garage," Mayo said. "Arkenstone said they leave around mid-morning, which keeps them in the ballpark. The garage must have electronic records of entry and exit for their card keys so we need to get hold of those."

"Okay. Were you aware that Hurst and Arkenstone are listed at the same home address in Denver?"

"That's interesting. They didn't mention it." Strange thing to leave out, Mayo thought. Why should she care if they lived together?

"As for Mason," Gumble went on, "he drives a Volvo. No match on the tread. And Kate Russell's car wasn't in the lot."

"Let's keep them on the radar anyway."

Gumble pulled a notepad from his pocket and handed it to Mayo. "I made a few calls while I was waiting."

Mayo skimmed his notes. "I can't read your writing, Gumby. What's it say?"

"You can't read that?" He shook his head. "All right. Let's see. My pals around town don't know of anyone in the area owning an Enfield bayonet, but my re-enactment buddy says they're not that rare. You can get one online for a hundred-fifty bucks."

"So much for the unique murder weapon," Mayo said. "We're having rotten luck on the forensics front. What else?"

"No current address yet for Joanna Selig."

"Okay. Next on your list — and you won't be too surprised — Heather may have met some partners for kinky sex in hotels. We need to canvass — I'm thinking Boulder, Nederland, and Black Hawk. Bring a picture of Heather. Bring the police artist's sketch for the hell of it. Maybe she used her real name and maybe not. Get McKern to help."

Eleven

Heather's funeral took place on Saturday afternoon inside an old stone church in North Boulder. With permission from Delia Holloway, Mayo brought equipment to film the service—standard procedure in a murder case—but the turnout was so light, Mayo asked Gumble to take it back to the car. Mayo and Gumble sat on hard wooden pews in the rear of the church. Gumble was squirming. His legs were so long, his jiggling knee rattled the pew in front of them.

Finally, Mayo nudged him. "What's your problem?"

"Funerals," he whispered. "I don't care for 'em." A faint line of sweat glistened along his upper lip.

"Anyone ever tell you you're in the wrong business?"

"Most bad guys are still alive."

Mayo, Gumble, and McKern had spent the past several days fruitlessly canvassing hotels and motels in the area with a picture of Heather and the police artist's sketch, hunting down false leads reported by various citizens who called after seeing the sketch, searching Heather Holloway's house for the diary, and trying unsuccessfully to contact Patrick Hull, the father of Toby Hull. He had not returned their phone messages and there was never an answer at the Boulder house on record as Toby Hull's address. Finally, that morning, Mayo had sent McKern to watch the Hull place while she and Gumble went to the funeral.

Meanwhile, the lab reported that the note from Heather's door was printed on regular white copy paper using a standard laser printer. There were no fingerprints although they confirmed that bits of paint on the note matched paint from the doorway. Only Heather's fingerprints were identified from the front doorknob. The sex toys had never been used, but Heather's fingerprints were found on several of them. Heather's car revealed nothing except fibers from her own clothing.

They still had not determined a use for the key that Mayo found in the plastic tub at Heather's house.

They had not located Joanna Selig, but did get hold of the police report for Toby Hull's disappearance. His father, Patrick

Hull of St. Louis, had become concerned that Toby did not answer his phone or return his emails so he had the police do a welfare check. No one answered the door at Toby's house and the police had no reason to force their way in. Patrick Hull drove out from St. Louis, broke into his son's house and found it apparently abandoned. Toby Hull's belongings were there but he seemed to have vanished. The father went to the police again and this time they checked Toby's bank and credit card records and found no activity for over a month. At the bottom of the police report under comments were scrawled two notes: "Interviewed Carl Mason at CWU, problems with Hull—dead end." And the second note: "Presumed dead."

Up front, Heather's body lay inside a closed casket. There was a single arrangement of lilies, but no portraits or other mementos of Heather on display. Jody and Delia sat in the first row. Patty Field sat a few rows back.

Turning in her seat now, Patty waved briefly. She wore a dusty-looking black dress and had worked her hair into long curls that somehow looked drab and forlorn.

Mayo tapped Gumby's knee, which stopped jiggling.

"Sorry," he said.

Mayo shook her head, trying to soothe her own urge to jump up and get the hell out of there. She hadn't been to a funeral since Glen—an ordeal during which some of the hundreds of officers present had kept a distance from her. At least it seemed like they did. Sometimes she wasn't sure.

Now, three elderly women came slowly up the aisle, two of them using walkers. They approached Delia Holloway and whispered to her before finding seats. Mayo noted Jody's apparent lack of friends, felt a flash of curiosity and pity for the girl. Jody seemed reasonably normal—she was gentle and sweet, the type who should have devoted pals and a worried, protective man hovering around. But there she was all by herself, the fix-it member of this off-kilter family, perched next to her rancorous mother, gazing impassively forward as though she were afraid to turn around and get an eye-full of the sparse turnout at her sister's funeral.

Soon, two men came in—though not together—and both immediately caught Mayo's eye. The first was in his early 50s, well over six feet tall, thin and attractive, long wavy hair streaked with silver, sharp cheek-bones, gunslinger moustache. He dressed western-style—cowboy boots and jeans, a starchy white shirt, black vest, and a black colonel tie. He found a seat near Mayo and Gumble, then peered around the church, his eyes resting longer than usual on Mayo. She returned the lingering inspection and, after several beats, he casually looked away.

The second man was a stiff blond in his thirties. He walked tentatively up a few rows and slipped into a seat next to the aisle. He had a strange manner of turning with his whole body, as though he couldn't twist his neck or waist. He wore a mask-like smile, showing off teeth that looked amazingly perfect. He gazed around, taking in the stained glass windows, altar, ceiling, the thin aisle carpeting, but he skimmed over the other humans in the room.

Mayo tried to picture either of the two men having a raucous time in a hotel room with Heather but despite what Maggie Hurst had told her, the image was hard to conjure.

The minister soon appeared. He was a chubby man with thick white hair and a sonorous voice. He delivered a sorrowful eulogy for Heather, whom he had never met, but about whom he had heard many wonderful things from his congregant, Mrs. Doug Holloway, whose husband had preceded their daughter in death.

At first he tip-toed around the manner of Heather's death, saying only that it was sudden and tragic. At one point, he heated up and lamented how "macabre" it was that a young lady could be "bayonetted to death in this day and age." He asked what was wrong with society, suggested that the internet might lay at the root of it. He warned about the sins of anger and vengeance, and went on at some length about the state of mankind, whose prospects did not look promising.

Mayo tuned him out, keeping an eye on the stiff blond and the cowboy.

The blond sat rigid in his seat. He didn't look merely self-conscious and ill-at-ease, he seemed to be in abject torment. He was listening intently, occasionally tilting his head in a bird-like manner as though trying to hear better. He didn't seem absorbed by the minister's words but determined to endure every punishing syllable.

The cowboy showed no sign of grief or any other distress. In fact, he seemed to be holding back a smirk as he checked out the others at the service. He met Mayo's eye again. He winked.

The wink surprised her enough that she cracked a smile before she could catch herself.

Gumble's nudges brought her out of this reverie and he nodded toward the front of the church. The service had ended and Delia Holloway was making some sort of scene. Jody and Patty jumped up, crowding around her, while the church ladies moved into a fretful clump behind them. Mayo and Gumble headed up to help just as a young man arrived with a glass of water.

"I'm all right!" Delia barked. "Don't crowd in like that!"

As the group got Delia into a seat, Mayo caught sight of the cowboy disappearing out the door.

"You take the cowboy," Mayo told Gumble. "I'm with the blond."

Mayo's target hadn't moved from his seat during the Delia Holloway ruckus. He continued to remain perfectly still when she slid into the pew next to him.

She told him her name and he smiled, swiveled toward her, and shook her hand, which was not a pleasant experience. His hand was cool and damp. His hair had the texture of a baby's, with blond wispy curls around his ears, and pale blue eyes.

She kept her manner friendly and mild. "Are you a friend of Heather's?"

"Hmm?" His expression suggested that she might need to try another language.

"Do you speak English?" she asked.

"I do."

"What's your name?"

"Donal Chestnut." A thick, undefinable accent.

"Donald?"

"Donal. *Nal.*"

130

"Do-*nal*. Okay. Sorry. Um, Do-*nal*, how do you know Heather?"

"She was girlfriend." The accent sounded vaguely Russian, but not quite.

"Oh, I see. How long was she your girlfriend?"

"How long?"

"Yes. How long. Months? Years? Weeks?"

"Ah!" He smiled broadly, showing the perfect teeth again. Mayo had a sudden vision of Do*nal* ripping the flesh off something with those grinders. She shook the image away. It was Heather, toxic Heather, making her crazy. Making her really, really nuts. And this guy was making it worse.

"Ah, what?" she prodded, trying to clear her head.

"Ah, well, about four years."

She narrowed her eyes—his accent had suddenly vanished. "Say that one more time for me, would you?"

"Of course. We've been together four years. We seemed together to me anyway."

She narrowed her eyes at the guy. "Interesting accent, Do-*nal*. Comes and goes, does it?"

"I apologize." He now spoke in midwestern American English. "I am actually called Donald, and I confess I have some unusual habits that are beyond my control. I get very nervous around strangers and I sometimes find that the only effective way to prevent myself from bolting is to act as if I'm someone else. Please forgive me. Don't take it personally, but this is a strange and difficult situation. I'm sure you think I've escaped from somewhere but honestly, it was my psychiatrist's idea."

She sat back and sighed. There wasn't much point in even being annoyed with the fellow. He was simply daft, the perfect sort of character to encounter at Heather Holloway's funeral. "You know," she said, "the trouble with trying to fool people is that you can lose sight of where real ends and fake begins. You can forget there's any difference at all. And once you've gotten to that place, what comes next is the idea that it doesn't really matter. And then what have you got?"

Donald's blue eyes were very bright but he didn't look away. "That is an excellent analysis," he said. "And please be assured, I know it matters."

Mayo felt herself softening, and a strange sense of calm and patience came over her. His oddness was soothing. "Was she really your girlfriend or was that statement a part of your therapy too?" she asked.

"I considered her my girlfriend but I don't know if she reciprocated. I mean, I don't know if she described me to others as her boyfriend. I suspect she didn't describe me to others at all. For example, I can see that her sister and mother over there don't know who I am. I've seen no evidence that they're looking around, anxious to meet the boyfriend they've heard so much about. They don't know I exist. I mean, they can see that I exist— or they would if they looked over here—but my existence doesn't mean anything to them."

Mayo shoved away the unpleasant sensation that she understood exactly what the fellow was saying.

Donald rolled his eyes in her direction without moving his head, a move that reminded her of Heather. "I've discussed this with my psychiatrist and as strange as it may seem, I'm quite ready to reveal how our relationship was."

"Okay," Mayo said. "I'm interested."

"It wasn't intimate in the way that most people think of those things," he said.

Mayo was surprised at this sudden revelation. "You're saying there was no physical intimacy?"

"That's precisely it."

This didn't fit, Mayo thought. Not at all. Maybe Heather had just been trying to shock Maggie Hurst after all. But the ME hadn't said anything about Heather being a virgin.

"Was that your choice or hers?" she asked.

"It was what brought us together. Two solitary souls who have, I suppose, issues about the human body and its various animal functions. Heather had her issues and as for me—well—" He gestured at his own overly-soft body. "I would prefer a life that wasn't confined to these physical trappings."

Mayo finally gave in and smiled. "You'd be happier as a floating ball of light?"

He returned the smile. Those teeth. "That would be a huge relief to me."

"Forgive my saying so, Donald, but you don't seem exactly grief-stricken over Heather's death."

The smile vanished now. "Oh, that does seem like a bad thing to say."

"Can't help it. Right now the world consists of Suspects and Not Suspects. It's really not a bad way to be. It simplifies life. Don't take it personally either. I'm not judging you, I'm just making an observation."

Mayo paused. She wasn't sure why she was blurting out these philosophical statements, except that it seemed to her that Donald needed to be addressed that way. And she was enjoying herself.

"I think I'd rather be a Not Suspect," Donald said plaintively.

She resisted the urge to give him a comforting pat on the knee. "That's why we're here—to make sure you're in that category."

"Of course, your observation is correct," he said quietly. "I'm not grief-stricken, but I would give anything if I could be. Last night I stood in front of the bathroom mirror and tried to cry. I tried for a very long time. I thought about Heather lying alone, stabbed to death. I imagined it in great detail. She lay in the dirt with sticky blood all over her. I imagined the ripping pain she felt. I imagined her trying to speak before her last breath left her body. I imagined the crazy thoughts flashing through her mind, when she first realized that she was going to stop living, and perhaps she even felt excitement that she would soon discover the nature of that other existence or non-existence—don't you agree that non-existence is by definition just another form of existence? I think I spent an hour in the bathroom working on this. In the end, I failed to cry."

Mayo took a moment to absorb it all. Aside from his immoderate remarks, the fact that he incorrectly described Heather's wound—which had not bled much at all—worked in his favor. Of course, he might be fully aware of that.

"How did you know Heather was stabbed?" she asked.

"I read it on the internet. There was a very long story about it on the local paper's website. It said she had been stabbed in the stomach."

"I have to say, Donald, I don't believe the usual boyfriend would ponder his lady friend's death with such philosophical intrigue."

"I can't deny you're correct but I was obliged to go through that in my efforts to cry, which seemed like an important thing to do. If you've never had this difficulty, it will be hard for you to understand."

"Is there any reason you couldn't?"

"Yes, I'm emotionally defective."

Mayo faltered here, and took a short break. She wasn't exactly sure if he was pulling her leg, but she suspected not. He sat very still, looking down at his hands in his lap. Like the rest of his body, his hands looked soft and unused.

"What do you do for a living, Donald?"

He nodded quickly, as though the question confirmed some thought he'd had. "I am a professional gambler."

She wouldn't have been more surprised if he'd said he was a jet fighter pilot. "You make a living by gambling?"

"Sometimes I make a lot of money; other times I lose money." He smiled with unabashed pride. "Mostly I make it. I believe my presence at the table causes the other players to lose their concentration."

"I can imagine." Mayo wondered if he wasn't trying to use the same ploy on her. "Is that your only source of income?"

"Oh, no. I also have a trust fund. My father back in Indiana runs a spray paint company. Spray paint is very lucrative but the smell of the place made me quite ill. I came out here for college and stayed."

"You live alone?"

"Yes."

"No regular job, you live alone. You must enjoy solitude."

He nodded earnestly. "I spend an embarrassing amount of time online. I have some online friends, at least they seem like friends. My father calls them my imaginary friends. There are several websites where I spend a lot of time entering comments."

"What kind of websites?"

"Mostly poker or forensics." He angled toward her in his rigid manner. "I also enjoy those forensics programs on TV. I admire you being a detective. I wouldn't mind doing that sort of thing every day."

"Did Heather gamble too?" Mayo asked.

"Heather and I met at a poker table in Black Hawk. She's a good player—very good. We met and seemed to become excellent friends within a few moments. That has never happened before to me and I expect it will never happen again. I always return to the same table now because of the good luck it brought me of meeting Heather."

To Mayo's surprise, a hint of moisture suddenly appeared in his eyes. He noticed it at the same time and carefully dabbed at it. He then held the finger before him, examining the tiny smudge as though it were liquid gold.

"Did Heather make money?" Mayo asked.

He took a deep breath, collected himself, and nodded. "She won quite often. Both of us win more often than we lose."

"So you and Heather regularly gambled up in Black Hawk. Every weekend? Or how often?"

"Maybe a couple times a week."

"Why did Heather take the job at Zippy's?"

He smoothed his pants, apparently thinking. "It was shocking and discouraging when she announced it," he said. "But I understood. Her concentration disappeared in the last few months and she began losing. A few weeks ago, things went very wrong for her at the table and she wouldn't stop. She lost a great deal of money. I offered to give her some but she said no, she didn't like to owe anyone anything.

"When exactly did this downward slide begin, do you remember?"

"Back in early summer. Not long after she graduated. I don't know what happened. I asked and she said it was nothing. She wouldn't discuss it. And then she suddenly moved to Sugarloaf from Denver, I don't know why."

"Did you ever go to her house in Sugarloaf?"

"We never visited each other's homes. It was just the way we preferred it. We met in restaurants and went to Black Hawk together."

"Did you ever go to hotels together?"

"No." Donald looked down at his hands. "We didn't have that sort of relationship, as I said."

"Can you think of anyone in Black Hawk who might have something against her?"

He shook his head. "I doubt they were pleased to see us coming, but you know, they make enough money off all the bad poker players and those poor old folks at the machines. They expect a few people will win. We've never had a problem."

"Did she go without you sometimes?"

"I don't believe so."

"Do you mind telling me your email address?"

He looked surprised momentarily, and then a crafty smile appeared on his face. "You've been searching her computer! Of course! How interesting. You'll have found some emails from 'fivecardstud.' That's me, I'm a little embarrassed to say. I realize I don't actually look much like a stud."

Mayo fought back another smile. "When's the last time you saw her?"

"A few weeks ago, the day she lost so badly."

"Have you talked to her since then?"

"We both have a dislike for the telephone so we used only email. And in answer to your next question, I think Saturday was the last email I got from her. She was upset about what happened at Zippy's and wanted me to stay away. Are you the officer who didn't believe her about the attack?"

"I had my reasons."

He nodded. "I am sure of that."

"What do you mean?"

"Nothing. I am sure you had your reasons."

Mayo brought the sketch out of her briefcase and showed it to him. "Have you ever seen this man?"

He took the sketch. "Is this a police artist drawing?"

"Yes. Do you recognize him?"

He pulled out a pair of wire-rimmed glasses with all the speed and determination of an elderly turtle. He positioned the glasses carefully on his nose and spent another minute or so gazing at the picture. Then he handed it back. "No. Who is it?"

Mayo put the picture away. "Were things generally good between the two of you?"

"Yes. We never fought, mostly because I let Heather have everything her way. There was the one demand that she never made, and that was the only thing that was critical to me."

"You mean, the physical intimacy thing?"

"Yes."

"I'm sorry to ask you this, Donald, but do you know if Heather had relations with anyone else?"

"I don't believe so."

"Do you know anything about her going with men to hotels?"

His eyebrows shot up — his first unpracticed gesture. "If that's what she told you then she was lying."

"Was she difficult? Did she make a lot of demands?"

"No, not demanding."

"Easy to get along with?"

"No. I couldn't predict what she'd do next. She was suspicious of everyone and got worse lately. I was worried about her all the time. But she also started to talk more and tell me things. The day she lost her money, she told me some stories. I was happy because she didn't like to tell me much. I don't know why she was suddenly talking. I find people exceedingly difficult to read. It's possible she wanted to change things between us but I don't know how that would go. She told me about her father and other men who tried to hurt her."

"What exactly did she say?"

"She said that her boss at the museum attacked her and her teacher in college attacked her, and that her father raped her. And then later she sent me an email that said she'd been attacked at Zippy's."

"And did those stories seem true to you?"

"I am fairly sure that none were true."

137

Mayo was surprised. Donald seemed like the type who would accept whatever Heather told him. "Why is that?"

He laced the fingers of his hands together as though he were preparing to pray. "I doubt it's statistically possible that so many different men all want to assault the same woman. But I still could have accepted this about her. My psychiatrist feels that my relationship with Heather was not terribly healthy, that she was not entirely available, emotionally. Of course I've argued that I'm not exactly Mr. Wholesome Family Fun myself. I have encountered very few people who come back for more once they've met me and recognize ... well, see how I am. Except for my psychiatrist, who is extremely well paid. But Heather came back for more, even once she realized I had certain impairments. She liked me. In fact, I believe she loved me. She is the one person on this planet who loved me."

Donald dabbed at his eyes again.

Mayo looked up to see Gumble come puffing back into the church. He hesitated, giving her a questioning look. Mayo stood and fished out her card.

"Thank you for your time, Do-*nal*. Please call me if you think of anything." She handed him her notepad. "Could you please write down your phone number and address for me."

He took his time carefully printing the information. "Can I ask you one question?"

She put her notepad away. "Of course."

"Where did it happen? I mean, I know about the ghost town, Wolftongue, but where exactly?"

"We found her in the ruins of a broken down cabin."

"Was it painful for her? I mean, how long did she ...?"

"I don't think she suffered, Donald. We believe it was very quick."

He gazed at her with unabashed gratitude—she wasn't sure why. "I was wondering if perhaps I could visit the spot where she died," he said. "Could you draw me a little map? I want to put some flowers there."

"Sure," she said. "I don't see a problem with that."

Gumble fell in beside her as they left the church. His face was red and damp. "I lost the cowboy."

Mayo gave a light shake of her head. Back to the world of the sane. "Was he trying to lose you or was it an accident?"

"Don't know. When I got outside, he was nowhere in sight. I jumped in the car and drove around awhile but didn't spot him. Sorry boss."

As she and Gumble headed back to their cars, she saw "Donal" watching from the church doorway.

"Run a check on a Donald Chestnut," she told Gumble in a low voice. "Check his license plate against Nutt's list and we'll need to look at his tires."

"That's him?" Gumble asked.

"Yeah. His car is probably right here in the lot, but he's still watching us." She waved at him, but he didn't wave back.

Twelve

After Gumble left to check on the last few hotels on their list, Mayo called McKern. Dressed in plain clothes, he had parked his personal SUV across the street near Toby Hull's house and pretended to work under the hood.

"What're you, psychic?" McKern said when he picked up. "A guy just drove up and went into the house. I've been dinking around with my belts for a two hours and someone called the cops. Patrol car pulled up a while ago, I had to explain. Then the guy arrived not two minutes ago, went into the house—"

Mayo kept her voice neutral. "You didn't let the local P.D. know what you were doing?"

"Was I supposed to? Wait, he's coming out of the house again... garage door opening. He's going into the garage."

She waited. "What's he doing now?"

"A cardboard box just flew out of the garage. Another. Hang on ... The dude is wigging—he's opening crates in there—garage full of boxes and crates. He's searching for something."

"What's he look like?"

"Tall and skinny. Older. Cowboy boots."

"Is he wearing a vest and a white shirt?"

McKern made an unpleasant noise into the phone. "How'd you know that?"

"What kind of vehicle?"

"Older model Ford truck. Probably 1980s."

"What color?"

"Brown. Needs paint. Oops—looking my way ..."

She waited again. "You still there?"

"Okay, he's back in the house ... Hang on. Coming out again. Has his keys. Gotta go."

When Mayo hung up, the message light on her phone was on. It was from Jody Holloway, who said she was at her mother's and would Mayo please phone. Instead of calling, Mayo made the ten minute drive to Delia Holloway's house in Table Mesa. Parked in front were the "Every Knee Shall Bow" Saturn and a blue Forester, which was Jody's. She recognized another car parked across the street—Patty's.

Before heading in, she made a quick tire inspection on the Holloway cars. Neither looked close.

Jody answered the door. Her face looked thin and lifeless, and the effect was to make her eyes enormous.

"How are you holding up?" Mayo asked carefully.

"I'm okay." Jody stepped aside and beckoned her into the house.

Patty sat stiffly at the dining room table with a glass of iced tea in front of her. Stationed in the same oversized chair as before, Delia now wore sky blue polyester slacks that clung to her legs in a fit of static, and a neat white button-up blouse with lace at the neck. An overheated glaze in her eyes, she watched Mayo as she entered the room.

Jody glided past her mother and took a seat on the sofa. Mayo continued to stand while they all angled their heads at her.

Jody pulled her legs up onto the sofa and hugged them. "I think the man who was following me and Heather was at the funeral."

"Which man was it?" Mayo asked.

"The skinny tall guy in the vest."

The winking cowboy, and probably the same guy that McKern was now tailing.

"Are you sure it was him?"

Jody picked at a nub of cotton on one of her socks. A tear suddenly spilled down her cheek. "I'm not positive but it looked like him. I didn't realize he was even there but at the end when Mom was ... I looked up and I saw him heading out the door. I don't know if he was there the whole time or just came in to gloat or what."

Jody stopped picking at her sock and pulled her knees tighter. She shoved the ball of her hand against her eyes to swipe away the tears.

"Jody, do you feel up to answering some questions?" She ignored the disapproving look Patty was giving her.

"Okay."

"Does the name Toby Hull mean anything to you?" Mayo asked gently.

Jody's face changed momentarily. "I don't think so."

She did think so, Mayo decided. "You sure about that? He was Heather's professor at Colorado Western U. Heather accused him of assaulting her."

"I don't know him," said Jody.

Mayo paused. Jody's supposed ignorance about so many details of her sister's life wasn't entirely believable. The email Heather had written to Jody about her latest job did not seem particularly secretive. On the other hand, Jody seemed like she wanted to talk. She just needed the right approach.

"How about any enemies your grandfather might have had in Sugarloaf?"

"My grandfather? I don't know anything about him. I was a baby when he died."

"Do you know where the Alonzo Holloway diary is?"

"You think that's what this is about?"

"We've got to check into it."

"I think she kept it in a safe deposit box. I don't have it." To Mayo's surprise, Jody actually sounded relieved. Relieved, perhaps, that Mayo was now barking up the wrong tree?

"Do you know what bank?"

"No."

"Do you have a family plot where all the Holloway ancestors are buried?" She glanced at Delia, who may or may not have been listening.

"No," Jody said, "but Heather was always trying to find Alonzo's grave. That was her big thing—finding his grave. She was writing a book about him and her search for the grave."

"But she hadn't found it."

"No."

"Did she ever tell you anything about having a tombstone made for him?"

"What?" Jody's voice was unexpectedly sharp.

"I found a tombstone for Alonzo Holloway in her closet."

After a moment, Jody spoke again. "Oh. I don't know anything about that."

"God save us from our children." Delia reached over and rummaged through a drawer in the coffee table. Her hand emerged with the familiar pad and pencil. After concentrating for some moments, she produced a set of zig-zag lines.

Jody watched her mother with undisguised hatred.

Mayo sighed. She did not want to get tangled up in the Holloway family net of dysfunction, but here she was. "Did you know about the Colorado Western charges, Jody?"

"No."

"Professor Hull lost his job and a grant after Heather's accusation. His father, Patrick Hull, reported him missing last June and he's still apparently looking for him."

Delia snorted.

Jody lowered her head and covered her face with her hands.

Patty left the table and sat next to Jody, draping an arm across her back. She gave Mayo another disapproving look.

Mayo waited a minute or two. Jody finally groped through her pockets for a tissue, and blew her nose.

Mayo started again. "Were you aware of the other accusations Heather made? These were against her boss at the history museum in Denver."

"Ah ha!" Delia put in. "I never hear about none of this."

"It's not true!" Jody said sharply.

Mayo didn't believe Jody, but she decided to keep that to herself for the moment. "I'm sorry to have to tell you these things, but last week at Zippy's was the third such incident we've found."

Jody's eyes closed momentarily. "Okay, so you think my sister was crazy and you don't really give a damn if someone killed her."

Patty was working her lower lip between two fingers, giving Mayo a look that said "Back off."

"I think you know that's not true," Mayo pressed on. "I'm trying to get at the truth so I *can* find who killed her. Were you aware Heather had a boyfriend, Donald?"

"Was that the weird looking guy you were talking to at the funeral?"

Mayo nodded. "Did you know about him?"

"Not really. I mean, Heather mentioned having a friend a couple times, but not a boyfriend."

"Heather never told me nothin'," Delia put in.

"He was Heather's actual boyfriend?" Jody sounded hopeful, as though the existence of a boyfriend would prove that Heather wasn't so bad.

"He seemed to think so. He was very fond of her."

Jody spoke to Patty instead of Mayo. "Heather was so excited when the museum hired her. She only just graduated and already she got a job in the field. She couldn't talk about anything else. But after a few weeks it seemed like something was going wrong. She stopped bringing it up and changed the subject when I asked her how work was going. And then suddenly she told me she'd quit. She said her boss was just using her to get the diary."

"She never told you about the attack then?" Patty asked.

"No."

Mayo addressed her next statement to the general room. "Please don't misunderstand me. I'm not saying women don't get assaulted and harassed, because they do. But it's unlikely that one woman would be attacked three different times by three different men in three different unrelated situations — all within one year."

"That's what I been sayin' ever since this attack baloney started way back when," Delia said.

Mayo turned to her. Progress at last. "What do you mean, this attack baloney?"

"Oh, she come up with this twaddle way back in high school," Delia said in a matter-of-fact tone. "She went after a couple boys in her class. All kinds of nutty accusations."

"I'll tell you when it started," Jody shouted. "When Heather and I were just little girls and our dad molested her every chance he got."

"Oh, for God's sake!" Delia tried to get up but didn't make it out of the chair.

"It's the absolute sickening truth!" Jody shouted.

"I've heard just about enough of that crap to last me a lifetime," Delia snarled. "Heather was a born liar, the daughter of the devil from the second she took her first breath. Everything about her was one big fat godless lie. I can assure you that girl is facing the holy music right now for all the damage she's done to her family. And she knows it too — why else would she go on with all that cutting business? You didn't know I knew about that, did you? She was a real loon — I can hardly say she's my own daughter — slicing her flesh like she couldn't stand it. The shrinks told me so, that she cut herself because 'self-loathing,' they called it. I could see they figured it was all my fault but I am telling you, I got nothing to do with that cutting stuff. And right now, that girl is on her unholy knees, begging for mercy and forgiveness. We can only hope the Lord sees fit to give it to her."

Jody jumped up from the sofa and leaned crazily over her mother. "I was in the room, Mother, lying in the upper bunk, listening to every disgusting second of it."

Delia opened her mouth and closed it again. "Sit down. I don't like people standing over me."

"Year - after - year," said Jody.

Delia looked away from her daughter, stroking her throat with rawboned fingers.

"He tried to get his hands on me too," Jody went on. "If it hadn't been for Heather, he would have."

Delia dropped her hand abruptly and narrowed her eyes at Jody. "What do you mean?"

Jody edged away from her mother. "When Heather turned 12 or 13, he got sick of her and decided it was my turn. You never noticed how I always refused to be alone with him, how I practically lived at friends' houses. I never came home from school unless I knew you or Heather was going to be there. Even if he wasn't there, I was afraid to go home because he might show up. And Heather made sure he never got to me. He tried to get us to switch bunk beds but she wouldn't. A couple times he touched me in the hallway and I ran away."

She moved in once again, pressing her face up close to her mother's. "He was an evil pig and you knew it and you let him do it."

Delia waved her bony hands. "Get away!"

"Heather saved me from him," Jody shouted, "and I was glad when he was dead!"

"You're as bad as your sister," Delia screeched.

145

"We were both glad, Mom," Jody hissed in her mother's face. "And you're even more of a devil than him for letting it happen."

Jody moved back then, picked up her purse and keys from the dining room table and ran out the front door.

Mayo gazed after her, wondering if there was more to the story of how Heather had saved Jody from the "evil pig." It occurred to her that she believed Jody, which would mean that Heather had been telling the truth about at least this one thing. Which still didn't mean that the rest of it was true.

She sighed, felt Patty watching her, perhaps expecting her to somehow fix the Holloway family mess. After a few moments, she groped through her pockets for her keys, absently considering whether there would be any weather that afternoon, or if she might be able to make it back up the mountain in time to take the dogs for a hike. It would be fine to vanish into the wilderness, if only for a couple of hours. She wanted to watch the dogs sniff along the trail, bound into the brush. She wanted to get all this Holloway crap out of her head.

No one spoke as Mayo said a quiet good-bye and headed out of the house. Patty seemed frozen in her seat. Delia had lapsed once again into her waking coma, staring out the window at the washed out September sky.

Thirteen

Mayo did not head up into the mountains for a quick hike with the dogs, but rendezvoused instead with McKern, who had been following the man they presumed to be Patrick Hull on an erratic journey around Boulder. After shopping at a hardware store, according to McKern, Hull visited a flower shop—from which he emerged carrying one tulip. He then stopped at an art supply store and a pet store, after which he headed to a well-known hamburger joint on North Broadway, where, McKern reported, Hull ate a house special bacon cheeseburger with onion rings and drank one beer, all the while keeping up a garbled banter with the bartender. McKern stationed himself at the far end of the bar, nursed a single beer and coped with a middle-aged, purple-lipped woman who had taken an interest in him. After that, Hull moved on to another, dingier bar further north, where McKern had been sitting in the parking lot for an hour and a half, until Mayo slid into the passenger seat of his SUV. It was 4:30 p.m.

"I've been following this freak around for hours," McKern said. "I'm not really sure why."

Mayo watched the door of the bar. It was a wooden rectangle of a building, peeling blue paint, no windows and a single black door. Probably not up to code. Cheap beer, floozy waitresses, pot-bellied pool players. Depressing as hell.

"Which one is his car?" she asked.

McKern pointed at a dark colored Ford truck amongst the Harleys and pickups.

"I don't particularly remember asking you to follow him," she remarked presently.

McKern shook his head, watching the road, where rush hour traffic was building. "Sometimes I feel like my job title should be 'mind reader.'"

How about whiner, Mayo thought ungenerously. "Why'd you call him a 'freak?'"

McKern squirmed in his seat. "Because I finally figured out what the hell he was tellin' the bartender back at the other joint.

He was gettin' all fixed up to go down to Trinidad and get himself changed into a woman."

"Uh-huh." Mayo fought back a rise of laughter. She was aware that McKern flailed and needed guidance, and that, despite a hint dropped here and there by Davy Brown, she hadn't spent much effort on that little project. Her idea was that it wouldn't be quite right for her to lead him around on a leash. It would be much better for him if he sniffed things out on his own. Theoretically.

"You sure he didn't spot you?" she suggested. "Maybe he was yanking your chain a bit?"

McKern's young face tightened into a scowl. "Hell if I know."

Then again, she thought, maybe she was just waiting for McKern to screw up so badly she could get rid of him. She opened the door and climbed out. "I've got dinner plans, McKern. Let's talk to our man — or woman — in the morning."

They walked through twilight down Geese Lane. A brilliant spray of orange and pink stratus clouds stretched across the western horizon and recent winds had washed the sky above Sugarloaf into a rich, flawless blue. They turned up Lower Tungsten Lane, Monte keeping up easily despite his ankle.

The Dumpling Cottage was a small building, at least 80 years old, sided in whitewashed wood shingles, with white window grids and a planter box of petunias on either side of the front door. The final storefront at the western end of Davy's Sugarloaf Road walkway, it was run by chef Analiese Zimmerman, a stern woman in her early 70s who had never relinquished her treasured German accent despite many decades in the U.S.

The Cottage only seated about a dozen parties, and the place was full when they entered. They headed for their reserved table by the front window. Much of Zimmerman's business came from loyal clientele down in Boulder, but Sugarloaf residents traditionally got the window seats.

"We're having champagne tonight." Monte snatched the wine menu from Mayo. "And dinner's on me."

"What are we celebrating?" Mayo asked.

"Nothing," Monte said. "My foot. My foot is better and I'm no longer cranky."

Mayo checked out the room. Patty Field and her husband, Corey, nodded from the other window table. Mayo did not miss the amused smile on Corey Field's face—the same goading look she always got from him. She knew what Corey and a few of the other town dinosaurs said about the idea of a female marshal. She wondered where McKern was, if he kept himself hidden on nights like this when his lover ambled about town with her lawfully-wedded spouse.

Patty rose and walked over to Mayo's table.

"Hey, folks." Patty shook Mayo's hand first. "Monte! It's so good to see you out and about. How's the ankle?"

Monte demonstrated his physical abilities by standing up and sitting down again. As he sat, he gave Mayo a luminous smile.

Mayo took this in with an unexpected rush of affection. Monte's hair was getting long and it fell charmingly across his face, making him look younger than he was. He had a whimsical quality that Glen had lacked somehow, even though he was also a joker. Glen's jokes tended to be dark, sarcastic.

Abruptly, it occurred to her that maybe she'd been wrong about Monte's reasons for watching her. But that was a thought stream she did not want to follow.

Patty turned to Mayo. "It was a weird funeral, wasn't it?"

Mayo nodded.

"I stayed with Mrs. Holloway for a little longer after you left. Even though it was pretty uncomfortable and she didn't seem to care if I was there or not. Still, I bet she's absolutely shattered and so is poor Jody, who is such a nice kid. I hope you'll be able to find that guy Jody was talking about."

"We're working on it." Mayo made a point of picking up her menu and scanning the entrees. She glanced up to find Patty still watching her expectantly.

"She's off duty." Monte pointed at Corey. "Back to your husband, woman."

"Oops, sorry," Patty said good-naturedly. "Keep us posted, okay Marshal? We're all just sick about what happened."

Corey kept his eyes on his wife as she returned to their table. He was a short, athletic man with exceptionally thick black hair, and startling eyes that seemed both wary and surprised. He supposedly had some sort of disability that kept him from working, but it wasn't clear exactly what. He was well known in town for his noisy public drinking. Reportedly attractive as a younger man, he now looked merely psychotic. Mayo reminded herself again to have a little chat with McKern before things got out of hand.

After the champagne arrived, they made a toast in favor of Monte's ankle.

"I want to thank you for putting up with me," he said. "It won't go unrewarded. When you're old and infirm, I'll return the favor."

"Monte, I never saw any sign of crankiness," Mayo said. "You're thanking me for nothing."

"You plumped my pillow a couple times," he said.

"Did I? That may have been an accident."

Mayo paused. Were they flirting? It was strange how something could, at the same time, feel all wrong and all right.

At the next table, Sigi Zimmerman pulled up a cart and cleared off dishes. He nodded at Mayo and left without speaking. Within a couple minutes, Analiese Zimmerman came out of the kitchen.

"Monte Mayo!" She shook his hand, pointedly ignoring Mayo. "You are all better now?" She wore an expensive-looking dress underneath her neat apron. Mayo had heard that she'd been unusually beautiful as a young woman, though Mayo could see little evidence of it through the cosmetics she applied to her heavy face.

Monte saluted her with his champagne.

Analiese flashed a brief malignant smile in Mayo's direction. "I see you got your 'not-a-wife' with you this evening."

Monte frowned. "Feeling cantankerous tonight, Analiese?"

Analiese focused on Mayo now. "Speaking of cantankerous, Davy says the town might be sued by this dead girl's mother. He says an attorney phoned him about it."

Mayo felt her face warming further. "That's the first I've heard of it."

"Davy claims he doesn't want to bother you with it," Analiese went on, "but I think you've hardened up a bit finally. No marshmallow, eh?"

Mayo didn't bother coming up with an answer.

Analiese bent over and kissed each of Monte's cheeks. "Order the Wiener schnitzel tonight. It's best."

After Analiese departed, Monte leaned toward Mayo. "Marshmallow?"

Mayo shrugged. "I believe it's derived from 'Marshal Mayo' and comes from the idea that I'm not liable to inspire fear and trembling in any bad guys, I suppose on account of being female."

"It's a cruel world we live in," Monte said. "I've had the burdensome name longer than you, and was subject to the torments of vicious children."

"Mrs. Holloway didn't say anything about a lawsuit this afternoon," Mayo went on to change the subject.

"Forget it." Monte refilled his glass again. "She won't have a case."

The bread basket arrived and Monte pulled apart a thick slice of chewy German farmer's bread. "And I order you to ignore the insults of our Teutonic hostess. She sees women as competition."

"She hates me," Mayo said. "Don't ask me why."

"I know why," Monte said. "You probably don't know that Analiese and Davy Brown were once a big item and still are on occasion?"

"I didn't know," Mayo said. "What's that got to do with me?"

"Davy likes you," Monte said. "He has taken you under his old buzzard wing."

"How stupid. She isn't going to poison our food, is she?"

"I have a question for you. Were you upset about Patty going to Heather's funeral?"

"Why would I be upset?"

"You didn't look happy about it just now when she asked you about it. I'm getting used to your expressions."

Mayo picked up the bread basket and picked out a slice. "Not at all."

Monte leaned forward and said softly, "Do you still think Heather wasn't raped?"

"I still think she wasn't raped. Her story had timing problems that she couldn't explain. And she has made allegations against three different men. Does that sound believable to you?"

"Something for the Guinness book if she was."

Sunday morning, Mayo and McKern drove back down to Patrick Hull's house in Boulder. Mayo didn't want Hull reacting to a police unit pulling up so they took McKern's SUV. She had also told McKern to dress in street clothes again.

Sticking to single-syllables and keeping his eyes on the road, McKern was obviously upset. Mayo did not ask why and didn't mention seeing Patty and Corey out together the night before.

Toby Hull's address led them to a modest red-brick ranch house on a quiet street lined with oak and walnut trees. The leaves were just beginning to turn, and a breeze lifted a swirl of dust from the front walk. While McKern knocked on the front door, Mayo checked the tires on the truck in the driveway. Possible match, she decided. In the truck bed, she spotted a dented toolbox and a scattered bunch of pinecones. She pulled out Deputy Nutt's list of license plate numbers—Hull's was not on it.

"I know he's here, damnit." McKern was working the doorbell when she joined him on the front step. "That's his truck."

Mayo sidled behind a bank of juniper bushes clustered around the front picture window, cupped her hands around her eyes, and peered in. "Someone's in there smoking." She rapped on the glass. "Hello? Mr. Hull?"

She untangled herself from the junipers, brushing off her arms on the front step. Behind the screen door, the main front door opened slowly. Mayo was not surprised to find the winking cowboy from the funeral staring at them from behind the screen door.

"We're looking for Toby or Patrick Hull," Mayo said.

"A peeping Tomasina," the man said. "Do I need to call the cops?"

They produced identification and McKern spoke up. "We're investigating the murder of Heather Holloway."

"May we come in, please?" Mayo said.

He opened the screen door and gestured them into the stuffy room. Swirls of cigarette smoke moved through a stream of sunlight coming in from the big window.

"Are you Patrick Hull?" Mayo asked.

"Last time I checked," he said. "I saw you at the funeral yesterday. Was it my imagination or were you guys chasing me when I left?"

Mayo met his gaze. "Was it my imagination or were you running?"

"He was at the funeral?" McKern asked.

"He was," Mayo said. "And I wouldn't mind knowing why."

Hull closed the front door and bathed them in a suddenly friendly smile. An L-shaped scar highlighted his right cheek — she hadn't noticed it at the funeral. He looked like Wild Bill Hickock. As a young girl, she had read everything she could find about Wild Bill, had drawn pictures of him and tacked them on the walls of her room. She had begged her parents to take her to Deadwood, the place of his death, a special gift they'd given her on her tenth. Best birthday ever.

Mayo felt an unexpected rush of nostalgia. She shoved it away.

He dropped into an armchair upholstered in brittle-looking faux leather and gestured vaguely toward a matching sofa. "Have a seat."

Mayo and McKern sat at opposite ends of the sofa, its cushions crackling unpleasantly. Mayo didn't particularly want to keep looking at Hull's face, so she surveyed the room. Mounted over the fireplace were an antique musket and saber. A male mannequin stood in the far corner, dressed in a double-breasted Civil War-era shell jacket and pants, in Union blue. On the opposite wall, to the side of the picture window, a glass museum-style display case offered an array of Civil War memorabilia.

Hull picked up a picture from an end table and leaned over to hand it to McKern, who sat closest to him. "That's my son, Toby. Missing for three months now."

McKern took a quick look and passed it on to Mayo.

It was a shot of a young man, around 30 years old, with a scruffy half-beard and the vague beginnings of a Fu Manchu moustache. He wore a grey and orange striped t-shirt that gave him a puckish air. Toby Hull was extravagantly attractive, with dark eyes much like his father's and a rowdy smile. Mayo could see why Kate Russell called it a "full-time job" to keep from falling in love with the guy.

More interestingly, he was also the man in the dark vest who showed up in so many pictures from Heather's photo album.

"It's my belief that Heather Holloway was somehow involved in Toby's disappearance," Hull said.

"What makes you think that?" Mayo asked.

Hull puffed deeply on his cigarette. "I'm sure you already know the story of her phony charges against Toby, or you wouldn't be here, right? The girl was obsessed with my son, and out of this great love did her best to ruin his life."

"Is that why you've been following her?"

He sat up straight — an exaggerated motion. "Who says I've been following her?"

"We have a witness." Mayo pointed at an Indiana Jones hat sitting on the kitchen table. "You weren't wearing your distinctive hat yesterday."

He relaxed again, smashing his cigarette out in the ashtray. "Nothing distinctive about my hat, though I am quite fond of it."

"Another thing mentioned was a big moustache." Mayo met his gaze. "And a wink, kinda like the one you gave me at the funeral."

He favored her with a sly smile. "Look, I read about her death in the paper and went to the funeral. I knew about her charges against my son and I thought I might find out something about what happened to him. Hell, I even had the wild idea maybe he'd show up. But I didn't and he didn't. Silly me. I'm a desperate chump."

"A brown truck was also mentioned," Mayo said, adding a small fib about the color, "so I'm thinking maybe I'll take a picture of yours and show it to my witness. I'm guessing it will be identified." Jody hadn't been clear on the color and Mayo doubted the girl would know one truck from the next, but Hull might buy it.

"Lots of brown trucks around," Hull said.

"You live alone here?"

"For the moment. And since I know you're trying to figure out a clever way to ask, I was with a lady friend the night before your victim was killed—all night and into the morning. Mostly in bed. There was some food and coffee in the morning too. She left around ten."

"Can anyone verify that besides your lady friend?" McKern asked.

"Only our videographer."

Hull returned McKern's sneer with a pleasant grin.

"Her name's Vivian Something." Hull found a piece of paper, wrote down the woman's name and number and handed it to Mayo.

"How did you know when the murder took place?" Mayo asked.

His face did not change. "I read it in the paper."

Mayo got up and went to the display case. Three worn-looking forage caps were neatly arranged against a black velvet background. One shelf was filled with brass insignia—miniature crossed sabers, artillery cannons, bugles. Another velvet plate displayed brass buckles and an array of chevrons, buttons, and epaulets.

"Quite a collection you've got here," she said.

"It's Toby's."

She turned. "This isn't your house, then?"

He crossed his leg, resting an ankle on his knee. His foot jiggled—perhaps nervously, she thought.

"I live in St. Louis," he said. "I came out last June when he disappeared."

"What exactly happened?"

"As far as I've been able to figure, he loaded his mountain bike up in his truck and took off for a weekend in the high country. Something he did often, except this time he never came back. A week or so later, they found his truck in Keystone—that's it sitting in the driveway. I found a spare key in the house."

"What steps were taken to find him?"

"Cell phone records, bank account, credit cards, social security number, tax records, license, insurance—all the usual. His computer was hosed so we got nothing there. We searched in the area where his truck was found but he and his bike were gone."

"You seem familiar with the process," Mayo said.

"St. Louis P.D. Homicide. Retired."

Great, Mayo thought, he'd been running his own investigation—although he didn't seem to have gotten anywhere.

"So what do you think happened?" she asked.

Hull suddenly got up and headed into the kitchen. "Can I get you folks some coffee?"

Mayo followed. Hull pulled three mugs from a cupboard and poured from a coffee maker.

"You want cream or sugar?"

"None for me, thanks," Mayo said. "So what do you think happened to your son?"

He poured a stream of sugar into his own coffee mug, then finally looked at her. "I think he's probably dead. If he were alive, he would have contacted me. He wouldn't put me through this hell. Does your deputy want any coffee?"

"No he doesn't," McKern said, scowling from the kitchen doorway.

"You still went to Heather Holloway's funeral looking for him," Mayo pointed out.

He gave her a stark look. "We parents are full of all kinds of ridiculous contradictions."

She recognized the ragged quality of his tone—he was still getting up every morning and somehow functioning through another day but it was not the same as actually living. The strain of it showed in his voice and on his face. Despite his quips, deep shadows gave his eyes a distant, vacant quality. Like Jody Holloway, Patrick Hull was shattered.

Mayo also knew how it went—fitful nights, forgotten meals, booze and hangovers, surprise meltdowns, lurid thoughts that wouldn't go away. Torture. There was nothing to do with it but try to survive. Or not.

Back in the living room, Mayo gestured at the musket and sabre over the fireplace. "Anything missing from the house that you know of, Mr. Hull? Like that kind of stuff?"

Hull gazed at her, his expression blank. "Not that I know of."

"What's in the garage?"

He shrugged. "Toby's stuff. I don't know what all."

"Like maybe a Civil War era bayonet?"

He shrugged again.

Mayo took a thoughtful sip of coffee. "Let me summarize the situation for you," she began. "Your beloved son is ruined by the wicked Heather Holloway. He disappears. You are seen following Heather in the days before she gets murdered. The murder weapon is a Civil War antique. Your house is full of Civil War antiques. You show up at Heather's funeral. You see us there and rush out. You hurry home and make a mad dig through your garage. You apparently spot my man here, watching you from across the street, so you decide to lead him on a wild goose chase around town. Next day we show up to talk to you and you don't feel like answering the door and when we insist on coming in, you just don't seem all that interested in talking to us. Do you follow, Mr. Hull?"

Hull smiled at McKern. "I'm not really getting an operation in Trinidad."

McKern sent a scowl in Hull's direction while Mayo went on.

"So here's what I'm thinking. I'm thinking how easy it's going to be to get a search warrant. I'm thinking maybe I'll just send my deputy over to pick it up right now while I wait here for him. Of course, it would put me in a better mood if you would just sign a Consent to Search."

Hull worked on his moustache with his fingers and smoked a cigarette for a while. "Just because one thing happens right after another doesn't mean the events are related."

"Slick answer," Mayo said. "I'm betting you were a great cop. Even so, allow me to repeat that you are looking mighty interesting to us, isn't he, McKern?"

McKern nodded with obvious relish. "Mighty interesting."

"Why don't you go grab a Consent to Search from the car," Mayo told McKern.

THE TROUBLE WITH HEATHER HOLLOWAY

After McKern left, Hull fixed his gaze on Mayo with a disconcerting frankness. The disquiet behind his smile was hard to look at. A retired homicide detective with a wronged and missing son would be capable of anything, she thought. And he was letting her know it.

He rose and went to the front door. "Right this way, Marshal."

She followed him outside and Hull pulled up the garage door, revealing a single car garage packed with three neat rows of cardboard boxes and wooden crates. A couple of empty boxes lay strewn in a messy pile near the door, and one crate lay open, revealing a mound of shredded paper.

"So what were you looking for yesterday?" Mayo asked.

He looked older in the morning sun, his L-shaped scar showing clearly in the light. Mayo wondered how he got it. He dropped his cigarette on the cement driveway and smashed it with his boot. "The preacher at the funeral said she'd been bayonetted. My son's collection includes at least a couple bayonets and I had a feeling the garage had been burgled last month so I came out to check."

Convenient story, she thought. Maybe too convenient. "And?"

"And..." Hull went to the open crate. "There's only one of 'em in here. Should be two."

Mayo pulled on some gloves and pawed through the shredded paper. Nestled within the crate was a bayonet in a leather scabbard. She lifted it and slowly drew the bayonet out from the scabbard. The handle was gold colored, the blade long and flat.

"That sure looks familiar," McKern said behind her.

It sure did.

"You say there were two?" Mayo asked.

"Yeah." Patrick Hull shifted on his feet. "I remember 'cause Toby used to have these mounted on his wall in an 'X.' Looks to me like someone got in here and took the one that was missing a scabbard."

"When was this burglary?" Mayo asked.

"Alleged," McKern put in.

Hull ignored McKern's comment. "A few weeks ago. Early-to mid-August thereabouts."

"Did you report it?"

His left eyebrow rose. "Nope. I wasn't even sure it happened until yesterday when I saw one of the bayonets was gone."

"What made you think you'd been burgled?" Mayo pressed.

Hull pointed at a flimsy looking back door, which led into the back yard. "I came home one day and found it open. Not much of a lock on the door—easy to pick. Toby was kind of stupid when it came to that sort of thing, keeping all this valuable stuff out here. The problem is I don't know what all he had so I couldn't tell if anything was stolen. I didn't know what to look for."

Mayo surveyed the stacks of boxes and crates. "Who knows this stuff is here?"

He shrugged. "Toby had a lot of friends. He tended to throw parties and whatnot. He liked to show off his collection. I'm guessing any number of people would have known about it but of course, I don't know because I didn't live here."

Mayo tried to read him. She judged him perfectly capable of telling any sort of lie. Back in the kitchen, he had seemed pretty broken about his son, but now he had returned to a light tone.

Still, if he had known anything about the murder weapon, why wouldn't he get rid of this second bayonet?

"We're going to need to take this." She placed the bayonet back in its scabbard and into the crate. "Do you know a Joanna Selig? She was listed as his emergency contact at the university."

This time, something flashed through his expression. Concern, possibly. Shielding. Affection. "Toby's ex-fiancée," he said. "She lived here up until sometime last spring."

Gumble had finally tracked Joanna Selig down to a phone number in Vail, where a man informed him that "the bitch" had moved out still owing money for rent.

"You know how to contact her?" Mayo asked. "We'd like to talk to her."

Pulling out his cell phone, Patrick Hull pecked out a number. He turned and walked far enough away that Mayo couldn't hear. She watched as he had a brief conversation, standing at the bottom of the driveway. Looking up, he gave Mayo another wink, and she felt an involuntary rush of warmth in her face. Judging from his little smile, he noticed it. He would try to keep her off balance, but she wasn't going to let him.

He moved the phone away from his face and called up to Mayo. "You want her to come by?"

She nodded, watching him sharply as he finished his conversation. He snapped the phone shut and strolled back.

"She's on her way."

Fourteen

Joanna Selig had eyes the color of a noonday sky, and she put them to use right away, batting her lashes at McKern as she walked up the driveway. McKern was impressed enough to open his mouth and leave it that way.

Hull hugged the young woman. "You're buttering up the wrong party," he said in an exaggerated whisper. "The lady's in charge."

Joanna smiled at Mayo, a gesture that wasn't entirely friendly. She seemed frail, with very white skin, and at the same time tall and lanky, with the looks of a model. Young, too — probably in her early twenties.

Mayo reciprocated with the same sort of warning smile that only a woman would recognize, brought out a notepad and took down her contact information. "I wonder if I might speak to you in private," she said pleasantly.

Joanna shoved her thick auburn hair behind her ears. Small diamonds glittered from her earlobes. She looked quizzically at Patrick.

"I'm afraid we're on the suspect list," he told her. "At least I am."

"He didn't do anything!" Joanna said.

"How about we go sit somewhere quiet?" Mayo gestured at McKern's car.

Mayo got Joanna settled into the passenger seat and closed the door, pulling McKern off to the side. She lowered her voice. "Get Hull to sign the Consent. Include the house, the garage, and the truck."

"Yes, boss."

"When you get a chance — wait 'til he's in the house or otherwise occupied, and bag the pinecones from the back of his truck."

"Pinecones?"

"Just do it, McKern, and don't let him see you."

When Mayo climbed into the car next to her, Joanna dragged fingers through her hair, pulling it briefly into a ponytail, then letting it slink luxuriously around her neck. She gave Mayo a flirtatious smile, rolled down the window and stuck her arm out. "How come you don't have a regular police car?"

"Our town is cheap. You working, Joanna?"

More ponytail flipping. "I'm assistant manager in a boutique on the Pearl Street mall."

"What was your relationship with Toby Hull?"

Now she folded her hands in her lap, taking on a prim expression. "Toby and I were together two years and we were going to get married. But we broke up and so I ran off with a ski bum and lived with him up in Vail. After I figured out that the ski bum was a bum, I came back to Boulder."

Mayo had the feeling Joanna had prepared herself for this conversation—probably with some coaching from Patrick Hull.

"When was the last time you saw Toby?" she asked.

"I know he didn't kill that girl."

"I didn't say he did. When is the last time you saw him?"

"Last April. He and I had a fight and broke up and I left."

"What was the fight about, if you don't mind?"

Joanna narrowed her lovely eyes at Mayo. "I don't even know you. Why do I have to tell you about my private life?"

Mayo decided to go for the commiseration angle again—it worked on most people. "I know it just seems like I'm prying, Joanna. I can guess that you've probably suffered a lot and you have my sympathy, really. I know what it's like, believe me. Under normal circumstances, this is none of my damn business. But these aren't normal circumstances. One person is missing and another is dead. I'm not just trying to find out about Heather—I want to know what happened to Toby and I know you do too."

Joanna seemed to buy this for a moment, but then her features hardened. "You just want to arrest him for killing Heather Holloway."

"Help me prove he didn't do anything. What was the fight about?"

Joanna sighed, dragging her fingers through the ponytail again. "I finally figured out that Toby was cheating on me." She

THE TROUBLE WITH HEATHER HOLLOWAY

gave Mayo a "Can you believe it?" look, as though the notion were the most absurd thing in the universe.

"Go on," Mayo said. "Do you know who it was?"

She shrugged. "No idea."

"So how did you find out?"

"Intuition. For a long time, I had a feeling that he wasn't really *with* me anymore. He didn't *adore* me anymore. I mean, a girl needs to feel like she's adored, doesn't she? Anyway, Toby was kind of weak when it came to some things, like telling the whole complete truth, for example. He also had a little trouble saying 'No' to anything. He was all 'Yes, yes, yes!' to whatever came his way." She rubbed her eye with the ball of her thumb. "He was crazy about me and everything, but I guess he just couldn't behave."

Mayo actually felt sorry for her now. "Was he in love with this other person?"

Joanna frowned. "I didn't stick around to find out. I asked him if he was being true to me and he admitted he wasn't and I told him to go cram his head in a cement mixer and left." Joanna's eyes grew shiny.

"Sounds rough."

She shrugged again. "I'm over it I guess." Her hands, lying in her lap, twitched.

"Did you speak to him after that?"

"Yeah. I called him a few times just to see if I still gave a damn about him. That's when the whole Heather thing happened at the university."

"What did Toby say about it?"

"It was out of the blue," Joanna said indignantly. "Suddenly Toby gets called into that old fart Mason's office and he's blabbing at him about some supposed sexual assault. There was never any evidence and the police never filed any charges against Toby because the bimbo couldn't prove anything. Toby said that jerkoff Mason believed every word of it because he hated Toby and because Mason was screwing Heather."

"How do you know this?" Mayo asked.

If true, it could explain Mason's contentious attitude. Depending on school rules, he might not lose his job for having an affair with a student, but the fact that he sided with Heather against Toby—with no evidence—made his dismissal of Toby highly questionable.

"Toby said he saw them together—Mason and Heather. I mean, gross! Have you met that guy, Mason? He's a real slug. I had to sit next to him at a dinner once—God, what a freak. He drank about two barrels of wine and started slobbering all over me. Gak. His wet dishrag of a wife kept watching from across the table like it was all my fault. I was, like, hey, get your old slob of a husband under control. But Mason already hated Toby, even if he wasn't screwing Heather. He was jealous because Toby was beautiful and brilliant. Mason is just a worm squirming around in his nice cozy university apple. He must have been jumping for joy to find an excuse to get rid of Toby."

Mayo wondered if Joanna realized she was still in love with Toby. Hell, Mayo had never even met the guy and she was half in love with him herself—when she wasn't busy being a moron about his father.

"I gather Toby decided not to do anything with this information?" Mayo asked.

Joanna smoothed an imaginary wrinkle out of her slacks. "He said he was still trying to figure out the best way to handle the whole thing. Patrick and I even thought maybe Mason had something to do with Toby disappearing. Maybe Toby went after him and something happened. So we told the cops about it and they went and talked to Mason but Mason was at some conference in Denver that weekend with a million other people."

Mayo remembered a note about a talk with Mason in the Denver P.D. police report. She also remembered that Mason hadn't mentioned any of this.

She wondered if she could get Joanna to admit what Patrick Hull would not.

"Then you and Patrick decided maybe Heather had something to do with Toby's disappearance?" she suggested.

Joanna gave her a sour look. "Who said we decided that?"

"Patrick. He said he thought Heather was involved."

"But we didn't do anything to her," Joanna protested. "Besides, Toby's not the only person she's gone after."

"Who else did she target?"

Joanna paused, apparently afraid that she had revealed something but not quite sure what. "I read the papers. I know about the thing at the gas station, whatever the store was called."

"You mean Zippy's." Mayo pondered this. Patrick hadn't mentioned anything about Zippy's either—he said he'd read about Heather's funeral. Could be a simple oversight, but she doubted it.

Her eyes on Mayo, Joanna screwed up her mouth as prettily as anyone could. "I get the feeling you're trying to trick me into saying something."

"I'm not, Joanna," Mayo lied. "I'm just hoping to get your help in sorting out everything that happened here. So you and Patrick took turns watching her or you did it together?"

Joanna narrowed her eyes. "Neither."

"No?"

Joanna shrugged stiffly, avoiding Mayo's gaze. "Not that I know of."

Joanna wasn't a very good liar, Mayo decided. She pulled the Holloway assailant sketch from her briefcase. "Do you recognize this man?"

Joanna looked at the picture, then shook her head. "Is that a picture of the supposed Indian guy from the gas station?"

"That's him.

"Never saw him before," Joanna said.

Back in the garage, McKern was replacing the lid on a wooden crate. Hull leaned against the garage doorway, a cigarette dangling from his mouth.

"We're almost out of your hair," Mayo said. "Just a couple more questions."

He shrugged as though to indicate he might answer and might not.

Mayo pulled out the sketch again and showed it to Patrick. He shook his head.

"Doesn't ring a bell?" Mayo prodded.

"Nope."

"Joanna tells me that she read about Heather's Zippy's antics with great interest," Mayo said. "It seems a little odd to me that you didn't mention knowing about it."

Hull massaged his chin for a moment. "I can see how you might read more into that little omission than you should. Is that what the sketch is from?"

McKern finished closing the crate and pulled off his gloves. "You knew what the sketch was from," he said. "You lied."

"I didn't lie," Hull said. "I just wasn't completely thorough. Listen, I'm cooperating. I told you about the missing bayonet, didn't I? I'm letting you stick your grubby paws into my son's things, aren't I? Search all you like. Search the house. Search my pockets. Here—" He opened his mouth wide. "Check between my teeth."

"Jesus H.C.," McKern said.

"I see you have gold fillings," Mayo remarked. "Were you following Heather?"

"Why would I kill her?" Hull said. "I figure she was the only person who knows where my son is."

"Did either of you send an anonymous letter to the Denver police?"

Hull glanced at Joanna. "No, but that sounds interesting. What kind of anonymous letter?"

Fifteen

The door to Mason's office was closed and he didn't answer Mayo's knock. She found a petite Latina typing into a computer in a miniscule room two doors up the hall who said he was usually in around ten o'clock. Mayo caught a hint of disapproval in the woman's voice.

At 10:15, Mason turned a corner and when he spotted Mayo came to an abrupt halt. Catching himself, he nodded and continued toward her.

Mayo, who had been leaning against the wall, stepped up and held out a hand. "Dr. Mason," she said cheerfully. "Thought you were about to turn and bolt for a second there."

His palm was damp and she picked up the metallic whiff of hangover breath.

"That's what you get for thinking." He pulled a set of keys from his pants pocket and got his office door open. "What can I do for you?"

She followed him in as he switched on the fluorescent lights and put his things on the desk.

"I'm here because I'd like to re-start our conversation about Heather," she said, closing the door. "Maybe we can get it right this time."

He responded by picking up a piece of paper and pretending to read it. "I don't know what you mean."

"Heather Holloway. You. Or should I say, you and Heather. The intimate relationship you neglected to mention."

Mason coughed out a phony laugh and said, "I never had an intimate relationship with that woman."

Mayo waited, her eyes fixed on him.

He put the paper back on the desk, took a quick look out the window, then sat. "Who the hell has been gossiping about me? That little yap dog, Kate Russell?"

"A friend of Toby's mentioned it. Someone not connected with the university and who therefore has no reason to make up such a story."

"They call that hearsay, don't they?"

"Did Toby confront you about it?"

"Of course not. There's nothing to confront."

"I guess this is a good time to point out," Mayo said, leaning on his desk, "I don't particularly care for it when I get lied to and you already wasted my time with a pack of lies last time I was here. Now, when I know I've been lied to, or when I smell an obfuscation, I get extra-specially attuned to the possibility of more lies and more obfuscations. And my lie and obfuscation alarm is going off big time right now."

Mason glared, moving toward her, chest-first.

"Put your chest thumping away," Mayo said, "and allow me to clarify how annoyed I'm feeling, Dr. Mason. I am going to call your wife and ask her what she knows about it. I am going to call the chancellor and the president of the university. I am going to call the press. I am going to tell them that you fired Toby Hull because your student-lover asked you to. Did I mention I've got a witness, Dr. Mason? Someone saw you together."

"I don't believe you," he bellowed. Then he moved back around his desk, sat in his chair and stared out the window.

She waited quietly while he pouted. She felt revulsion, and a warm sense of justice. He had helped destroy Toby Hull, apparently without much thought, and now it was coming back to him. This created balance and Mayo loved balance.

"What do you want?" he growled finally.

Mayo wanted to twist the knife just a bit. "Does your wife know about the affair?"

"No."

"When did it start?"

"When she came to see me about Toby."

"How did it start?"

"She kept visiting my office to talk and told me she trusted me and then one afternoon suddenly she came around the desk and ... well, I went along."

"Did you have a physical relationship?"

"Yes."

"Intercourse?"

"My God." Mason's face was red. He mopped his forehead with his sleeve.

"Answer, please."

"Yes. The answer is yes."

"Here in the office?"

"Of course not. We—we left and went to a motel. It only happened a few times."

"How many times?"

"Maybe three or four times. It only lasted a few weeks."

"When did it end?"

"Right after Hull left."

"Who ended it?"

"She did."

"What was her reason?"

Mayo saw a flash of real pain in Mason's eyes.

"She didn't bother coming up with a reason," he said. "She said it was a mistake and it was over. She wasn't pretty about it."

"I see. That must have been hard to take."

"I didn't enjoy it, if that's your next question, but I quickly realized that she was a deeply disturbed young woman who needed professional help."

"You only noticed that after she dumped you?"

Mason moved his jaw. "Of course not. I knew she had issues."

"Yet you helped her go after Toby Hull?"

"I didn't see it that way. I believed her."

"When's the last time you saw her?"

He dropped his hands in his lap. "Not since spring, when she graduated."

"When is the last time you talked to her?"

He had loose, dry-looking lips and Mayo fought away the image of young Heather kissing them. The guy was old enough to be Heather's grandfather.

"She called me last week," he said. "She claimed someone was stalking her."

This caught her attention. "Did she say who it was?"

"No."

"Why did she call you? What did she want you to do about it?"

"Hell if I know," he said. "She didn't make any sense and it was a brief exchange. I wasn't incredibly keen on listening since she basically blackmailed me into recommending her for the goddamn museum internship last summer. I mean why the hell—"

"What do you mean she wasn't making sense?"

"She said Toby was after her."

"Why did she think that?"

"I told her she was crazy, that he was missing and probably dead. She said it didn't matter if he was dead, he was still after her. I told her she was crazy."

"Why did she think that?" Mayo asked again.

"Hell if I know. She's crazy, remember? The fact is, I'd had a few drinks and didn't pay much attention."

Mayo took a moment to absorb this. Toby Hull—an abandoned truck in the mountains, no credit card use, no contact with friends and family. All circumstantial indicators that he was dead. Still, no body.

"Do you remember how the conversation ended?" she asked.

"She hung up on me." He licked his lips, scanning the ceiling. "And now she's dead. So, okay. Maybe there was something to it. Maybe Hull is still alive and took care of her. And maybe I'm next."

"Do you have any actual reason to conclude that?" she asked, though she agreed it was possible. "Someone following you?"

Mason glared at her. "No, but still."

"Did you ever hear of anyone threatening Heather about her ancestor's diary or her Sand Creek theories?"

He shrugged. "She whined about it."

"Any whining in particular?"

"Some resentment from other students."

"I'm going to need a list of all Heather's classmates. In particular, I'd like you to mark the names of American Indian students." Mayo jotted down her email address and pushed it across the desk at him. "I'd appreciate it if you could email me that information by the end of the day."

Mason looked sideways at the slip of paper. "I don't know if I can pull that off."

"Sure you can."

Mayo hoped he wouldn't mention this little chore to Kate Russell, who would try to put a stop to it. For now, she had Mason exactly where she wanted him.

"You know, Dr. Mason," she said. "I've met Heather. In the very short time I knew her, she told me so many lies my head is still spinning. She was more than just a little disturbed."

Mason looked almost grateful as he stared at Mayo. "I don't know how the hell I got mixed up with that mess. I made a mistake. A big one."

"I wouldn't blame you if you felt just a jot relieved to find out she was dead. She can't tell your wife now."

He narrowed his eyes. "You're fishing for a confession, eh? Don't hold your breath. I don't know what happened to her. I thought we agreed it was probably Hull, back from the dead."

Mayo went to his window and looked out over the tidy university lawn. A pair of young men were walking across the grass. One pecked something out on his phone while the other talked, oblivious to the fact that his companion wasn't listening.

"I don't remember agreeing on that," she said, turning. "Last Saturday morning, where were you between 12 midnight and 10 a.m., please."

His mouth opened but it took him a moment to begin speaking. "Fergawdsake, all right. I'll play along. I went to bed my usual time, around 11, got up at seven as usual. I had breakfast and puttered around the house."

"Can anyone vouch for that?"

"My wife sleeps late. Our cleaning woman came in around seven-thirty or eight. You can speak to her if you wish."

Mayo gave him a piece of paper and a pen. "Write her name and contact information, please."

He scribbled on the paper and handed it back to her. "You're wasting your time, but go for it."

She studied Mason as she put the slip of paper in her pocket. He was a man of rotten character, hiding in a stuffy little office with his title and his comforting flask. She considered him perfectly capable of murder.

After leaving Mason's office, Mayo checked her messages. She had one from Len Belka, the computer forensics guy, and another from Maggie Hurst at Colorado Frontier Museum.

She called Belka first, who gave her the name of a bank in Boulder where Heather kept a safe deposit box.

"Good job," Mayo said. "Anything else from the computer? What about chat room activity or surfing history?"

"Yeah. Online poker, a bunch of history sites. Your girl had several obsessions: pioneer cemeteries, the Arapaho and Cheyenne Indians, the Sand Creek massacre, and a ghost town called Hellfire."

"Where's that?"

"Summit County, near Keystone."

Keystone, where Toby Hull's truck was found.

"Thanks, Len." Next, she called a judge in Boulder to ask for a search warrant on Heather's safe deposit box, then she dialed Maggie Hurst's number.

"I'm supposed to let you know that Felix asked one of our part-timers to search the collection for missing bayonets," Maggie said when she came on the line. "Nothing missing, we're happy to report."

"Okay. Thanks."

"And I've got a confession," Maggie went on quickly. "I mean, Felix and I do. I hope it won't make you too terribly cranky with us."

"I'm listening."

"We talked about it and decided we'd better let you in on our little secret. No one at the museum knows about it, but Felix and I are married and we have been for a long time."

"Okay. That explains why you're listed at the same address."

"Oh!" Maggie said. "You knew about it already. You must have been thinking bad things about us all this time."

"Why keep it a secret?" Mayo felt impatient with Maggie's chatty routine. What did she really want?

"It's not too complicated," Maggie said. "When Felix was hired as curator the assistant curator position was also open. He wanted to hire me but we knew there'd be issues—people

172

whispering about cronyism and so on. You understand how people can be."

Mayo sighed. "Yes, especially when they get lied to."

"Uh-oh, you are cranky. I'm sorry, really. We both are."

"So one day you'll announce to your colleagues that you've fallen in love and eloped to Las Vegas."

Maggie made an unidentifiable noise at the other end of the line. "Something like that."

Mayo held the Alonzo Holloway diary in her hands. Hardbound and faded, the front cover hanging on by a few threads, it had been stored in Heather Holloway's safe deposit box.

Inside, the writing was an elegant cursive in faded ink. She paged through it briefly, read a few entries:

"Our colonel is a preacher and he says we must clear out the country for Christian civilization."

"We are all going mad with doing nothing. On night watch last night. Yesterday they hung a horse thief. Fellow asked for it, I say."

"We rode all night, had little to eat. My feet nearly froze by morning. Still, our mood is excellent. We are finally moving. No more Bloodless Third."

Tucked between the pages were two folded pieces of paper. The first was a homemade map, drawn using a computer graphics program. It showed a road running alongside a river, with a couple of dotted paths heading away from the road with tiny hiker icons. Other icons indicated a campground, some ruins, a bear, a rabbit, running water, numerous mines, and a strange oblong shape dotted with three black circles, like a barbell with three bells. One of the mine icons was flanked by a circled tombstone and a star, which seemed to be the destination. The map title read "Hellfire."

Len Belka had mentioned Heather's web search for information about Hellfire.

The second piece of paper was a muddy-looking picture that had been printed by a laser printer on regular letter paper instead of photographic paper. It showed a tombstone on a bare rocky mountainside next to a tunnel opening. The tombstone read, "Alonzo Holloway 1845 - 1920." It looked a lot like the tombstone Mayo had found in Heather's closet.

Sixteen

Mayo called Gumble and McKern on her way back to Sugarloaf and they met in the office. Mayo cut herself a slice of lemon cake that Emlyn had brought in and led the deputies back into the conference room.

"What's the latest?" Mayo said, settling at the table with the cake.

"We've gotten a few more calls from people who've seen the Indian guy," McKern said.

Mayo sighed and ate another mouthful. They'd been getting a lot of calls from people who'd seen the Indian guy, and not one of them had sounded sane. She'd been showing the artist's sketch to everyone as a matter of routine, but did not particularly expect it to lead anywhere.

"All right," she said. "Let's hear it."

"Old Mrs. Poe came in," McKern said, "and says she saw the guy walk by outside Daffodils." He checked his notes. "She said he was wearin' a hatchet—" he glanced up "—or something like that, tucked in his belt."

Gumble groaned.

"This sort of assistance from Mrs. Poe is unavoidable," Mayo said. "What else?"

"Two phone calls." McKern paged through his small notepad. "A couple kids saw a guy doing something strange up at Wolftongue last night."

"Like what strange?" Mayo said.

"They called it 'jumping around the fire.' They said they got scared and drove off."

"Jumping around the fire," Mayo repeated, keeping a smile out of her voice. "You mean like on the warpath, I presume. Did they mention a vehicle?"

"No."

"Okay. Probably needs to go in the same category as Mrs. Poe. The other call?"

McKern cleared his throat. "The last one sounded pretty wacko. Not sure who it was. Said he saw an Indian but he was also rambling on about the president being a terrorist and so on."

"That's great, McKern." Mayo said.

"So do we follow up on those or not?" McKern asked.

Mayo sighed and made an effort not to look at Gumble. "You really think they're worth following up on, McKern?"

"Look, these aren't the best tips but I still don't get why you're so skeptical about it. I figure this Indian guy is our best lead."

"Fine," Mayo said, putting her fork down. "Fax the sketch to the Arapaho and Cheyenne tribes. There's the Wind River Reservation in Wyoming—I don't know where else. Our friend Dr. Mason has promised to email me a list of American Indian students in Heather's college classes by the end of today. I'll forward that to you, McKern, as soon as I get it and I want you to run checks on them. Okay. Let's go over our suspects again." Mayo went to the white board and began to write down names.

"Let's start with Danny Pitt who works at Zippy's," she said. "He had some kind of kinky little thing going with Heather in the few days they knew each other. He thought he might get laid, but it didn't happen. He's got rampaging hormones—maybe they got out of control."

"I have a hard time seeing Danny Pitt figuring out the Alonzo Holloway history and writing the note and getting hold of a bayonet," Gumble said.

"I agree it's extremely unlikely." Mayo drew an unhappy face next to Danny's name.

She wrote another name: "Patty Field."

"No way," McKern declared.

Mayo drew another unhappy face. "No motive, and she actually seemed to like Heather. Anyone else in town?"

Gumble spoke up. "Her neighbor, Honeysuckle No Last Name. She's chanting for Heather's soul even as we speak. I wouldn't put her on this particular list. The other people I talked to had no fond memories of old man Holloway, but nobody knew Heather."

"I'd say that angle's a zip," Mayo said. "Moving on to the family—Jody Holloway. I'm guessing she's one of two people on the planet who actually gave a damn about Heather. There's the mother, Delia. Heather had disowned her. Not much apparent physical strength. Has hired a lawyer to sue the town of Sugarloaf for whatever they can get away with. I don't see either one of them as killing Heather." Mayo drew unhappy faces for Jody and Delia.

"Who's the other person who gave a damn about Heather?" asked Gumble.

"Donald Chestnut, the boyfriend or whatever it was. Did you run a check on him yet?"

"Yep. No record. I drove down early this morning, had a look at his tires. No match and he wasn't on Nutt's list either. His car was dusty though. He'd been on a dirt road recently."

"He said he wanted to take flowers to the spot where she died," Mayo said. "I should have asked him to delay that. We now know Heather had a brief affair with Carl Mason over at the university. Looks like she was using him to get at Toby Hull. Maybe Donald found out about it, and maybe he's not as incapacitated by weirdness as he seems. I've learned he likes to play-act and knows how to psyche out other players at a poker table." Mayo gave Donald a happy face.

"I also swung by Hull's place and took some pictures of his tires," Gumble said. "I emailed those over to Troy this morning. I'd say they're a possible match but only a maybe."

"Good job," Mayo said. "Happy face for Hull. There's also Heather's gambling at Black Hawk," she went on. "McKern, call Donald and find out which casino they played at. Go up there and sniff around."

Mayo scanned the list of names on the board. "Okay, now. Colorado Frontier Museum. We've got Felix Arkenstone, who neglected to mention that his assistant is his wife."

"I say he's a nice suspect," Gumble said. "If only because he's one of Heather's targets and we know he's alive."

"Capable too." Mayo gave Arkenstone a happy face. "I wouldn't want to mess with this guy. Not the type to forgive and forget, in my mind. He and Maggie Hurst left for Sand Creek that morning sometime after rush hour. Gumble, did you find any record of them entering or exiting the museum garage that morning?"

"Yep." Gumble dug around in his pocket for a small notepad and flipped through it. "Let's see. Felix Arkenstone's electronic key was used to enter the garage at 9:34 a.m. No exit on that day. Maggie Hurst's key was used to enter at the garage at 8:41 a.m. and exited at 9:52 a.m., same morning."

"Maggie, the secret wife," Mayo said. "Possible motive is revenge for the accusation against her husband—a bit flimsy, but what the hell." Mayo gave Maggie a happy face.

"You can get to downtown Denver from here in about an hour and a half," Gumble said. "With traffic, probably more like two hours."

"Saturday morning, no rush hour," Mayo said. "Say Heather was killed just after 6:30—someone could have buried the stuff and driven back to Denver by 8:15 or 8:30. We may need to run a test on that."

She looked back at her list. "Moving on to Colorado Western U. Carl Mason, Dean of the History department. Lied about his affair with Heather until confronted. Cheesy, miserable character, not lovable. Snarls when cornered. Drinker. Your basic basket case. Gumby, did you call the housekeeper?" She had given Gumble the contact information over the phone earlier.

"Yep. She says she was there that morning and chatted briefly with Mason when she came in, but she doesn't remember exactly what time. She said she usually goes in around eight."

"Okay. He said seven-thirty or eight, which isn't entirely the same thing. We may need to revisit her. I'm keeping him high on the list. Heather had her claws into him enough for a possible motive. Oh, and there's one other person of interest at the university—Kate Russell. A friend of Toby's, possibly more. Let's keep her on the happy list just for giggles."

Mayo scribbled notes on the board. "Okay. Moving back to Boulder. There's Joanna, the disgruntled ex-fiancée. Says Toby Hull was seeing someone else, but doesn't know who it was. Patrick Hull already has a happy face. We've got some pine cones out of his truck—I'm having those compared with pinecones from the scene. A long shot, but what the hell. He supposedly has an alibi, which he volunteered without being asked. But he's an ex-cop." She dug around in her pocket and handed Gumble the piece of paper Hull had given her with Hull's lover's name and number.

"Says he was in bed with this lady, Vivian. Run her down, would you? The murder weapon likely came from his garage, though we haven't confirmed it yet. He says it may have been burgled."

Mayo paused a moment, gazing at Patrick Hull's name. "He's in a very bad place right now. Capable of anything."

"And he's a dick," McKern put in.

"His son is missing and he's got us — the police — sniffing around in a murder case," Mayo said. "You'd be a dick too."

"Okay! Okay!" McKern said. "No need to bite me."

Mayo felt an unwelcome churning inside, took a breath.

"Which brings us to the man himself, the charismatic Toby Hull," she continued, "who lost his job and a grant because of Heather. Disappeared last June. No evidence that he is actually dead but nothing to indicate he's alive either. If he is alive, he's got the strongest motive and said he was going after Heather. If he's dead, we want to know how and why."

She drew a happy face next to Toby's name, then went on. "We still don't know any more about the SUV at Zippy's, which was also seen by Monte. I'm guessing the truck that Jody saw outside the grocery store was Patrick."

She examined their list. Too many suspects. She dug around in her briefcase and pulled out pictures of Heather's mutilated head and of the piece of Heather's scalp they'd found buried in the hole. She tacked the pictures to the bulletin board.

"Why *was* she scalped?" Mayo asked.

"Well, sorry if I'm so stupid," McKern said, "but they say the Indians used to run around scalping people. You forgot to put the Indian up there."

"Oh, yes." Mayo wrote 'American Indian' on the white board and drew a neutral face next to it.

"That guy is probably a descendant of someone who got clobbered during the massacre," McKern said. "These people don't forget stuff like that."

"It's possible," Mayo said.

She pulled out the map and picture of Alonzo Holloway's tombstone from Heather's safe deposit box and tacked them up. She wrote "Recurring Themes" on the board and underlined it. "One, we have a map made using a computer program, tucked into the Holloway diary. It gives directions to something represented by a tombstone, located in a ghost town called Hellfire, which is near Keystone, which is where Toby Hull's truck was found. Heather was doing web searches on Hellfire. Toby Hull disappeared in June. Heather's pseudo-boyfriend says Heather began acting weird in June."

She scribbled notes on the board. "Another recurring theme: the tombstone. I'm fairly certain the one in that picture is the same one we found in Heather's closet."

Gumble scratched his chin. "The tombstone stuff is a muddle as much as a theme. Someone lures her up to Wolftongue on the promise of finding her ancestor's grave. Meanwhile, she's got a picture of his grave in her safe deposit box, and the tombstone from the picture in her closet. That all just seems like crazy noise — doesn't make any sense at all."

Mayo put the cap back on her marker. "Gumble, I'd like you to get up to Black Hawk this afternoon. McKern, you're working on the American Indian angle."

"What are you going to do?" McKern asked.

"I am going up to Hellfire."

McKern snorted and shook his head, making notes in his notepad.

"You got something to say, McKern?" Mayo asked.

"Don't get me wrong, boss," he said. "I realize you know what you're doing, but it's just a stupid map stuck into a book. I don't get what you figure on finding there."

Mayo put the marker down. "I believe I may find out something about Toby Hull." She felt extremely patient.

"I got news for you: he's *dead*. You'd need fifty thousand people to search those mountains for a body."

"Maybe," she said mildly. "Nevertheless, I think he's somehow connected to our dead girl and I think this map is connected to both of them. And unfortunately for you, McKern, I'm in charge of this investigation. If you can't handle that, the door is right over there."

When Mayo arrived home, the house was quiet. Too quiet. Monte's absence somehow felt louder than his presence.

She leashed up the dogs and set out for a hike. The details of the case churned in her head. She needed to step back, get a clear picture. It occurred to her that she was sucked into it now, forgetting about everything else. The way she used to be.

It felt as though her withering life had found fresh water after a long drought. She was finally moving on.

The dogs trotted at her side, stopping here and there to sniff. They headed west out of town, up the Orange Blossom trail, where Heather used to run. Once into the trees, she unclipped their leashes and let them roam. She pushed the case out of her thoughts and absorbed the sharp clarifying scent of the forest.

They hiked for over an hour, then turned back as the sun began to set. The trip down went faster and they were back on Geese Lane in no time. She was famished. If Monte wasn't home yet, maybe she'd run over for a cheeseburger at the Peregrine—

"I heard the town of Sugarloaf is being sued now."

Mayo stopped in her tracks and turned. She was just three doors away from the sanctity of her home, but Brin Beedle had found her.

"Brin, what a delight."

"Yeah, right. You've been avoiding me again."

Tinker, an 85-pound greyhound, shoved his long nose into Brin's privy parts. She pushed him away.

Mayo pulled Tinker back and gave him a congratulatory scratch around the ears. "I would never avoid you, Brin."

Brin stepped closer, a thrill showing in her dark eyes. "I hope you realize what people are saying."

Mayo took a deep drink from her water bottle.

"They say you're ignoring the obvious. You don't want to admit you're wrong about her being raped at Zippy's. The girl had all kinds of problems with the Native Americans, she was scalped and eviscerated by a bayonet from the Indian Wars era. Can't help wondering why you refuse to investigate that aspect of it."

"Where'd you dig up those so-called details?"

"You said you were going to give me the real story. You said it was going to be a hot one. And then all I get is a whole lot of nothing."

"I'll give you the story when I know what it is. Come on, Brin, how many days has it been?"

"If you don't know what it is, how do you know it's so hot?"

Mayo shook her head and started to move on. "Oops. Caught me there."

"I've got to print something, you know. I might print what I found out about you."

Mayo stopped and turned.

Brin smiled. "I thought that might get your attention. I've been wondering about you since the day you got handed that marshal job without even a search for candidates. I wonder if anyone else in town knows that you killed your own husband in a car wreck. Forgive me for being blunt, but I understand you were barely injured and that you left the Denver P.D. very suddenly right after. Why is that?"

The greyhounds whined. They were hungry, wanted to get home and eat, then curl up for a nice snooze. Mayo did too.

"So that's how it's going to be, eh?" she said.

Brin took a step closer, and Mayo caught a whiff of jasmine. Such a pleasant scent.

"So you don't deny it?" Brin said.

Mayo drank again from her water bottle. "I can't tell you what to print and what not to print. However, if you run off with some cockamamie crap about this case, I will make a point of contradicting you and making you look foolish to every news service I can get hold of." She pushed past Brin and made clicking sounds to bring the dogs along.

"I will not be kind," she said over her shoulder.

When she got home there was a message from Monte on the answering machine that he was heading for dinner at a vegan joint in Boulder if Mayo wanted to meet him there. Mayo didn't feel like driving down the canyon and sensed that the Peregrine might not offer a relaxing question-free meal at this particular stage, so she ate a tuna sandwich in the kitchen and fed the dogs. Afterward, she dug through her briefcase and pulled out the Alonzo Holloway diary. The perfect escape. She wouldn't let Brin Beedle mess with her head. She had a case to solve.

In the morning, Mayo sat at the kitchen table nibbling a cheese and mushroom omelet. After another rotten night's sleep, she felt drained, worried. The nighttime conversation with Brin Beedle had made her feel exposed again, even claustrophobic. In no time, the "Glen" story would be dogging her. She wouldn't be able to breathe. It would be like it had been back at the Denver P.D. — people watching and wondering what really happened that night in her SUV. The hang-up phone calls might start up again. Maybe she would have to move once more, leave the state, try to start over in some place where she could be invisible.

Maybe she'd never be able to move on.

Monte sat across from her, paging listlessly through an art magazine. As though feeling Mayo's eyes on him, he looked up. "You okay?"

"Sure, I'm great."

He rattled the magazine. "A great liar anyway."

Mayo told him about the conversation with Brin Beedle. When she finished, he got up, came around the table and hugged her.

"Just do your job, marshal. Keep your eye on the ball." With that, he left the room.

Mayo sipped her coffee. On the table in front of her was the police artist's sketch. The man's features were stiff, unfriendly, but attractive too. He looked worn, tough, solid. The bad eye stared off to the side. She wondered if she'd been wrong in not taking the sketch seriously.

She pushed it aside. After staying up too late to finish the Holloway diary, she felt bleary-eyed and she wasn't sure she had learned anything of much use. Toby Hull had been right about it—the Alonzo Holloway who wrote the diary was just an immature boy of 19, fixated on John Chivington, the mastermind behind the Sand Creek massacre. Holloway obsessively admired another cavalryman as well, Major Ned Wynkoop, until Wynkoop "went turncoat" and tried to make peace with the tribes. This happened after a fateful meeting between Wynkoop and a Cheyenne chief named Lone Bear, whom Holloway described as "an evil-eyed demon of the plains who bewitched Major Wynkoop and who slashed my leg down to the bone with his knife during the battle." Holloway went on for another page about how he had been crippled during the "great battle" at Sand Creek, how he resented the rumors about "mutilations and scalping," which "never once happened to anyone he saw on the battlefield."

It was all very interesting from a historical perspective, but she couldn't see anything worth killing over.

She picked up her fork and began to eat. She was swallowing the last bite when Monte returned to the kitchen wearing his hiking gear.

"Going up Arapaho Pass today," he said. "Gotta test my ankle. I won't invite you because I know you're too busy."

Arapaho Pass—one of Mayo's favorite hikes—was a vast semi-circle of rugged blue peaks, a lush valley below dotted with beaver ponds and impenetrable banks of willows.

"When I'm done," Mayo said. "And thanks for being a good friend. I never realized it before—back when Glen was alive."

"Why didn't you come down and join me last night?" Monte had come in around ten o'clock the night before, tired and happy after a "stunning" meal at the best vegan house in town.

"I've been up and down the canyon too much lately."

"Beth..."

"Yes?"

"I don't want to upset you again after the Brin stink bomb."

"Okay."

"But I decided I better tell you, I stopped by Bartleby's last night for orange juice and heard some junk."

"Go on."

"Pete Nipper said Deputy McKern was in there earlier jawing off about the case. He said you aren't following up on the Indian sketch thing. He said your past history with the hate crimes unit has got you too scared to touch it and that he's the only one in the department who believes Heather Holloway was actually attacked by this Indian guy."

"I see."

"He, meaning McKern, also said you don't really want to be marshal and don't pay close attention to things. He said some other crap too."

"Let me guess. He called me a 'marshmallow.'"

"Can't you fire the little twit for insubordination or stupidity or something? I mean, we all love Davy but coddling his nephew in the middle of a murder case is above and beyond."

Mayo sighed. This was an issue she really didn't feel like dealing with at the moment. But sooner or later, she would have to. "I probably could fire him," she said. "Davy knows his limitations. The timing's not great right now though."

Monte suddenly smiled. "I stuck up for you."

"Did you?"

He reached over and tapped her arm. "Of course I did. You know I did."

"Sometimes I wonder."

"Wonder what?"

"I sometimes wonder if maybe you're thinking, 'Howcome Glen is dead and you're alive?'"

"What the hell?"

"Beedle was right about one thing," she went on. "I did leave the Denver P.D. suddenly and there were people who thought I did something bad. People who blamed me."

"Cut it out, Beth. Just stop. You're making this up."

"You think I'm being paranoid?"

"No, you're not paranoid. But you're not yourself. You're overly wary now. Wary of everything and defensive, and you've got that survivor guilt thing going."

"I didn't imagine the phone calls," she said coldly.

"Phone calls?"

"Dozens of them. Hang up calls after Glen died. And the looks. My own commander in the department. He loved Glen. Everybody loved him. I've seen that expression on your face too. I am the person who killed your brother."

"No, Beth," he said. "Just no." He moved toward her but stopped himself. "I've said this before, maybe you could find someone to talk to. Get some of this garbage aired out so you can see it for what it is."

"And I've said it before, I don't want to." She picked up her dishes and headed into the kitchen to wash up.

After Monte left with the hounds, Mayo picked up the phone and called Patrick Hull. "What are you doing today?" she said. "I might have a lead on your son."

Seventeen

Mayo drove, with a gloomy Patrick Hull in the passenger seat next to her. He seemed hungover, barely grunting out a greeting when she picked him up, and had been unhappy about the tombstone icon he saw on the "Hellfire" map that she'd pulled from Alonzo Holloway's diary.

"What the hell is Hellfire anyway?" he asked as she headed up I-70 into the high country.

"I assume it's a ghost town."

"Is this tombstone supposed to be my son's grave?"

"All I know is that it was important enough for Heather to hide away in a safe deposit box. But I admit, it might be nothing."

"You don't think it's nothing."

"I hope it's something."

He sighed and stared out the window at mountainsides dotted with autumn patches of yellows, reds, and orange.

It occurred to her suddenly that she was getting better — she actually noticed the fall colors. Maybe it was the contrast with Patrick's obvious suffering. She had been like that for many months. But now, the presence of the mountains was a balm for her. This had always been her favorite time of year — hers and Glen's. Every September, they made a backpacking trip into the high country, driving their truck up this same highway, leaving shop talk behind. On the trail, Glen filled the woods with ridiculous stories and laughter. They ate beans and tortillas and freeze dried soups. They hiked up thirteeners and fourteeners. When she lagged, he waited patiently, and sometimes pulled her by hand to get her going again. It still made no sense to her that such an animated human, such a dynamo, was abruptly dead. The shattering event had come out of nowhere. But maybe she was starting to accept it.

After two hours of driving, they passed through the Eisenhower Tunnel. In recent years, the mountains on the west side of the divide had taken on the dull hue of dead trees — millions of lodgepole pines killed by the pine beetle epidemic. It seemed a fitting backdrop for today's mission.

At Silverthorne, they turned off I-70 and headed south. After stopping in Keystone to buy sandwiches and bottles of iced tea, they continued on, soon turning onto an unpaved county road that led toward Hellfire Pass. They drove by a corral where horses swished their tails and munched on rich-looking grass. A couple of Jeeps passed by heading out, leaving clouds of dust in their wake.

"We're looking for a trailhead." Mayo rattled Heather's map. "Something to do with a bear. If we come to a campground, we've gone too far."

"I recognize this road," Patrick said, finally sitting up straight. "We searched around here."

"I thought you might."

"Didn't find a damn thing though."

Mayo spotted a trailhead marker. She pulled over and Patrick got out to read the tiny sign.

"Ruby Mountain," he said, climbing back in.

They continued on and within a few minutes they came to another trailhead — Bear Trail.

"This is the one," she said.

"Let me see that map again," he said.

The first part of the trail was a steep uphill climb across a field of thick autumn grass, then into a grove of aspen trees that were still turning color. As they entered the grove, they were enveloped in a shimmering golden light cast from millions of autumn leaves. The eerie effect was heightened by the serpentine soil, which gave the ground a reddish tint—a recent rain darkening it to near purple.

They soon emerged from the aspen, crossed another open meadow, then headed up the mountain into a pine forest. Mayo was glad the area had not been hit by the pine beetle disease — yet, anyway. Horse tracks marked the trail, and Mayo spotted a pile of elk droppings.

The trail crested a hill and headed downward for a while. They came upon a brooklet and Mayo paused to dip in a couple of fingers. The water was shockingly cold, fresh off a snow-crusted peak somewhere. Someone had placed a log bridge over the brook and Mayo stepped across easily, with Patrick behind her.

After the brook, the trail widened into what must have once been a mining road. It skirted the mountainside, just uphill from the brook, and the pleasant sound of the gurgling water rose up the valley as they hiked. The path mellowed into a gentler slope and they entered a clearing, where Patrick called for a halt.

"Cripes," he said. "You're a hiking machine." He sat on a log and took a swig from his water bottle.

Mayo had a drink too, and scanned the surrounding woods. From deep in the trees, a twig snapped. She held a finger to her lip. The faint sound of rustling branches reached them. She caught movement in the brush alongside the stream. As they watched, a female elk emerged from the trees and made her way along the brook. She stopped suddenly and looked up in their direction before ambling off into the dark forest.

"Nice spot," she said.

Patrick pulled a candy bar from his pack and took a big bite. "Toby's kind of place," he said with a mouthful.

"I don't know how he did this on a mountain bike," she said, pointing at the narrow trail heading uphill. "Assuming he did."

"That kid could do whatever the hell he wanted."

Mayo pulled a baggy of trail mix from her pack and ate a handful. "So I hear. I got the impression he was quite the character."

Patrick chuckled without humor. "Driven, you could call him. Obsessive. But he knew how to stop and enjoy too. And he knew how to survive."

The word hung between them for a moment.

"You were close," she said presently.

"Actually, not really," he said. "Not when he was younger. I was a crappy father, if you must know. Just another stupid cop obsessed with the job—St. Louis, as you can imagine. A tougher town than Denver. Toby was close to his mom."

"Where is she? Back in St. Louis?"

"Nope. Gone. That's what happened to bring Toby and me together. My wife died and I couldn't cope. I just couldn't get on with it. So my son came back to St. Louis that summer and kicked my butt. I kept wondering why the hell he bothered." Patrick finished his candy and stuffed the wrapper back in his back, averting his face.

"Seems like an odd thing to wonder," she suggested. "He's your son."

"Sure, and I was pretty well worthless as a dad. I didn't earn it."

"But you appreciated it."

He smiled, and she caught a glimpse of the winking cowboy she'd first seen at Heather's funeral. "I did for sure. Sounds cliché but I think he saved my worthless butt that summer. Pestered me back to the living."

She nodded. "I can relate."

Before he could insist on an explanation, she hoisted her pack back into place and started heading up the trail. She heard him follow behind her.

They hiked in silence for another hour or so. Lulled by the rhythm of their footsteps, breathing in the sharp alpine air, Mayo had almost forgotten about their mission when Patrick stopped and pointed at a split in the trail.

"Which way?" he said.

She pulled out the map and they clustered together to look at it.

"There's a split where we go to the left," Patrick said, putting a long finger on the map. "What's that rabbit about? And what's that thingie supposed to be?" He pointed at a rectangle filled with three bulging circles.

They scanned the area, and Patrick made a guttural noise and ran over to a tree. It was a pine tree, its trunk marred by three swollen galls.

He was excited now and started briskly up the path to the left, past the diseased tree. "What the hell! I think we're onto something! Come on!"

Another hour later, they passed timberline and the trail vanished.

Patrick was panting heavily from the steep slope. "Where the hell are we?"

Mayo had been worried for a while that they might have missed a smaller path going off to the left. The map said they should have encountered some mine ruins before hitting timberline. Now there was nothing in front of them but scree and talus.

It was past noon now, and to the west, a wall of heavy clouds had settled over the peaks. The wind had come up a bit and the air felt cool and refreshing. They turned and headed back down into the trees, looking for the turnoff they'd missed.

Ten minutes later, Patrick pointed at a trail heading sharply up to the left. "How come we didn't see that?"

"Looks a bit overgrown. We don't know how old this map is."

They were quiet as they headed up the new path. Soon, they arrived at a closed up mine shaft, now just a dent in the earth next to a pile of rubble that someone had dug out of the earth more than a century before. Among the trees lay pieces of rotted wood and the rusted remains of an old bedspring. Mayo checked out the map again, and wondered if the ruins were the abandoned settlement of Hellfire. According to the map, they would soon hit timberline again, then find another mine along with something else, represented by the tombstone icon.

The trail headed up more sharply now as the sun disappeared behind the clouds. The western peaks were completely hidden, and it smelled like snow. They pulled jackets from their packs and Mayo put on a pair of gloves.

After another quarter hour, they arrived again at timberline and once again the trail vanished into a scree field.

And it was snowing.

"What the hell," Patrick puffed. His hair was sprinkled with snowflakes. "Do you have a clue where we are? Did we screw up again?"

Mayo scrambled up into the scree, sending a small cascade of rocks down the mountainside. He followed.

After a few minutes, she stopped and surveyed the area. It seemed untouched by humans—nothing more than a desolate plain of rocks stretching endlessly up. No sign of a path.

"What the hell," Patrick said again. "I don't see how even Toby could pass over this mess on a mountain bike."

The sky was dark, and the snow thickened. Mayo continued up into the scree field. After hesitating a moment, Patrick followed.

She wiped snowflakes from her face, stopping again to scan the scree for signs of a path. She moved on, lost her footing on the slick rocks, slipped and fell, banging her elbow.

She felt Patrick's hand on her arm, pulling her up.

"You okay?" He pushed a bit of her hair away from her eyes.

"I'm thinking we better find some shelter," she said.

He looked tired and cold. He had only brought a light jacket with him. It was snowing hard now and she looked around at the rocks and the clouds. She spotted something on the mountainside—the edge of something dark, partially hidden behind a ridge. And something gleaming in the faint light.

"Over there!" She pointed.

They picked their way across the talus. Just beyond the ridge were the crumbled remains of what used to be a wooden retaining wall built into the steep mountainside. Above it, a tunnel opening. Leading out from inside the tunnel was a series of rotting railroad ties. A pair of gleaming rails reached out and ended abruptly in space. Below the extended rails, the mountain fell sharply away, its slope littered with wood debris and rubble.

A flimsy wooden gate blocked the entrance to the tunnel, patched with three "No Trespassing" signs.

They made their way up the treacherous slope to the tunnel opening, where Patrick yanked the gate out of the way. They crept in.

A few feet inside the tunnel, they stood shivering. Mayo's skin tingled with cold and excitement. They turned and watched the snowstorm—it had abruptly thickened into a white-out. Behind them, the tunnel issued musty air from its depths, and the rusted narrow-gauge tracks disappeared into the dark.

Mayo stepped back outside and surveyed the area surrounding the tunnel. She pulled out the picture of Alonzo Holloway's grave and showed it to Patrick.

"I found this along with the map," she said. "This is the place. See? The configuration of rocks matches the picture."

"But no grave," Patrick said. "I'm still confused."

She moved back into the tunnel, took out her flashlight and scanned the interior. It headed upward into the mountain at a gradual angle.

"Not much friendlier in here than it is out there," Patrick commented. His voice sounded low and hollow.

He turned on his cell phone flashlight and together they ran their beams along rock walls. The tunnel did not go straight back, but veered left.

Damp and cold, they moved slowly along the tracks. The light from the mouth of the tunnel quickly vanished behind a turn. After veering off to the left, the tunnel switched to the right again, then back to the left, all the while heading gently upslope. Mayo understood just enough about hard rock mining to know that the miners had followed a meandering vein into the depths of the mountain.

Patrick stopped and Mayo nearly ran into him. The scrabbling sound of falling rocks echoed from somewhere. They slowly moved on, the soles of their boots crunching against the rough ground. The universe had become blackness, Patrick's breathing, a queer musty scent, train tracks gleaming in the narrow light beams, the feel of damp against her legs.

"I can't hear anything except my breath." Patrick's voice sounded faint now — more resigned than afraid.

The upward angle of the tunnel leveled off. It seemed like much longer, but Mayo guessed they were only a few minutes in when Patrick stopped again. "What's that?" He played his flashlight beam across the ground up ahead.

Mayo added her beam.

The tunnel widened in front of them. Along the wall was a large pile of rocks. It looked all wrong, and Mayo could not think of any good reason for it to be there. It was man-made.

She scanned the surrounding ground. Faint lines showed in the dirt, as though it had been swept with a tree branch.

"Are you thinking what I'm thinking?" Mayo said.

"Dear God, I don't know," he said.

They found elevated spots to position their flashlights and went to work, lifting rocks off the pile, one by one. The work seemed to take a very long time.

Mayo stopped suddenly. She picked up her flashlight and trained it on the rock pile.

Sticking out from among the stones were the shrivelled remains of a human hand.

"Holy mother..." Patrick staggered backward into the dark.

Mayo ran her flashlight beam across the thing. She saw the cuff of what she guessed had once been a white long-sleeved shirt.

"It could be Alonzo Holloway," she said hopelessly, turning to check on Patrick. As she did so, her light passed over the far wall, deeper into the tunnel. She caught a flash of metal.

"What was that?" Patrick said. "Did you see that?"

He trained his own beam of light across the cavern, and it glittered against what looked like a fan of white sticks.

Spokes on a bicycle tire.

"Oh God," Patrick said. "It's Toby. My boy Toby is here."

Eighteen

Patrick Hull had not moved in a while, except to suck on a cigarette. He stared out the big picture window in his son's living room. Though he seemed more hung over than drunk, Mayo suspected he had not been sober since he returned from Hellfire, two days earlier.

She had talked to him on the phone several times since then, and none of the conversations had been particularly lucid. She considered the possibility that his drinking might have been getting in his way for a long time now and could explain his months of camping out in Toby's house without making much progress in finding out what happened to his son. Or, there was another possibility.

Back on the mountain, she and Patrick had scrambled down the trail through the snow, despite the dicey conditions. When they hit cell reception, she began making calls. The storm was bad enough that CBI and local officials decided to wait until it passed, so she and Patrick found a hotel for the night. Without saying much, he had gone to his room with a bottle of scotch. The next morning, when the weather cleared, Joanna Selig drove up to take Patrick back to Boulder. Mayo led a local rescue team back up to the cave. A crew of four carried the remains down the mountain through snow and slush and mud, then put Toby Hull's body into the coroner's van that was waiting at the trailhead.

The medical examiner successfully fingerprinted the body — despite its advanced state of decomposition — and confirmed his identity. The CSIs also found a wallet in the pockets, had removed an amazingly well-preserved driver's license from the wallet with Toby Hull's name on it. The preliminary report determined that he had been dead for several months — probably since the time of his disappearance. He had died from multiple blunt force injuries, cause of death either a beating or a fall down the mountain — most likely the latter. Which meant someone had carried him into the tunnel.

They fumed the bike with superglue and discovered only Toby Hull's prints.

One significant finding was that body fluids were detected in the soil beneath the body but not on the rocks piled around it. Which meant the rocks were not present when the body decomposed. Which meant that someone came along later — weeks or months later — and piled rocks over him.

Which was what Mayo wanted to discuss with Toby's father — that other possibility.

Hull sat by the window, the day bright outside. He stroked his chin with his fingertips, humming faintly and rocking in the recliner. Instead of his dead son, he might have been thinking about lunch. His rocking was rhythmic, hypnotic, and Mayo thought inexplicably of the golden colors on the trail up to Hellfire, the path damp and mulchy from autumn snowstorms. She thought of the elk poking amongst the grasses by the creek, the drowsy silence of the valley, the beautiful bleak mountainside.

And then the horror in the tunnel.

She stood quietly for some moments before speaking. "You been sitting here boozing for the past two days?"

One side of his mouth twitched. "Sobered up for your visit."

She sighed. "You have someone who could come over? Where's Joanna? Or didn't you have a girlfriend around here somewhere? Vivian?"

Mayo was surprised to find that she felt awkward bringing up the subject of these women.

He did not respond.

"How about I make some coffee? Anything to eat in the fridge?"

He looked at her. "What're you, my wife all of a sudden?"

Her skin prickled and she cursed herself for falling into the trap of trying to bring a drinker around. Patrick Hull wasn't her problem. She didn't even know why she was thinking this through.

"Sorry," he said abruptly.

She looked up to find him watching her.

"I thought I had accepted that he was probably dead," he went on. "I obviously hadn't. Didn't mean to zing you."

"Don't worry about it."

"Forgive me?"

"Forget it."

He massaged the back of his neck. "Jesus. I got a hangover. Did you say something about coffee?" He hoisted himself out of the chair and walked into the kitchen, where he filled the coffee maker with water and brought a sack of coffee out of the cupboard. "You want some?"

"No thanks." Mayo tried to organize her thoughts. She had some questions for him—she needed to ask them and go. But this man had finally—absolutely—lost his son, and she felt reluctant to push.

He got the coffee maker going then filled a glass with tap water and drank it. "Did you say it looked like he'd been beaten?"

"The ME said it looked more like a fall, probably down the mountainside. He had a number of broken bones and his clothing was torn in the corresponding spots. And based on the injury to his skull, there's no way he crawled back up and into the tunnel on his own."

He rubbed his face. "Oh, God. Toby."

"I'm so sorry, Patrick," Mayo said.

Hull leaned over the sink, staring out the window into the back yard. After a few moments, he looked up. "Did you tell me all this already?"

"I mentioned it, yeah."

He turned on the kitchen faucet, splashed water over his face and dabbed it dry with a grimy dish towel. He turned around and faced her. "This isn't some goddamn biking accident, is it?"

"Nope."

"What the hell." He leaned against the counter, shaking his head.

Mayo chose her words carefully. "CSI says someone came along later—probably at least 50 days later—and buried him."

His face changed. "Huh?"

She explained about the decomposition and the rocks, keeping the details to a minimum. Hull was a homicide detective—he could fill in the rest for himself if he needed to.

When she was finished, he poured two cups and handed her one, even though she'd declined it.

He slurped loudly at the rim of his cup. The suave cowboy from Heather's funeral was long gone.

"So you think it was me," he said.

"Me - what?"

He flashed a humorless smile. "Me who buried him."

"Was it?"

A trace of his previous swagger showed now as he straightened up and swallowed more coffee.

"So," he said after a moment. "You think I'd leave my own son up in some god forsaken tunnel somewhere?"

"It's possible — if you had good enough reason."

It had occurred to her that maybe Patrick Hull had been putting on an act during the whole journey with her up to Hellfire. Maybe he had already found a copy of the map. He had mentioned that Toby's computer was hosed, but maybe he lied or maybe there was another printed copy. Maybe he used the map to discover his son's body, buried him, and then decided that Heather was responsible so he murdered her. It was a workable conclusion.

"Well, I didn't," Hull said. "But am pretty sure I know who did. Heather Holloway."

"That's possible too."

"Of course she did," Hull went on. "She killed him, got paranoid about him lying there, and went back later and buried him."

"It's possible."

"Stop saying that." He put his coffee down suddenly. "You still got that picture? The tombstone one?"

Mayo found the picture in her briefcase and handed it to him.

"Follow me," he said. "I need you to see something."

Out in the garage, he opened an oversized cardboard box and plunged his hand into a pile of shredded paper. It came out with a fist full of chiseling tools.

"Toby's stone carving tools." He nodded at the box. "My wife gave that stuff to him when he was in high school." He dug around again, with both hands this time, and from out of the depths lifted a piece of blue-tinted granite.

Mayo stared at the thing. The size, shape, and color matched the Alonzo Holloway tombstone from Heather's closet, and it said "A-l-o" with a chip marring the "o."

"A-l-o, as in Alonzo Holloway," Mayo said.

"Toby must have made it," Hull said. "This thing was the first try. He made a mistake on the 'o' and had to start over with a fresh piece of granite."

"Has this been out here the whole time?" Mayo asked.

Hull shrugged. "I looked through this stuff when I first came out from St. Louis and I noticed it then. Didn't think anything of it at the time." He flashed another empty smile. "Guess that brilliant deputy of yours must have missed it during his search, eh?"

"No comment," Mayo said. "You mind if I take this? I'd like to get them compared."

They put the unfinished tombstone back in the box and carried it out to Mayo's SUV. Back in the kitchen, they found their mugs and sipped coffee for a while. Mayo was beginning to understand.

"Heather was obsessed with Alonzo Holloway and finding where he was buried," she said. "She talked about writing a book, all about this big grave-searching adventure. Toby must have known that. Oh, one other little thing we found in his pocket — it's no good now, but he was carrying a small tape recorder."

"Jesus," Hull said. "What was on it?"

"Tape was no good," Mayo said.

"Last time I talked to him," Hull said with sudden energy, "Toby said he was going to get her to fess up somehow."

"So he cooked up this scheme," Mayo said. "He made the tombstone, propped it up in a believable setting — up at Hellfire — and took a picture. He sent it to her, along with a detailed map so she could come and find it."

"And he went up there and waited for her to show up," Hull continued. "He left his truck in Keystone so she wouldn't see it at the trailhead and rode his bike up."

"Along comes Heather, following the map to the tunnel," Mayo went on, "thinking she's going to find her ancestor's long lost grave, and instead she finds her former professor, whom she had got fired —"

"Tape recorder in pocket," said Hull. "Planning to record their conversation."

"Precisely."

It occurred to Mayo that Hull was becoming more of a collaborator than a suspect, which wasn't necessarily good. But perhaps not necessarily bad either. It wouldn't hurt to let *him* feel that way — as long as *she* didn't actually feel that way.

"Does this seem like something your son would do?" she asked. "Come up with this complicated scheme to get her to fess up?"

"It's exactly the sort of thing he would do," Hull said. "Toby would never settle for something simple. You sure there's nothing on that tape?"

"Lab says it was irretrievable." She left out what the forensics people said — that Toby's body fluids had ruined both tape and machine.

"But we can surmise that the conversation turned bad," Hull said.

"Maybe they fought and he fell."

He scratched his chin, which he obviously hadn't shaved in days. "Or maybe she shoved him."

"Maybe," Mayo said. "But I see two problems. Why would Heather go all the way back up there a couple months later and bury him? Why take the risk?"

"And the second problem," Hull said. "Assuming he did fall far enough down the mountain to get killed, how the hell did that scrawny little gal drag 180-pound Toby back up and into the tunnel?"

Mayo folded her arms and watched while Hull rummaged around in the cupboard and came out with a packet of soda crackers. He stuffed two into his mouth, then opened the refrigerator and grabbed a brick of cheese.

"Jesus, I'm hungry," he said, spewing a flake or two of cracker. "I don't think I've eaten anything for a few days."

"How'd you know?" Mayo asked.

He pulled a knife from a drawer and sliced a chunk of moldy-looking cheese, then made a sandwich of it between two crackers. "You want any? How'd I know what?"

"That Heather was a 'scrawny little gal.'"

He stuffed the food into his mouth and chewed for a moment, then swallowed. "You caught me there."

"How long you been following her, Mr. Hull?"

"C'mon, we've been through so much together. Call me Patrick."

"How long?"

He made himself another cracker sandwich and ate it before answering. "Off and on, all summer. Ever since Toby disappeared. Don't tell me you wouldn't have done the same. And you know damn well I didn't kill her either. The last time I saw her was two weeks ago in the supermarket parking lot, the day her sister saw me — something I allowed to happen."

"Why'd you do that?"

"Because I was tired of the game and wanted to up the tension. I wanted her to know she was being watched."

"Do you think you were noticed before that day?"

"No."

"Were you always driving Toby's truck?"

"Yeah," he said. "Why?"

But Mayo didn't answer. She was thinking about the dark SUV.

Nineteen

Jody's front door was open, and Mayo knocked on the screen. She had called first and Jody gave her directions to a condominium complex in northeast Boulder, not far from Toby Hull's neighborhood.

Jody appeared presently from a hallway, wearing a simple black Japanese style housecoat decorated with gold embroidered letters. Underneath the open housecoat, she wore baggy pants, a wrinkled t-shirt and flip-flops. Her hair was oily and tangled, and she shoved it out of her eyes as Mayo entered.

She gestured Mayo into a large, sunny living room. The floor was rust-colored ceramic tiles, and half a dozen oversized tropical plants were clustered around a picture window. Lined along the wall was a double row of taped cardboard boxes. There was no furniture.

"You moving, Jody?" Mayo asked.

"Yes." Jody appeared to have shrivelled since Mayo last saw her. She seemed stranded right where she stood, as though she didn't quite inhabit her body enough to make it move.

"Can we sit somewhere and talk?"

Jody shrugged. "I've sold all my furniture. Sorry."

"That's all right." Mayo stepped forward and touched Jody's arm. "You don't look so hot."

"I'm moving," Jody repeated. She looked around as though trying to remember what she'd been doing. She picked up a stack of newspaper, headed into the small kitchen. Mayo followed and watched while Jody pulled plates from a cupboard, wrapped them in newspaper and stuck them into a box on the counter.

"Patty is worried about you," Mayo said. "She said she gave you a call but you didn't get back to her."

Jody looked up, her eyes shiny. A couple of tears spilled over, but she quickly wiped them away. "I really don't feel like talking to anyone."

"Where you moving to?"

Jody wiped her eyes with a sleeve, then pulled another plate from the cupboard. "I don't know. I don't really care. I'm just getting out of here."

"What about school?" Mayo asked, recalling that Jody was a nursing student.

"I quit."

Mayo watched helplessly while Jody continued packing dishes. She ought to try and stop her, make her take a deep breath, convince her not to do anything rash while she was in such a bad frame of mind. She remembered her own refusal to return to the Victorian—her grandmother's beautiful, beloved old home—to their cheerful kitchen with ferns in the window and fun-filled snapshots on the fridge. Mayo had also abandoned her home, left her job, withdrawn from old friends.

She understood exactly what Jody was doing.

"You said you had something to tell me." Jody did not sound particularly interested.

"I've ruled out one of my main suspects."

Jody pulled an expensive looking wine glass from the cupboard and briefly held it up to the light before wrapping it. "You mean the cowboy? The guy at the funeral?"

"I meant the cowboy's son, Toby Hull. Heather's former professor."

Jody didn't look surprised or disappointed. She didn't look like anything except a woman who was packing up a stranger's kitchen.

"You remember me telling you about Toby Hull the other day?" Mayo pressed.

Jody nodded but didn't look up from her work.

"I got the feeling that you already knew about him."

Now Jody glanced at her. "Heather kept secrets from me too, you know."

"But you knew about the other claims of rape before the Zippy's incident, didn't you?" Mayo said.

Mayo waited, but Jody kept working and did not respond.

"Jody," Mayo went on, "it's not a betrayal for you to recognize your sister's problems. You said she had a monstrous childhood. It would be a miracle if she *didn't* have issues."

Jody stopped then, staring into the empty shelf in front of her. She turned to face Mayo. "I didn't believe her either, don't you see? I figured she just wanted to get me to move in with her. But I should have taken it more seriously because I saw that guy watching us. I should have protected her."

Jody was crying now, and Mayo stepped forward and took the girl into a hug.

"It's not your fault, Jody," Mayo said quietly. "You couldn't stop any of it from happening." A part of her felt like she was talking to herself.

They stood like that for a time, with Jody sobbing into Mayo's shoulder. Finally, Jody sniffed and gazed up at the ceiling.

"You know, sometimes they seemed like they had a good relationship," she said. She pulled away from Mayo and groped around the kitchen counter until she found a box of tissues. She blew her nose.

"Who did?" Mayo asked.

"We'd all be watching TV or eating dinner," Jody went on. "And they would make jokes and laugh."

Mayo realized she was talking about Heather and her father.

"She was a couple years older than me," Jody said. "She was so pretty and dainty and smart. She liked to teach me things, like jigsaw puzzles and origami. She was really good at cards too. I think she might have had a photographic memory. We spent a lot of time together in our room. We had bunk beds and she let me have the top bunk.

"It was always the early morning—just when the birds started—and I'd hear our bedroom door open and close. He was so quiet about it. He'd whisper to her and the bed would creak and I'd hear the sound of his belt buckle." She shivered. "I still hate that sound. And then later the door would open and close again and I'd listen really hard but I never heard her crying or saying anything. We never talked about it, not once.

"Then, one afternoon, when I was nine—it was after school. My mother was at work and he was home for some reason. I had just come up the stairs with some animal crackers and there he was, waiting for me at the top of the stairs. I think I stopped and he told me to come here. He squatted down and I went up the stairs. He touched my hair. I was so scared I didn't know what to do. I just froze. He said my dress was very pretty, and he touched each of the buttons down the front. Then suddenly Heather was there."

Jody splayed her fingers in front of her and her lips moved as though she were counting them.

"He went flying down the stairs," she said finally. "They said he broke his neck."

After a moment, Mayo remembered to breathe. "I understand."

"Not really. You can't really understand."

Mayo noticed that her own heart was pounding. She *could* see, quite clearly. She saw Glen's face, his look of surprise and frustration as he opened his mouth and it filled with blood, as he lay in the ditch, his head in her lap. He had coughed and his blood covered his chin and went into to her jeans....

"You're right, I can't," she lied. "But I think I can try to imagine how tough it was for you. And how none of it was your fault."

She wondered if she ought to do something with this unexpected disclosure. Probably not, she decided. Both parties were dead, what was the point?

"In high school," Jody went on, "Heather started accusing boys of touching her. I think she did it because it made her feel powerful. The boys would get into trouble. And then they got on her case about it, you know, the school administrators, and they kicked her out of school. After that, they took her away to a hospital and I didn't see her for a year. They wouldn't let me visit her. When she finally got out, she seemed better. She even seemed happy. My grandfather had left us some money and the house in Sugarloaf. Heather and I would go spend weekends there, just to get away from Mom. That's when Heather found the diary in an old crate. She was so excited! We used to drive around Colorado visiting ghost towns and looking for Alonzo Holloway's grave. Heather said that was her mission—finding this grave. I don't know why it was so important to her and I didn't care. We had so much fun. I think that was the only time when we were both actually happy.

"When she got into the history program at Colorado Western U, I really thought Heather was all better. She had these plans to write a book—she was going to call it 'The Search for Alonzo Holloway's Grave.' It would be about our adventures looking for the grave, intermixed with the story of his life and his diary. It seemed like the story of Grandpa Holloway was the first really good thing that had ever happened to her. But then..."

"But then something went wrong?"

"The thing with her professor happened—Professor Hull. And then she got involved with this other professor, the dean. His name was Mason. She was secretive about it at first but then began to tell me things. He was an old man and madly in love with her. She said he'd do anything for her. She got a huge kick out of it. It was that feeling of power again. Heather wasn't an evil person—she was just sick because of what happened before." Jody dabbed her eyes again. "She just couldn't help herself."

"What you're saying makes sense, Jody. I understand."

Jody sighed. "I wish I did."

"I'd like to show you something."

Mayo brought out Heather's photo album, opened it to a section with multiple street shots. "Do you know why Heather was taking pictures of Professor Hull?"

Clutching a tissue, Jody seemed spellbound by the photos. "Was she following him?"

"Apparently so. Can't really say I blame her. He's extremely nice looking, isn't he?"

"Yes, he is," Jody said quietly. "I can see why she liked him."

Mayo tapped the page. "Can you explain to me how you know which one is Toby?"

Jody pressed the tissue against a nostril, her eyes glued to the pictures.

"You also haven't asked why I ruled him out as a suspect," Mayo prodded.

Jody still did not speak.

"You want me to find out who killed your sister, don't you?" Mayo asked.

"Yes."

"Then you need to come clean with me. Heather's gone; nobody can hurt her any more. Now you and I both want to find out what happened to her. Let's work together."

Jody closed the photo album and handed it to Mayo. "I knew he couldn't have killed Heather because I knew he was dead."

Jody's eyes brimmed over again and Mayo waited for her to continue.

"One day last June," Jody said finally. "Heather got an email. She didn't know who it was from, didn't recognize the sender's email address. All it said was 'Location of Alonzo Holloway's grave,' and there were two attachments. She couldn't talk about anything else. I told her not to go. I told her there was something wrong, but she went the next day."

"Did you see the attachments?"

"Yes. There was a picture of Alonzo Holloway's grave next to a tunnel and the other was a map."

"Did you go with her?"

"No."

"So what happened?"

"Next thing I know, she calls me — this was before she turned against phones. I was at school. She was crying and I could barely understand her. She said she was up in the mountains, some place called Hellfire, and she was in trouble and could I please, please come and help her. So of course I left school and drove up there. She gave me these complicated directions and it took forever. I had to go through a ski area — Keystone — and then drive on a dirt road. I finally found her car at a trailhead, and I had to hike for another couple of hours up this trail. It was almost five o'clock in the afternoon by the time I got there."

"And you found her?"

She nodded. "I was hiking along and she suddenly jumped out from behind a tree. She took me up this mountain and there he was, lying there on some rocks."

"Toby Hull?"

Jody hung her head and covered her face with her hands. Mayo waited.

"Yes," Jody said finally. "He was all bloody. He was dead."

"Did she tell you what happened?"

"She said he wanted her to write a letter saying the rape accusation was a fake. But she told him no way, she wasn't going to write any letter..." Jody paused to blow her nose.

"Go on," Mayo said after a few moments.

"Anyway, she realized that the whole thing was a trick to get her up there where he could threaten her. He had a tombstone lying in the dirt. It was a fake. There wasn't any grave. She said they had a big argument on the mountainside and somehow he ended up falling."

"She said he fell?"

"Yes."

"Jody, did Heather push him off the mountainside?"

Jody ran the tips of her thumbs across the tips of her fingers, her eyes averted from Mayo's. "I wasn't there. I don't know what happened."

"But you have some idea."

"Her story was a little confused. I thought it might have been just like ... "

"Just like what happened with your father?"

"Maybe."

"Okay," Mayo said after a few moments. "So what happened next?"

"I helped her drag him up into the tunnel and then we left."

"You didn't bury him?"

"I know it was awful, but there wasn't time. It was late and started to get dark. I don't know why I—I mean, I didn't know what else to do." She covered her face and Mayo waited while she composed herself. "It was horrible. He was so bloody. But she was my sister. I didn't want her getting into trouble. There was a kind of gate thing at the mouth of the tunnel that had 'No Trespassing' signs on it, but we moved it and carried him into the tunnel. We put his bike in there too. Heather grabbed the tombstone and we left. You're going to have to arrest me now, aren't you?"

"Did you go back later and bury him?"

"No."

"Jody, we found him buried under a pile of rocks."

Jody's eyes were red and puffy. "You couldn't have. We put him in the tunnel and left."

"Exactly how did you leave him?"

"We just put him down in a dark spot where nobody could see him if they looked into the tunnel."

"Are you sure Heather didn't go back later on?"

Jody shook her head. "No way! I know we shouldn't have left him there but we were just so scared. A few weeks later I told her we should at least go back and bury him or something. I couldn't sleep, I was having these terrible nightmares. But she said there was no way she would do it. And I couldn't do it on my own. I just couldn't."

Jody began crying in earnest.

Mayo poured a glass of water and stood watching while Jody got a grip on herself.

"Am I under arrest now?" Jody asked.

Mayo hadn't given it much thought. "No," she said finally.

"I know I should have called the police," Jody said. "I guess I'm not much better than my mother—keeping horrible secrets like that. But you see, I would do *anything* for her. She saved me from *him*."

Twenty

Toby Hull's memorial service took place at a non-denominational hall in Boulder. The place was packed. Mayo guessed at least 300 people had crammed in, filling every seat and lining the walls.

Mayo and Gumble were among those standing and she had Deputy Nutt stationed in the back with the department's old video camera. After the service, she planned to tell Patrick Hull in person what happened between Heather Holloway and Toby Hull up in Hellfire. She had brought Gumble along mostly just to have another body in the room.

"I did a test run yesterday morning," Gumble whispered. "From Wolftongue to downtown Denver."

"And?"

"One hour and fifty-two minutes at rush hour."

"Hmm," said Mayo. "That would rule Mason out if the housekeeper really talked to him at seven-thirty or eight."

"I don't think we're going to get anything more precise out of her." Gumble pulled out a notepad and skimmed it. "I ran a background check on Mason, came up with a DUI a few years back, but nothing else. Let's see ... Patrick Hull's alibi checks out. This woman, Vivian, says she met him in a bar, came to his house around midnight, stayed for eggs and toast, and left around mid-morning."

Mayo scanned the room and spotted Patrick in the front row. He had cleaned up nicely, wearing a tidy black suit, his hair trimmed and combed. Joanna Selig sat primly next to him in a sleeveless black dress.

"The lab called," Gumble continued. "They said the murder weapon does match the one from Hull's garage, and that his back door does appear to have been tampered with."

As Mayo watched, Joanna rested her cheek against Patrick's shoulder. He turned his face slightly, and pressed his lips against her head.

Mayo looked away. "I guess he didn't like Vivian enough to invite her to his son's funeral."

Gumble made an unpleasant noise in his throat. "We've sent faxes of the sketch to a long list of tribes — did you know there are over three hundred reservations in this country?"

While Gumble talked, Mayo scanned the crowd. A few rows from the front, Kate Russell sat next to a man Mayo didn't recognize.

Gumble went on. "I'd like to officially lodge my opinion that this reservation thing is a wild goose chase."

Mayo straightened up, tried to get a better look. The man had his arm across Kate's shoulders. A gleaming black ponytail draped down his back.

"Agreed," she told Gumble. "I don't think we need to take it any further."

"Good," Gumble said. "I ran checks on three American Indian students from the list your university buddy sent us — from Heather's classes."

Mayo kept her eyes on the man with Kate Russell. She caught sight of a high cheekbone, a sturdy, whiskerless jaw.

"All of them have out-of-state addresses now," Gumble went on. "One in Las Vegas and two in Oklahoma. I'm thinking this is a waste of time too, by the way."

She tried to move so she could see more of the man's face, but the hall was too crowded.

"You're right," she told Gumble. "Drop it." A heavyset man stood up, blocking Mayo's view of Kate and her companion.

"Seems like our leads are drying up," Gumble observed.

Mayo gave him a sour look. "When the prime suspect turns out to be dead since before the fact," she said, "I'd say it's a setback."

Gumble kept his eyes straight ahead. "Did you really think he was alive?"

She thought for a moment. "Without the murder of Heather, I would have said probably not. But in light of Heather's murder, the fact that she destroyed his life and that he was conveniently missing, yes, I thought he could be our guy."

The heavyset man sat again so Mayo got a better look at Kate's companion. Even from the back, he looked Native American.

"If we had something solid on someone," Mayo said, "we could have checked the road debris in their fenders and tire treads and tire wells."

"You mean test for minerals?" Gumble asked.

"Exactly," she said. "Colorado soils have a distinct mineral content, and we might have been able to see whether a car has been on Wolftongue Road. But it's probably too late. That kind of stuff disappears in no time and it's already been over two weeks."

Gumble leaned close and nodded toward the front of the room. "I'm liking the father at this point. He was following her and the murder weapon came from his garage. He had motive."

"Maybe," she said. "But I don't think so."

She sensed that Gumble was giving her a look, but she ignored it.

Up front, the ceremony was about to begin. Toby Hull had been cremated and a white urn containing his ashes sat on a multi-colored Navajo blanket. The urn was surrounded by several dried flower arrangements and a dozen or so framed photographs.

She thought she saw Donald Chestnut in the crowd, except this man had dark hair and black rimmed glasses. Still, she was sure she recognized the stiff way he held himself, turning his whole body to look around.

A man approached the dais and introduced himself as a school chum of Toby's from the history department at University of Colorado in Boulder where Toby earned his degree. The man was loud and enthusiastic, telling predictable stories about their college parties, their skiing and biking adventures in the high country. He then introduced Patrick Hull.

Patrick stepped up to the dais holding a piece of paper. Without making an introduction, he read the poem, "I Did Not Die." His voice was strong and sober, and he did not look up from the paper while he read. By the time he finished, many in the audience were weeping. Without saying more, Patrick sat down. Toby's college friend returned to the dais and invited others to come up and speak. For the next two hours, people from Toby's past filed up front and told stories about what Toby Hull meant to them.

Mayo had received the final ME and forensics reports that morning. The lab confirmed what they already knew — that the rocks used to bury Toby were not in place when the body lost its fluids, a process that occurs during the first three weeks after death. There were also signs of predation, which would have been difficult had he been under the rocks the entire time. The team also reported evidence of recent activity in the cave — aside from the disturbances left by Mayo and McKern. They speculated that someone had trudged in and out with rocks to bury the body, then used an aspen tree branch to brush away the footprints. The dried remains of some aspen leaves were found in the tunnel that could not have gotten there on their own.

When the service ended, Mayo and Gumble positioned themselves by the exit while people filed through. The man who looked like Donald Chestnut in disguise disappeared into the crowd. Mayo watched for Kate Russell and her companion. When she caught sight of them, they were heading straight for her. Kate's eyes were red from crying.

Kate shook Mayo's hand and nodded at her companion. "This is Daryl Sweezy. He was a good friend of Toby's. Daryl, this is Marshal Mayo."

The man was tall and lean, mid-30s, American Indian. His eyes looked normal. He was not the man in the sketch.

"This is Deputy Gumble," Mayo said.

"They're investigating — are you investigating Toby's death as well?" Kate asked.

Mayo shook Daryl's hand. "It's not officially my case, but I'm sniffing around. I wonder if we could find somewhere to talk."

The four of them edged out of the way while others filed past.

"How do you know Toby?" Gumble asked Daryl.

Daryl shoved his hands into the pockets of his jeans. "We taught together at Colorado Western."

"Daryl resigned in protest on Toby's behalf," Kate put in.

A large bald man passing by suddenly stopped and gave Daryl a bear hug. "Long time no see, Sweezy! Where you been? Can you believe this about Toby?"

"Hey!" Daryl squeezed the man's arm. "I'll catch you out front in a minute!" After Daryl gave the bald man a meaningful look, the man moved on.

"Resigned in protest?" Mayo prompted.

"I didn't like the way he was treated by the administration so I decided to look around for something else." He shrugged. "And I found it."

"I wonder why nobody has mentioned you before now." Mayo gave Kate a look.

Kate smiled. "I guess it didn't come up."

Mayo realized that Kate had been trying to protect Daryl as much as her students. There was a spark between the two of them.

"Where do you live?" Gumble asked Daryl.

He smiled pleasantly. "Lawrence, Kansas. I teach at the university there."

"When's the last time you were in Colorado?" Gumble went on.

Daryl glanced at Kate. "I came back last June when I found out Toby was missing. I helped search for him but had to return after a week to teach summer school."

Kate crossed her arms and edged closer to him, her fingertips resting against his arm.

An elderly couple stopped then and reached for Daryl and Kate. Mayo and Gumble waited while they finished their solemn hellos and the couple moved on.

"I'm sorry to intrude on the funeral," Mayo said when the couple had left.

"No problem," Daryl said. "I want to help if I can." He gestured toward the pews and they moved out of the crowd's path and sat. "We've got a big room rented at the university for a Toby-style wake, which means lots of booze and good food. You're welcome, of course."

Mayo pulled the sketch artist's picture out of her briefcase and showed it to Daryl. "Have you ever seen this man?"

He took the sketch, then shook his head. "He looks kind of familiar but I couldn't say whether I've seen him for sure. Who is he?"

"When is the last time you talked to Toby?" Mayo asked.

"I'd say early June sometime, after I left for Kansas. He called one morning and we talked for about an hour."

Mayo went on. "What was his state of mind?"

"Not great. He was preoccupied, trying to figure out a way to get his life back."

"Did he mention anything about an Alonzo Holloway tombstone or a place called Hellfire?" Mayo asked.

"No. Not that I remember."

Mayo sighed. Another dead end. She gazed up at the front of the room, where a few stragglers were looking at pictures of Toby.

Kate's cell phone rang and she answered it. "We're heading over in a minute," she said into the phone. "Sure, no problem. Take your time." She hung up. "That was Toby's father," she said. "They're stopping by the house to pick up some things. He asked if we could grab the pictures and Toby's ashes."

Mayo abruptly focused on Kate. "Toby's fiancée told us he was seeing someone else. I don't suppose that was you."

Kate looked startled. "Last time I checked, it wasn't."

Mayo pressed her. "Nothing more than a casual friendship between you?"

"I said, didn't I? We were just friends." Kate pulled a tissue from her purse and wiped her eyes. "We already discussed this, Marshal. Why are you bringing it up again?"

A man with a florid face and stringy hair appeared and pulled Kate up into a hug.

"Kate! You still at CWU? Hey, I'm so sorry about Toby, man. I know you guys were close" He glanced up at the others. "Excuse us, I haven't seen this gorgeous woman in five years. Where the hell have you been?" He dragged her aside and began lecturing her at close range.

Daryl watched absent-mindedly, then turned abruptly to Mayo. "You're right—there *was* a woman."

"What do you know about it?"

"He didn't tell me much, except that it was serious. He said he needed to decide if he ought to break off his engagement with

Joanna. And then he did. He told me he meant to be together with this other woman."

"Do you have any information about her at all?"

Daryl shook his head. "Sorry. He didn't like to talk about her."

Mayo's cell phone rang and she opened it impatiently. "Mayo!"

"McKern here."

"What's up?"

"Got two interesting calls in the last few minutes. First call was Troy, the tire casting guy. He says he compared the pix Gumble sent of Patrick Hull's tires and they don't match."

"Okay."

"But you might want to forget about that when you hear about the next call."

"Yeah. Go on."

McKern's voice rose. "A techie from the DNA lab just called. They actually got a DNA match on something you will not believe."

"What is it, McKern?" Mayo recited a quick, silent plea for patience.

"Those pinecones we got out of Patrick Hull's truck match a couple pinecones from the parking area up at Wolftongue, which means Hull's truck must have been parked underneath those pine trees. He was there, boss."

Twenty-One

By the time Mayo and Gumble headed out into the lobby of the church, it had nearly emptied out. As they drove across town to Patrick Hull's house in hopes of intercepting him, Mayo's cell phone rang again.

"Hey, boss," McKern said cheerfully. "You pick up Hull yet? You gonna need any backup?"

"Gumble and I are on our way over."

"Jody Holloway just called," McKern went on. "Had a helluva time talking to her. She was badgering me about the case, wantin' to know what all was goin' on. She was in a big dither, kept saying we weren't gonna do nothin'. Major meltdown. So, anyway, I was trying to get her to calm down and I told her about the pinecones in Hull's truck."

"You—what?"

"I—just thought—"

"What time did she call?"

"Right after I talked to you. Geez, boss. I thought you were all geared up to make the arrest or I wouldn't—"

"What did she say?"

"She hung up on me. That's why I thought I better call you."

Mayo hung up and dialed Jody Holloway's number. Jody didn't answer.

Joanna Selig's yellow sedan was parked in front of the house, and Patrick's truck sat in the driveway. Across the street was a light blue Subaru Forester—Jody's.

The picture window curtains were closed. The scent of juniper floated across the front step from the shrubbery.

Gumble stood to the side while Mayo rang the doorbell.

No one answered. They unsnapped their holsters. Gumble banged on the screen door.

"Mr. Hull!" Mayo called. "Can you hear me? Jody? It's Marshal Mayo!"

"Try around back?" Gumble whispered. "Call for support?"

Mayo pressed a finger to her mouth, hammered once more on the screen door.

Gumble bit his lip and for the first time since she'd known him, Mayo saw worry in his face.

The front door opened abruptly. Behind the screen stood Joanna, the whites of her eyes showing in the gloom. Joanna didn't speak, but flicked her gaze toward the room's interior. Mayo nodded. Her fingers closed around the grip of her Glock, her palm sweating.

"Jody?" Mayo said loudly. "I'd like to talk to you. It's very important."

Joanna stepped back. "She wants you to come in." Her voice was barely a squeak.

Mayo and Gumble drew their weapons, opened the screen door, and slowly entered the house.

The room smelled, as usual, of Patrick Hull's smoke. Mayo also detected another fragrance — Joanna's perfume. Joanna moved back as they came in. She looked slim and elegant in the black mourning dress but her eyes were wide with fear.

Jody stood next to what remained of the glass display case of Civil War memorabilia. The case and its contents lay in shattered bits across the carpet. Patrick Hull sat hunched in the leather chair. Jody stood over him, aiming a black 9mm Smith & Wesson at his head. Mayo spotted a red welt on his temple and a trickle of blood running down into his ear. With a jolt, she realized that Jody must have hit him with the handgun — hard.

Mayo edged slowly forward, her weapon aimed at Jody's heart. She felt her finger stiffen, and she calculated. Jody's finger was tight over the trigger. No way to shoot without losing Hull.

"Give me the gun, Jody," Mayo said. Her voice sounded far away, coming from someone else.

"He killed my sister," Jody said softly. Her hair was an oily tangle and she wore the same t-shirt and pants she had worn when Mayo last saw her. She did not move her eyes from Patrick Hull's head. "I don't care anymore. Just shoot. I want to die anyway, and I'm going to kill him too. That will finish it."

Mayo stopped. "Jody, listen to me. Don't throw your life away like this. Or Patrick's. You're a good person — I know that about you. This isn't you."

Jody's face was a blotched mess of red and white and her eyes were swollen from crying. Her weapon was about three feet away from Hull's head.

Jody's wrist twitched and her gaze flashed briefly in Mayo's direction. "He killed her for revenge and you won't do anything about it. You all just think she deserved it."

From behind her, Mayo heard a faint squeal coming from Joanna's throat.

"Give me the gun, Jody," Mayo said again. "Heather always watched out for you, didn't she? Didn't she do everything she could to protect you? Do you think Heather would want you to destroy your own life?"

She sensed Gumble moving behind her.

"It's already destroyed," Jody said. "There's nothing — it's not worth it anyway."

"I think Mr. Hull might disagree with you. Right, Patrick?"

Patrick Hull nodded briefly but otherwise stayed motionless.

Mayo took another step forward.

"Stay back!" Jody yelled.

Mayo stopped. "You're a smart woman, Jody. Use your head. You want Heather to have her day in court, don't you?"

"I want my sister's killer to be punished! I know you're not going to do it. You're all just thinking, 'Good riddance. Someone finally killed that crazy girl.'"

During the speech, Mayo had stepped forward again. She was about four yards away from Jody now. Gumble had fanned out to the right.

"But Heather would not want you to do this," Mayo went on. "Patrick, why don't you get up out of that chair and come over here."

Patrick gave her a quizzical look, then glanced at Jody. He moved his legs slightly, then a little more. Jody said nothing. He put his hands on the arms of the chair and began to push himself up.

"Don't!" Jody yelled.

Patrick sank back down but did not settle into the seat. Mayo tried to catch his eye, but he was watching Jody. In an instant he swung his arm up and slammed it against hers and the gun discharged into the ceiling. He bolted out of the chair and Mayo and Gumble were across the room, wrestling the Smith & Wesson out of Jody's hand. It fell onto the carpet.

"No - o - o!" Jody wailed. Mayo scooped up the weapon, removed the magazine and dropped it into her pocket. Gumble pressed Jody face down into the carpet and cuffed her.

Joanna, meanwhile, latched on to Patrick. "Thank God!" she yelled.

"Call 911," Mayo told her.

Mayo stayed at the house while Gumble took Jody in. If Jody was deemed fit by a doctor, she would be processed and transferred to Boulder County Jail.

After they left, Patrick Hull opened a bottle of brandy and downed a snifter full. His hand was shaking as he checked his watch. "We need to get over to Toby's wake."

Joanna stood over him, pressing a washcloth wrapped around ice cubes against his temple. "She just showed up at the door and said she wanted to talk to Patrick. So I didn't know, did I? I mean, I couldn't just slam the door in her face!"

Hull winced as she pressed the cloth against his head. "Stop it, wouldja?" He tried to stand up but she shoved him back into his seat.

"No!" Joanna barked. "You sit there and shut up. That wake'll be going on all night. So then she comes in and says she's Heather's sister and says, 'Why did you kill her?' and pulls out this humungous gun and says for him to sit down and shut up and she's gonna put a bullet in his skull and she shoots the glass case, and everything goes splattering all over the place and Patrick tries talking to her so she bashes him right in the head with this gun and she tells me if I move or say anything she's gonna shoot me. Then you guys start banging on the door and she starts freaking out about it and then suddenly she tells me to let you in. Then you guys come in with your guns and all, and I couldn't believe — I thought we were all goners."

Finally exhausted, she let Hull take over with the cloth and sank down in the chair next to him.

Hull swallowed some more brandy, then gave Mayo and Joanna both a painful grin. "One thing for sure, she certainly woke me up." He pulled the cloth from his head and examined the smear of blood.

"I still say someone needs to look at that," Mayo said. He had refused to go to the emergency room.

"Hold on, you're not doing it right." Joanna jumped up again, snatched the cloth and reorganized the ice cubes. "I hope she's going to jail, isn't she?"

"We'll make sure she can't hurt either of you," Mayo said, though she had no idea what would become of Jody. Whatever it was, it wouldn't be good. Yet another victim of Heather's mess.

Hull lit a cigarette and surrendered his head again to Joanna. Mayo leaned against the wall, folded her arms, and watched. It seemed to her that Joanna had plans for Patrick and herself and that he was happily going along.

She gave herself a brief, silent lecture about not judging, but it didn't have much impact.

"That maniac was really going to kill you," Joanna said. "And me too."

"Maybe at first." Hull glanced at Mayo. "But I think she changed her plans."

"That was my impression," Mayo said. "Suicide by cop."

"Yep," Hull said. "Saw you at the funeral by the way. Thanks for coming. It was a good service, I thought. Toby had a lot of friends."

"A million," Joanna put in.

Hull looked at his watch again but didn't try to get up. "We need to get over there." He drank more brandy, dripping a bit down his chin. "Jesus." He put the glass on the table and held his hand up in front of his face. "Man, look at that," he said. "Still shaking. You sure you don't need something to drink, Marshal? Those were some pretty quick moves you had there, you and your deputy. You manage to exchange your knucklehead deputy for a good one?"

"Not yet," Mayo said. "I was wondering, by the way, exactly when did you spot Deputy McKern the other day?"

He looked puzzled at the question, but answered readily. "It wasn't hard. When I left the house again, he hopped in his car and followed. Most miraculous broken SUV I ever saw. Why do you ask?"

"That really is a nasty welt you got on your head," Mayo said. "I didn't think she was capable."

Hull gave her a look. "How long you been a cop?"

She shrugged. "So I was wrong."

Joanna sank into a chair, dropping the washcloth on the table. "Sorry, Pat. I can't hold this thing up any more. I need to rest." She looked pale and overheated.

Hull poked at the washcloth but didn't pick it up. "She's the one who spotted me following her sister, isn't she?" He didn't meet Mayo's eye. "Is that why she thought I'm the one?"

"Uh, maybe." Mayo was not anxious to reveal the extent of her deputy's incompetence. "Listen, I wanted to let you know, we were right about what happened up at Hellfire."

Hull picked up his snifter and studied it for a moment before draining it. "Exactly which parts were we right about?"

Mayo sat down and recounted what Jody had said about her trip to Hellfire.

"So, if what you say is true," he said, "that it was like the business with her old man on the stairs, then she deliberately shoved my son off the mountain."

Joanna stood. "I'm going to be sick." She hurried out of the kitchen and Mayo heard a retching noise from the bathroom.

Hull moved into Joanna's seat, closer to Mayo. He reached across the table and, to her surprise, took her hand.

"Makes you wonder if there's hope for any of us, doesn't it?" He let go abruptly and leaned back in the chair. Lifting his head, he gazed at the ceiling. The L-shaped scar on his face had gone an angry pink. She thought she heard a low moan from deep in his chest.

Mayo still felt the place on her hand where he had touched it. "Of course, there's no evidence."

They sat in silence for a time. Finally, he spoke. "She's dead anyway."

Suddenly, he got up from his seat, placed his hands on the table and leaned over her. The St. Louis homicide cop was back. "There's something else, isn't there?"

Mayo cleared her throat. "Did you ever drive up to Wolftongue? The site of Heather's death?"

He gazed at her as though he didn't recognize her. "I've been in Sugarloaf, but not the ghost town—not Wolftongue."

"You absolutely sure about that?"

"Yeah, I'm absolutely sure about it. Why?"

"Pinecones."

"Huh?"

"The other day, when you gave us permission to search your house, the garage, and your truck—"

"It's Toby's truck."

"We found a couple pinecones in the bed of Toby's truck, which is your truck, as far as I'm concerned. The crime lab found a DNA match between those and some pinecones from the parking area at the murder site."

"That sounds like some bull," Joanna said dully from the kitchen doorway. "What are you talking about, pinecones?"

Patrick began pacing around the kitchen, his palm pressed against his injured temple. "Someone put 'em there. Listen, Marshal. I never went near Wolftongue and I'm sure there weren't any damn pinecones in that truck bed last week when I cleaned it out. I'm being set up here. I never went near the damn Holloway homicide scene. Anybody could have driven by here and tossed a couple pinecones into my truck bed. How about that deranged young woman who was just here? That charming young accessory to the murder of my son?"

"Take it easy," Mayo said. "I'd like your permission to do some further testing on your truck. I'd like to call the crime lab and have them come pick it up."

Patrick stood at the kitchen sink and looked out the back window. "Call. Test. Administer a polygraph. Let's do whatever the hell we need to do."

It was a still, moonless night and the sky was black with a spray of stars. Mayo soaked. The jacuzzi was surrounded by several lighted candles, and a glass of wine sat on the ledge. Sinking low in the water, she rested her head against a plastic bath pillow. The pillow had been a good investment, she decided. It was soft and comfortable. This was the perfect way to end a perfectly dreadful day.

Someone opened the sliding glass door and she heard the tinkle of dog tags as Chica and Tinker spilled out into the back yard.

"Knock knock." Monte came out.

So much for unwinding, Mayo thought. "Who's there?"

"May I approach?"

Mayo was nude, but it was dark. Besides, she liked the idea of getting Patrick Hull out of her head.

"You may."

"I promise not to peek." He positioned a lawn chair next to the jacuzzi and sat primly facing sideways. "You okay?"

"Last time I checked."

"You seemed kind of glum at dinner, talking about what happened with Jody today."

"Did I?" She draped a hot wet washcloth over the top of her head.

"Yep. I'm worried about you. I've got the feeling you're now taking on the blame for this Heather Holloway mess too."

She looked up at the sky and wondered idly if anyone had actually ever tried to count all the stars. She'd seen astronomy shows where they said how many there were, but she always figured they must have been guessing. Like almost everything else, like why did Glen die, it seemed unknowable.

"Am I bothering you?" he said when she didn't answer.

"Of course not," she lied.

"Well, talk to me then. Count me as a brother-in-law. Family. And a friend."

She sighed and dragged the cloth off her head. She met his gaze, though it was difficult to see in the faint candlelight and he wasn't supposed to be looking at her anyway. His features seemed soft, worried.

"I'm not really looking of course," he said.

"You better not."

"But prepare yourself for a slightly invasive question out of the blue: Do you sidestep me because I'm Glen's brother?"

The jacuzzi water suddenly felt uncomfortably hot and she wanted to get out. But she didn't move. "That's out of the blue, all right."

"Well, it comes from my general observation of your attitude. Or I should say, lack of attitude. I often suspect you'd be happier if I left you alone. Which of course doesn't stop me."

"I don't mean to give that impression." Another lie.

"Davy and I were talking about you ..."

"Uh-oh."

"We can't really help it. It's a quiet town, you know. One must find one's entertainment somehow. Davy is worried about you too. He feels bad for pushing you into the job. And now you're loaded down with this seemingly endless murder case."

"Double murder case. One of them is solved. But the other one...I just don't know."

"I'm worried. I said that already."

"Don't, Monte. Just don't."

"You aren't the same person you used to be, back when you and Glen..."

"Of course I'm not. I lost my husband. He's dead."

"It's more than that. Sometimes I think the old Beth got killed too. Or you've decided to kill her."

"Is that an accusation?"

"Glen once told me he married you because you were funny."

"Ha. Glen was the funny one."

"And because you were more social than him and you dragged his butt out into the world."

"Did I?"

"But now you give off the impression that people are kind of — that we're intruding. You're quiet and secretive and remote. You're insular."

"No, I'm not." She was glad it was too dark to see much. She didn't like having this conversation lying naked in the jacuzzi, with him sitting so close. She fought back a surge of annoyance that he had chosen this moment and this situation to start such a conversation—or confrontation, whatever this was.

As if reading her thoughts, he stood up. "I'm sorry. I didn't mean to—never mind, Beth. I'll let you finish your soak."

"Sit down, Monte. Let me explain something," she began. "I loved your brother. I loved him so much, it hurt. And I respected him. He was smart and kept me on my toes. We were happy. We were best friends. And the sex was amazing."

"Okay, okay," he said. "That's enough detail please."

Mayo scanned the sky again. "Did I ever tell you how it happened?"

"Just that you swerved away from something in the road and went into the ditch."

"We were driving home from a party," she said, "and Glen was drunk. I was the designated driver, you see. I wasn't drinking. He was telling me a crazy story about a time he had these terrible stomach cramps and that his guts hurt so bad he thought he was going to die and it got so bad he went to the emergency room but when he got there and got into see a doctor he let off this huge fart—"

"Holy cow," Monte said. "I know that story. That was the funniest thing I ever heard, the way he..." He shook his head, not laughing.

"He was telling me this story," Mayo went on, "and I was laughing so hard and I saw a dog or something in the road at the last second and we went into the ditch and Glen the jerk didn't have his damn seatbelt on."

She let the sorry facts dissipate into the cool night air. This was the longest speech she'd ever made about what happened with Glen. She was surprised at how good it felt, having got it out.

"And I'm telling you—again—that this wasn't your fault," Monte said presently.

"I wasn't drunk. I should have made him put on the fricken seatbelt. There were guys in the department who thought so too. You saw them at the funeral. They wouldn't look at me. And you..."

"You've said that before, but you're wrong." His hair looked almost white in the moonlight. It was getting so long, she thought. It looked soft, too.

"Monte, I saw it in your face. You blamed me—or at least wondered if you should."

"Okay," he said. "Maybe I wondered once. At first. I couldn't absorb the fact that he was gone. It didn't take me long to figure out how stupid that was."

"I won't ever love someone like that again," she said abruptly. "It hurts too much."

"I bet you're wrong."

"I doubt it." She let a few moments drift by. "What about you?" she asked finally.

"What about me?"

"You're always worrying about me. What about you?"

"What about me what?"

"I don't know. Just, What about you?"

"You mean my love life?"

"Yeah, sure."

"I didn't like that divorce stuff much. Never got a hankering to go down that road again."

"That was a long time ago. And here you are, pestering me to move on."

"I'm not pestering you to do anything."

"Aren't you?"

"Well, maybe. Look. How about you and I do something together sometime? Nothing amazing. Nothing threatening. We'll go get an ice cream."

She considered this. She and Glen's brother? Ice cream? "We live together, Monte. What do you mean by 'do something together?'"

"You know what I mean."

"Oh dear lord," she said. "I can't deal with this right now. I've got to finish my case."

"I know, I know. I'm sorry. Forget I said it."

"Thanks. I—I don't know."

"I suspect you know better than you think." To her surprise, he began to hum softly.

"Hey," he said abruptly. "I thought you *had* finished the case. I thought you were going to arrest the guy with the pinecones in his truck."

She shook her head. "I'm betting that when we test his truck, we won't find any sign that he was anywhere near Wolftongue. I think someone planted evidence to point at him."

"How do you tell planted evidence from unplanted evidence?"

Mayo reached for her wine glass, but it was empty. "You have a knack for asking unanswerable questions."

"It has caused me much misery for many years. Can I make a suggestion?"

"I'm listening."

"The father, what's-his-name?"

"Patrick Hull."

"You are smitten by Patrick Hull. When you talk about him, I can hear the affection in your voice. You don't *want* him to be guilty."

He was right, of course, but he still had no business saying it.

"Not true," she said.

She could see his grin in the dim light. He was no longer facing away from her.

"Listen," she said. "You need to give me a little more credit than that. I don't let my personal feelings interfere."

"Why are you ignoring the evidence then? You said you had forensics that put him at the scene. Your pinecones." He was leaning forward now, looking straight at her. "And you said the murder weapon came from his garage."

"Yes. And he was following her and he had a motive. But I have some questions, which I hope are answerable, unlike yours. I want to know why Patrick Hull would use the bayonet from his own garage to kill her, then leave the weapon at the scene and the matching weapon in his garage. The guy is a retired cop, not someone who would make such a sloppy move. Furthermore, why would he show up at her funeral and then, after hearing she was killed by a bayonet, frantically search the garage? That part wasn't for show—he didn't know McKern was watching him until *after* he had searched the garage. Besides, why not just get rid of the damn thing? And he's right—anybody could have dropped the pinecones into the back of his truck. And finally, why would he do a revenge killing in the first place if he didn't know his son was dead?"

"Maybe he did."

"Yes, maybe. But my gut is telling me No, he didn't. I think he was framed."

Monte was silent for a few moments. "Who?"

"I don't know yet."

Monte stood up. The small flickering candle flames revealed that he was not smiling. "Okay, I said my piece and you're not done with the case."

"Nope."

He briefly nodded, then headed past his sculptures and back to the house. Mayo watched him step carefully up to the sliding glass door, favoring his good foot. He was humming again.

"Did you hurt your ankle up at Arapaho Pass?" she asked.

He pulled the door open and turned. "Just a tad," he called across the dark yard. "And just a thought, did it occur to you it might be someone you haven't seen yet?"

Without waiting for an answer, he went into the house.

Mayo climbed out of the water and slipped on her bathrobe. She sat on the wooden platform and leaned back against the jacuzzi, gazing up into the night sky. Bit by bit, she went over everything she knew about Heather's life in the months, weeks, and days before her death. After a long time, she got up, smiling into the darkness. Monte was wrong. It wasn't someone she hadn't seen. It was someone who'd been right in front of her all the time.

Later, after getting ready for bed, Mayo pulled out Heather Holloway's picture album and went through it again.

Twenty-Two

In the morning, Deputies McKern and Nutt were in the office when Mayo arrived. It was Sunday and Gumble had the day off, which was a good thing. She didn't want him around for this.

She shook hands with Nutt, who was manning the front counter. She heard McKern in the back, cursing over the coffee maker.

"Deputy Nutt," Mayo said in a low voice. "Go get yourself a coffee over at Daffodils."

Deputy Nutt paused, his eyes bright and young.

"Ma'am?"

"Come back in half an hour," she said.

Without asking why, he took off. Mayo watched him out the window as he crossed the street. Then she headed back.

"Why can't we get a decent one of these things?" McKern muttered. Through the thin wall, she heard Davy Brown in the mayor's office next door, pecking at a typewriter—a favorite bit of "history" whose features he proudly demonstrated to anyone who was young enough to ask about it.

Davy wasn't usually in the office on a Sunday morning, but she had phoned him earlier, filled him in, and asked for a big favor.

McKern was wiping up a pool of brown water surrounding the coffee maker. As they shook hands, he kept his face turned away, but Mayo quickly saw a swollen and bruised eye, plus a purple stain at his left nostril.

"What happened to you?" she asked.

"Don't want to talk about it."

Mayo sat down at her computer and watched it boot up. She logged in and checked her email. She drummed her fingers on the desk. She kept her mouth shut for the moment, waiting to see if McKern had anything to say for himself.

Finally, while the coffee machine began to make gurgling noises, McKern came out and sat at his desk.

"What happened to your face, McKern?"

"Corey Field happened to my face."

"I see."

"No, you don't. Nobody *sees*. Besides, I don't want to talk about it."

"Is Patty okay?"

"I guess."

Mayo sat back and laced her fingers over her stomach. "You haven't asked me what happened with Jody and Patrick Hull yesterday."

"Look, boss, I didn't mean to—I just—"

"Jody showed up at Hull's house with a gun and bashed him in the temple. When we got there, she invited us in, held a gun to his head. Hull managed to punch the gun away and young Jody has been carted off to the psych ward. We are very, very lucky that something much worse didn't happen."

"Uncle Davy said you didn't arrest him, even though we got the pinecone DNA."

"Quit trying to change the subject, McKern," she said. "Can't you even begin to fathom what a colossal screw-up that was? You had no business telling Jody anything."

He kept his eyes determinedly fixed on his empty Denver Broncos mug.

Mayo let her words settle in for a few moments, then made an effort to inject a tone of reason and concern into her voice before continuing. "You know, McKern. Every human being has particular gifts. The trick to a fulfilling life is to find out what your gifts are and to use them constructively. And sometimes the thing you *want* to give is not the thing you're best at."

McKern's jaw moved noticeably forward. "What's that supposed to mean?"

"Sometimes it's a big surprise when you figure out what you really ought to be doing. And in your case, maybe it's not law enforcement."

"Just because I made that one mistake on the phone?"

"Try one long series of mistakes," she said. "Not the least of which is you running around town bad mouthing the marshal, and by extension, making the whole department look bad. If you'd like a review of all the other screw ups you've managed to pull off—just during the past week or so—then I guess I'll have to sit down and make a list. But I'd rather not do that and, besides, I think you know perfectly well what they are."

He twisted his mouth "Davy's really pissed at me too."

"One thing I'd suggest is get over this pathetic reliance you have on your Uncle Davy. He's a delightful man and I've got a soft spot for him like everyone else in town, but he doesn't do you any favors by coddling you."

McKern put his free hand up to his swollen eye and dabbed at it tenderly. "He doesn't coddle me."

Mayo appraised at his eye. "Corey found out about you and Patty, eh?"

"I seriously don't want to talk about it," he said.

"Fine." Mayo took this as an affirmative and refrained from pointing out that he was probably lucky to be alive, having escaped the wrath of a cuckolded Corey Field with only a couple bruises.

She sighed, and considered drinking some of the junk from the coffee pot. She decided against it. As soon as this little "interview" was taken care of, she would head over to Daffodils for some real stuff. She had another difficult interview to do after McKern and she was going to need something to get her through it.

McKern looked into the open door of their conference room where the notes from their last pow wow were still on the board. Mayo got up and closed the door so casual visitors to the office wouldn't get a detailed rundown. From now on, things would tighten up around the office.

"She dumped me," McKern said.

"Patty did?"

"Yep. We had a big blow out — all three of us — and Patty had to pick. She decided to stick with that crazy old bastard instead of goin' with me." He rubbed his neck. "Now why the hell do you think she'd do that?"

Mayo shrugged. "Habit, maybe."

"She said she loved him."

"Oh."

"She actually said it."

"Sorry, McKern. That's rough." Mayo sensed what was coming next.

"Give me a break, wouldja, boss?" McKern pleaded. "I promise I'll keep my big trap shut from now on. I totally promise it'll never happen again."

Mayo shook her head. "Sorry, McKern. You've already used up all your breaks. You're done here. Clean out your stuff. I'll need your badge, weapon, and keys."

As Mayo escorted McKern out of the station, she felt crummy, even a bit soiled. McKern wasn't a bad guy, and she didn't like delivering the blow. She hadn't enjoyed watching his dispirited process of gathering things into a plastic grocery bag, his pointed act of washing the Broncos mug and tucking it in with his other possessions. Maybe if she had made a better effort to train him and keep him in line, this wouldn't have happened.

But she kept these thoughts to herself as she locked the door and crossed the street to Daffodils. Behind her, she heard McKern's voice in Davy Brown's office next door. As she headed up the walkway, she knew Davy was breaking the news to his nephew. He was saying that he already knew all about it, that there was nothing he could do, and furthermore, that he had already agreed to come out of retirement as a temporary deputy—starting that same day—until Mayo found a replacement. McKern would be hurt, would feel betrayed, but he would get over it.

McKern was Davy's problem now, not hers.

Meanwhile, she had more pressing matters. To her surprise, she'd slept amazingly well the night before, had awakened refreshed and confident. A picture of what happened to Heather Holloway had taken form in her mind.

Mayo went into Daffodils for a double latte to go and to tell Deputy Nutt what happened.

"There were problems with Deputy McKern," she explained quietly, mindful that Candy McKern was chopping vegetables behind the counter a few feet away. "I'd like to just leave it at that."

Nutt looked uneasy but did not ask any questions.

After Nutt went back to the office, Mayo drove to Boulder, where she headed straight to Donald Chestnut's house. He lived in a rambling Victorian mansion in an elegant historic neighborhood—not too different from Mayo's old neighborhood in Denver, where her own rambling Victorian sat, still full of her dishes and furniture but otherwise deserted.

Chestnut's place looked very big for a man living by himself.

The door opened almost instantly and Donald was there, stiff and grinning. He wore a green plaid flannel robe and large sheepskin slippers. His baby-fine hair looked wet.

"Hello, Donald."

He beckoned her inside.

The front rooms of the house had been renovated into a giant open area with sparse furnishings—a large walnut table with a laptop computer, an easy chair next to the front window, a single floor lamp and a small television set.

Donald stood with his arms folded across his chest, twisting like a nervous ten-year-old.

"That was you at the funeral yesterday, wasn't it?" she said. "Brown wig?"

He tightened his grip on himself and shrugged.

"C'mon, Donald. I'm busy and don't have time for screwing around."

"I was just curious," he said. "I wanted to understand who Toby Hull was."

"Do you understand now?"

Donald bent his head to the side, as though he were stretching his neck. "He was one of those annoying enchanted types that everybody loves. You want to sit?" He nodded in the direction of the dining table.

"So, did you make it up to Wolftongue?" Mayo asked when she was seated.

"What?"

"Wolftongue," she said. "Please, Donald, sit down. You seem very anxious."

"Do I?" He took a seat across the table from her.

"You remember you asked me where it was? Where Heather was killed?"

234

"Yes. I asked."

"You said you wanted to visit there, bring flowers to the spot."

He tightened his eyebrows, arranging his face into something that resembled puzzlement. "Yes. I did go there actually. I left white roses for Heather. They're probably still there, unless the wind blew them away."

"What day was that?"

He put a finger against his chin in an exaggerated "thoughtful" pose. "I'm thinking it was after Heather's funeral. It might have been the same day."

"I see. And did you happen to pick up anything from the scene?"

"Like what?"

"Like, perhaps, a pinecone or two?"

Donald's eyes widened.

"A what?" he asked.

"You heard me. I also recall that you said you liked forensics. You said you watch forensics programs on TV."

"Yes, I watch those programs. I told you I did. But I only went there to put some flowers—"

"You're probably aware, then, that plants have DNA and that they've been used as evidence in criminal cases."

Donald scratched his whiskerless chin without enthusiasm. "Uh huh."

"C'mon, Donald. I know it was you."

"Me what?"

She battled away a rush of exasperation and kept her voice calm. "Listen to me. There's another victim involved in this story. There's a man who lost his son, who just buried that son after a long summer of wondering where the hell he was and worrying about whether he was alive or dead."

"He's no victim!" Donald said. "He killed Heather! I know he did!"

"And you decided to make sure he paid for it. You drove up to Wolftongue right after Heather's funeral, you grabbed some pinecones from the parking area, swung by Hull's house that same night and dropped them into his truck, which was parked in the driveway."

Donald spoke down into his chest. "You were never going find any evidence against him. He was going to get away with it."

Mayo looked around the barren room, shaking her head. "You shouldn't have done it, Donald. It was a really bad idea."

"He was following her."

"How do you know that?"

Donald's face was red. "Because I was following her too."

This caught Mayo's attention. "When were you following her?'

"I was worried about her because she told me she was being followed. I decided to be proactive for once in my sorry life and I spotted him. I followed him to a house in Boulder. I did a little research and figured out who he was. After I saw him at Heather's funeral, I knew he must have done it."

"Were you driving an SUV?" she asked.

"No," he said. "I was driving my Ford sedan."

"That your only car?"

"Yes."

Mayo narrowed her eyes at him. It was easy enough to check. "Did you see anyone else following her?"

"Of course not! It's him! Don't you see?"

"You're wrong about him, Donald, and you're just lucky it didn't go any further."

Donald looked uncertain. "What do you mean? You didn't arrest him?"

"No."

"Why not?"

Mayo got up and headed for the door. She was no longer amused by the eccentric antics of Donald Chestnut. "Because someone else killed Heather."

Twenty-Three

Hey you,

I have left this envelope for my father and asked him to put it in the mail if something happens to me.

I need you to do something. I've enclosed a map. Please don't give up if you don't find it right away – my computer crashed and I've drawn this from memory. You're looking for a tunnel and you'll have to go pretty far in. When you get there, you will know what to do. This is very important – it has to do with Heather Holloway.

I think you know it was real for me. We were. I am sorry. Sorry for everything. Well, almost.

Love, Toby

Mayo and Gumble perched on top of an oversized boulder on a mountainside. It was two p.m. Below them lay a field of talus, scree, and boulders, with a skirt of golden aspen further down the mountain. The height of fall colors had arrived and the entire valley was dotted with patches of reds, oranges, and gold.

Mayo barely noticed.

The previous afternoon, they had hiked up to Hellfire, pitched two pup tents, shared a basket of cold chicken and coleslaw, and gone to bed without a campfire. For most of the night, Mayo had lain awake, listening to the far-off sound of the creek down in the valley, the quiet rustle of trees moving in the night wind. Occasionally, she drifted off to sleep, only to be awakened by the yipping of coyotes.

At dawn, they collapsed the tents, packed up the gear and stashed it. Carrying only the bare essentials, they hiked further up the trail to an outcrop of rocks that afforded a view of the tunnel where Toby Hull had been found. There they sat down to wait.

They'd been waiting for six hours.

Gumble finished off his canned cappuccino and tried unsuccessfully to crumple the heavy tin. "Why do they make these so thick?" he muttered.

Mayo watched him work on it for a few moments. They hadn't talked about anything of much importance in the 24 hours they'd just spent together and Mayo had been content to let it sit that way. Gumble talked about his kids. She heard details about his nine-year-old son's big role as Pappy Yokum in L'il Abner at school, his six-year-old girl's success at a recent spelling bee, and a preschool brawl involving his four-year old boy. She had met the kids and his pediatrician wife and they all seemed inordinately well-adjusted. She occasionally envied Gumble his life—a world revolving around children, the house a constant din of activity, where holidays still brought excitement, where the family gathered to celebrate the small victories of each member.

Now, as he wrestled with the coffee can, he was making her uneasy. "You seem a little antsy, Gumby. You're kinda bugging me."

"Who, me?"

She looked around. "Don't see anyone else here."

"Well, we've been up here awhile now. What if no one shows up?"

"We stay here and keep waiting."

He chuckled. "Hope we brought enough food."

Mayo sighed. "Et tu, Brute?"

Gumble sighed back. "I'm not turning on you," he said. "I'm just not positively positive this secret lover is going to show up."

"You think we should have arrested Patrick Hull?"

He gave the uncrumpled cappuccino can a careful inspection before answering. "Yeah, maybe. Probably. Okay, the pinecones turned out to be planted, but that doesn't mean he didn't do it. We got a murder weapon from his garage. We got him following the victim before she was killed. We got motive. He could have paid off that Vivian woman to lie for him. I'm betting he came here and buried the body. I'm betting he found out that she killed his son and took his revenge."

"You think he buried his own son in that tunnel over there and just left him like that?"

"C'mon, you have to admit it's possible. Maybe his son kept a copy of the map and he found it. Or maybe they just stumbled across the tunnel when they were searching the area. Maybe he and those two from the funeral were in on it—Daryl Sweezy and Kate Russell."

A gust of wind slapped Mayo's hair across her face. She rummaged around in her pack, found a ball cap, jammed it on her head, and tucked away the unruly hair.

"Just trust me on this, Gumby. The lab guys are testing the dirt under Hull's fender and tire wells. They are going to call us up and tell us the mineral content isn't a match for the dirt from Wolftongue Road."

"How conclusive is that? It's been several weeks now—all the road dust could be gone. Think about it. Shouldn't we have our hands on him just in case? He could be in Belize or Outer Mongolia by now."

"If that happens, you can blame me."

Gumble smiled. "That's all I want out of life is to blame you."

"Speaking of which, how come you haven't asked me about McKern?

He finally gave up on the can and stuck it into his pack. "Call me cautious. I figured you'd tell me in your own time."

"Or maybe it's because you already know why I fired him."

He picked a couple of stray pebbles off his pants and dropped them in the dirt. "Pretty much, yeah."

"You have any questions about it?"

"No. I know why you did it and I also know it will cost you some good will around town."

Mayo smiled. "Maybe the citizens will gather a bunch of signatures to get rid of me."

"Tssst—" Gumble held a finger to his lips.

They watched, listening. Half a minute passed. Then, far off down the mountain, Mayo caught a flash of red through the trees. Someone was coming up the trail.

Grabbing their packs, they slid further back behind the boulder. Mayo peeked out. They had chosen their spot well—not only could she see the tunnel opening but she also had a view of the trail where it emerged from the trees. Several minutes went by before the hiker appeared. Mayo lifted her thumb for Gumble.

Moving briskly up the trail was the one person Mayo knew had been given total access to the Alonzo Holloway diary and, by extension, the Hellfire map tucked inside it.

She sat back behind the rock and beamed at Gumble. "Our fish has taken the bait."

Maggie Hurst had either lost weight or Mayo didn't remember her being so tiny. She wore baggy, lightweight hiking pants and a bright red shirt that dangled over her thin chest — a couple sizes too big. She wore a sky blue ball cap on her head and a white handkerchief around her neck. She carried a small backpack and used two hiking poles.

They waited behind the boulders while Maggie passed by and headed across the mountainside, picking her way through the talus, her hiking poles clicking. They crept around the back for a better view. She headed straight for the tunnel opening. There, she turned and scanned the area.

"What's she doing?" Gumble whispered at Mayo's back.

"Shh!" She looked again.

Maggie sat on a rock near the tunnel. She pulled a water bottle from her pack and drank. She untied the handkerchief and meticulously dabbed her face. She re-tied it around her neck and drank more water. Finally, she stood up, pulled on a pair of work gloves, and yanked the tunnel barrier out of the way. When it lay on the ground, she stared at it for a few moments, then put out a hand and leaned against the entryway. She stayed like that for a minute or so before pulling a flashlight from her pack and entering.

Mayo and Gumble moved quickly, scrambling across the rocks.

When they had positioned themselves on either side of the opening, Mayo cupped her hands and called into the tunnel. "Hello! Hello, Maggie!"

Within a minute, Maggie emerged, wiping her face with a sleeve. Mayo caught sight of the tears on her cheeks.

"Good afternoon," Mayo said.

Maggie looked back and forth between Mayo and Gumble. Her eyes were wet and bright. "What's going on? What are you doing here?"

"I don't believe you've met Deputy Gumble," Mayo said.

"We were wondering the same thing about you," Gumble said.

Maggie pulled the handkerchief off her neck again and dabbed her face. "I got a weird map in the mail. I don't know what it's about."

"Can I see it?" Mayo said.

After a pause, Maggie reached into a zippered pocket in her hiking pants and, turning away slightly, fiddled with its contents. She pulled something out and handed it over to Mayo. It was the map Mayo had drawn.

"No letter with that?" Mayo said.

Maggie's mouth opened slightly but her face was otherwise blank. "Did you get one too?" She pulled a letter from the pocket and gave it to Mayo. "I don't know what it's about but it was strange enough I had to check it out."

Mayo glanced at the familiar letter. With help from Joanna, who said that Toby always began his letters with "Hey you," she had typed it herself. Patrick Hull, who had been forging his son's signature to pay household bills, then signed it. Mayo had also hand-made a copy of Toby Hull's map, with a couple of important changes.

"Interesting that you found the place after all." Mayo folded up the papers and handed them back to Maggie. "That map is wrong."

"What?"

Maggie looked down at the papers in her hand, then looked back at Mayo.

Mayo pointed. "The map you have says to go to the right when you get to that spot there, where you see the tree with the galls, but you knew that was wrong, didn't you? You must have gone to the left on the smaller trail, or you wouldn't have made it here. Not only that but I took out the mine ruins at Hellfire. The trail that leads to those is quite overgrown by now, and hard to spot. I'm guessing you have a copy of the original map, which tells you to go left at the galls and then look for the mine ruins before hitting timberline."

"I don't know what you're talking about," Maggie said. "I followed this map."

Mayo took a step closer. "My deputy and I have a little mystery to solve. It's an interesting one. Maybe you can help us figure it out."

Maggie picked at the strap of her backpack with a fingernail. She didn't answer.

"It starts with a map made by Toby Hull," Mayo went on. "The man I mentioned before — the nice-looking fellow you thought you might have met at a conference or something. Anyway, our Toby made a clever little map to Hellfire, just like this one. Last June, he sent it to Heather Holloway, along with a picture of Alonzo Holloway's grave. He knew she couldn't resist the possibility of finding this grave. When Heather arrived, she and Toby had a confrontation, probably right here at this exact spot." Mayo gestured at the immediate vicinity, and Maggie reluctantly looked around. "This fight ended with Toby's death — he went over that ledge there."

Maggie peered down the rotted structure. She dabbed at her face with the handkerchief.

"Heather phoned her sister, who came to her rescue," Mayo went on. "They dragged Toby's body back up and into this tunnel. Then they did another terrible thing: they left him lying there, left him all alone to rot."

"How do you know all this?" Maggie whispered.

"Because Heather's sister told me about it."

Maggie turned away.

"A couple months later," Mayo said, "someone came along and found our Toby. This person, for some reason, buried him but did not notify authorities."

Maggie was very still.

"So of course the mystery is, how and why? And I have a theory. I'd like to run it by you and see what you think."

Maggie still didn't respond, so Mayo continued.

"I think the person who came here and found Toby was someone who cared deeply for him, who was specifically looking for him. I think that person had seen the map that Toby sent to Heather, the same map that my deputy and I used to find Toby for ourselves. I did mention that we found him, didn't I?"

"I heard..."

"So who could possibly have seen this map?" Mayo went on. "Heather kept it folded up inside the Alonzo Holloway diary, which is where we found it. Everyone I met was pretty clear about Heather's possessiveness around that diary. You and your husband both said she wouldn't let you read it without her being present."

Maggie finally smiled dimly. "Paranoid little twit, wasn't she?"

"But there was one person who had access to the diary and the map, if only for a short bit of time. Someone who got into Heather's desk at the museum and brought Heather her things." Mayo paused. "So what do you think?"

Maggie sighed. "I think it all sounds a bit flimsy. I still don't even know what you're doing up here."

Mayo pushed on. "Sometimes when you put a whole bunch of flimsy bits all together," she said, "you come up with something solid. I have some other bits and pieces. Would you like to hear them?"

"Were you here waiting for me?"

"There was the poster you were working on for the Sand Creek exhibit. I thought it was strange that you 'forgot' that you wouldn't have the diary when the exhibit opened. I think you knew Heather was out of the picture and that you might be able to get the diary after all."

"Oh, come on, Marshal," Maggie protested. "That's so weak. I don't even know what it's supposed to mean." Maggie gave Gumble an imploring look. "Deputy—I'm sorry, I forgot your name. What's this all about? I'm worried that maybe the marshal here is—"

"I also think you threw up some pretty good smoke screens when I came to talk to you," Mayo went on. "All that historical eloquence about how the native tribes see history—that was really very good. I wouldn't be surprised if it were true. But not that nonsense about Heather going to hotels with men. I think you saw that kinky package being delivered at the museum and figured we probably found some stuff along those lines in her house. You figured you could leverage that to point the finger elsewhere. It was a complete fabrication that wasted a lot of our time."

"I didn't fabricate a thing," Maggie said.

"Then there's the matter of your tires," Mayo said. "Deputy Gumble here had a peek at them and he thought they looked new. I'm betting that when we get hold of your credit card records, we're going to see the recent purchase of some new tires. When you drove up to Wolftongue, you felt free to leave tire tracks all over the place. Maybe you bought new tires beforehand and swapped them out later. Maybe you changed them that same morning you killed Heather, between the time when you arrived back in the museum parking garage and when your husband showed up. You had almost an hour."

Maggie was shaking her head through this speech. "What a bunch of crazy speculation. I can't believe you guys have been creeping around my car and I can't believe you just accused me of murder."

"What did you think you'd find here today?" Mayo asked.

Maggie looked at her abruptly, as though she had just realized. "Oh, my God. You sent me that letter, didn't you?"

Mayo let the question hang.

Maggie let out a long, slow breath, then seemed to collect herself. "I wanted to check it out. It was weird and I didn't know what it meant. Nothing illegal about that."

"I think anyone else would have been merely puzzled by it and would have given me a call, especially since it mentions Heather."

"Maybe 'anyone else' isn't as curious as I am."

"So how did you find the place? I mentioned the map was wrong, didn't I?"

Maggie pulled her water bottle from an outer pocket of her pack and took a sip.

"You made another tiny mistake," Mayo said. "We found foreign fibers on Heather's clothes. I'm guessing we've got a shot at coming up with something that matches among your possessions."

This wasn't entirely true—not even remotely true, in fact, but Maggie didn't know it.

When Maggie didn't answer, Mayo reached into her backpack and pulled out an enlargement of a picture from Heather Holloway's photograph album. She handed it to Maggie, who took the picture and examined it for a long time. It showed a close-up of Toby Hull standing in a crowd at a busy city intersection. He was smiling at a woman standing next to him. The woman had her hands folded on his shoulder. She wore a hoodie and sunglasses, which covered most of her head and face. Mayo had shown the picture to Joanna, who confirmed that it wasn't her. On the woman's wrist, mostly hidden by her cuffs, was the edge of a distinctive bracelet, just barely showing a swirl of beads.

"I recognized the jewelry," Mayo said. "It's your watch."

A single tear abruptly rolled down Maggie's cheek. She ran a finger across the picture of Toby's face.

"Toby gave it to me," she said. "I was wearing it that day you came to the museum, wasn't I?"

"Yes, you were."

"Where did you get this picture?"

"From Heather's photo album."

Maggie shook her head. "She *was* following him. He suspected she was." Maggie looked up at the sky. Then she looked back at Mayo. "That was a dirty trick, sending me that letter. You can't know what it felt like when I opened the envelope and saw his name signed at the bottom."

"His father is a pretty good forger." Mayo said. She decided not to mention Joanna's suggestion of a Toby-esque last line: *"I think you know it was real for me. We were. I am sorry. Sorry for everything. Well, almost."*

Maggie pretended to laugh. "You know, you come off very pleasant and concerned, but you're really incredibly heartless."

"Sure," Mayo said, "and it takes a lot of heart to point a finger at the father of this man you supposedly loved and at a nation of people whom you profess to admire."

"How did I point a finger?"

Mayo rubbed her chin. "Hmm. Let's see. Heather was scalped. Gee, it must have been an American Indian. Bayonet from the Hull garage? Gee, it must have been Patrick or Toby Hull."

Maggie sighed. "I didn't mean to ..."

Mayo waited, but Maggie seemed to have run out of words.

"Look," Mayo said. "I think I understand. You loved the guy and she ruined his career. And if that wasn't enough, she killed him and left him here to rot. I really can't say I blame you."

Maggie's eyes grew wet again and she took a deep breath. She pulled a tissue from her pocket and blew her nose, then began to talk. "Toby and I — we didn't mean to — it wasn't meant to be anything serious. I was married and Toby was engaged. I wasn't exactly throbbing with happiness in my marriage, but it wasn't bad. Felix is a good man — a little stuffy maybe. But somehow the affair with Toby ended up becoming the most important thing."

She glanced into the dark of the tunnel. "We met at a conference in New Mexico. Felix wasn't there — he had something going on that weekend. I guess we drank too much one night and ended up sleeping together. I felt pretty bad in the morning. We were awkward about it and agreed to forget it happened. But I emailed him a question a week or so later, just a history question, and we started up an email relationship. We opened secret email accounts. It was exciting and fun."

"He ended up breaking off his engagement for you," Mayo said.

Maggie swept fingers across her eyes and face, briefly massaging her jawline. She looked as though she were about ready to collapse, but then she went on. "One weekend, we got together again in Golden. He said he thought he loved his fiancée but they didn't have much in common. You know, the usual bull — she doesn't care about this or that important thing and so on. Of course, I was spewing off the same junk. We convinced ourselves we had earned our little treat on the side. This went on for a few months.

"One weekend we agreed to meet up in Keystone. I'll never forget that day — God, the sky was so clean and blue. It was one of those magical Saturday mornings when you realize life is really, really good. We were meeting at a coffee place and I got there early and bought my coffee and walked across the street to a little park. I was just sitting there on a bench and I looked up and found Toby standing front of me. I remember noticing for the first time how many freckles he had. Silly, isn't it? After that, he could have asked me to cut my head off and I would have done it. Have you ever been in love like that, Marshal Mayo?"

"I have."

Mayo felt Gumble's eyes on her.

"That weekend," Maggie went on, "he told me he had left Joanna. It was so strange, as though everything changed for both of us at the same time without the other knowing it. It was wild and mad and wonderful! I started making plans for how to end my marriage to Felix, which of course would mean losing my job too. But then a couple weeks later, the Heather Holloway business hit. And before I knew it, Toby slipped away from me. He lost his job and then the grant. He became swallowed up by it, thinking up complicated schemes, trying to figure out a way to fix it. He couldn't focus on anything else. I don't blame him really, except that he eventually withdrew and left me completely out of it."

"He never told you about his Hellfire plan?" Mayo asked.

"No. He just disappeared. Suddenly there was no response to my emails. I thought maybe he had decided to go back to Joanna and didn't have the guts to tell me. But then I found a couple stories on the internet saying he had disappeared. I drove to his house and parked across the street. I saw Joanna and Toby's father going into the house and they seemed wilted and upset. In the end I just drove away. I lived for weeks in a state of limbo, waiting for him to come back. I waited and waited. I kept checking the internet for news and I'd send him another email. But nothing."

Maggie lifted her hands and dropped them hopelessly. "He just ceased to exist." She paused, looking out across the mountainside, her eyes suddenly going blank.

"And then Heather showed up at the museum," Mayo prompted after a few moments.

Maggie nodded. "It was about a month later. I had reached the point where I was simply using most of my energy trying to forget about him. And then one day, a young lady showed up looking for an internship. I could hardly believe my eyes when I saw her resume. It was Heather Holloway. I recognized the name of course. And there she was, right in front of me, all polite and trying to kiss my ass. It seemed like fate was reaching out and yanking me back awake. I realized I'd been walking around dead. I needed to know if she had anything to do with Toby's disappearance. I convinced Felix that we should bring her on. It wasn't too hard."

"Your husband wanted the diary," Mayo said.

"Yep. Not one of Felix's more attractive traits—his willingness to use people. Anyway, Felix didn't seem to notice, but I could see right away that she was unstable. Of course, I already knew what she was capable of. And she was always nervous and chattering obsessively about the most inane things. Sometimes I found her watching me with those little bird eyes of hers. She reminded me of a bird, the scavenger carnivore sort that squawks constantly and pecks at roadkill."

Maggie shivered and wiped her face with the handkerchief.

"I was still trying to figure out how to find out what she knew about Toby, and one day—she'd only been there a few weeks—Heather accused Felix of trying to rape her! I was so stunned I almost laughed. I knew she'd been lying about Toby, but I didn't know that making up rape accusations was her hobby."

"And you sent the anonymous letter?" Mayo asked.

"I had to do something—I wasn't going to let her do to my husband what she did to Toby."

Maggie bent over and brushed dirt off her boots.

"And then she called you," Mayo prompted.

Maggie glanced up. "Yes, I told you that, didn't I?"

"She had left the Alonzo Holloway diary locked in her desk."

Maggie smiled. "God, that awful diary. I should have burned it. She considered me her friend, you see. I had made a point of being nice to her and she didn't know that Felix and I were married. Anyway, when I opened the desk and got the diary, of course I looked through it before giving it back. I found the map and the picture of the Alonzo Holloway grave."

"How did you know they had come from Toby?"

Maggie smiled. "Ah, I knew instantly. I mean, the hairs on my arm stood on end. You see, he and I hiked up here that weekend we stayed in Keystone. We saw something very unusual—a black jackrabbit running through the woods. And then there was the tree with the galls growing on its trunk. I remembered it vividly. And again, it was like fate reaching out. Why would Toby put that jackrabbit there unless he knew I would someday be looking at this map? I mean, what could it possibly mean to her? Nothing!"

Maggie raked her fingers down the line of her chin. "So you see? Somehow, he knew, and he put it there for me and me alone."

Mayo figured he put the jackrabbit there just because he liked it but kept this thought to herself.

"I knew his truck had been found in Keystone," Maggie went on. "And his mountain bike was missing. At that moment I *knew* Heather was connected with his disappearance and that Hellfire had something to do with it. So I made a copy of the map before giving it back to Heather. I took a day off, told Felix I had some shopping to do and I drove up here."

"And you found the tunnel," Mayo said.

She nodded. "I found my Toby. He was lying on the ground inside there. He was dried up—his beautiful hair—his face didn't look real. Of course the light was bad and all I could see was a small image in the flashlight. His cheeks were sunken in and the eyes—his eyes were his best feature, you know. I wasn't prepared for it at all. I just screamed and screamed. I don't know what—I ran out of the tunnel. I sat right here on the ground, whimpering, oh God, for the longest time. I don't remember how long. It was the worst moment of my life, a living death. My Toby dead and abandoned..."

Maggie dropped her head. Mayo found a tissue in her backpack and gave it to her.

"Maggie," said Mayo. "Why didn't you just phone the police?"

When Maggie lifted her head, her gaze had gone utterly vacant, as though her spirit had abandoned her. "Because I knew that Heather was crazy enough that she'd get off. She had told me during our little meeting that she'd spent time in a psychiatric hospital during high school. So I knew—I *knew* she'd just go back into the hospital for a while, then get out again. She would get away with killing my Toby."

She fixed her desolate eyes on Mayo. She was probably right, Mayo thought. It really wasn't so difficult to understand.

"So you buried him," Mayo said.

"It took me a long time, but I carried rocks—mostly from outside the tunnel. I couldn't look at him but I piled the rocks over him and covered him up." Maggie glanced back at the tunnel. "I had my own private funeral service for Toby in there."

Mayo waited while Maggie collected herself and drank some more water.

"What did you do next?"

"I started watching Heather. When we met, she gave me her new address in Sugarloaf and I drove up there a couple times and watched her house. I learned that she went out to jog in the morning."

Mayo glanced at Gumble. The dark SUV.

"And then I got the bayonet."

"You stole it from Patrick Hull's garage?" Mayo asked.

"Yes. I knew Toby had a collection, including some bayonets, and I knew he kept it in the garage. He was always talking about finding better storage for it. It was easy to get to—I picked the lock on the back door. I kept the bayonet and the knife in my car for a few weeks, I guess. I took vacation the week before our trip to Sand Creek and I was watching her. I thought it was pretty funny when she came up with her latest rape that week. The night before we went to Sand Creek, I slipped Felix a sleeping aid and left the house about three in the morning. I drove up to Sugarloaf and to Heather's house and stuck a note in her door."

"'Alonzo Holloway is buried at Wolftongue,'" said Gumble.

"I knew she wouldn't be able to resist—all she talked about was this drab little book she was supposedly writing about her search for his grave. She was constantly obsessing about it at the museum. And I knew it would seriously mess with her head, because it was the same ploy Toby used. I knew it would scare her and I also knew she wouldn't be able to resist going. It actually seemed quite beautiful — it felt like balance."

Maggie paused and smiled quietly, apparently remembering the pleasure of this trick.

"Anyway, I parked down the street and waited. Sure enough, right around 6:25 or so she came out with her jogging stuff on. She found my note in her door, went back inside. She came out again about two minutes later and got into her car. I followed her up to Wolftongue. It was all amazingly easy."

Maggie smiled and Mayo was struck suddenly at how beautiful she was. She and Toby must have made an alluring couple.

"How did you get her down into the cabin?" Gumble asked.

"Like I said, easy. She parked and got out and I pulled up right beside her and told her I was the one who found the grave. I thought she'd be surprised at my being there but she apparently wasn't. That's how narcissistic she was: It was perfectly believable to her that I would be looking for this grave on her behalf. I told her it was down the hill near the ruins of this cabin. I was wearing a raincoat and hiding this bayonet underneath it, which was not easy. I'm sure I looked stiff and clumsy but she was too busy scurrying down the hill to notice anything like that. When we were in the ruins, and I brought out the bayonet, she still didn't get it. Even after I told her, 'This is for Toby,' and even when I let her have it, and even as she went down, she still seemed to be looking around for that grave."

Mayo watched as Maggie's face brightened.

Gumble squinted. "Why did you bury the bayonet and knife so close by?"

Maggie frowned, as though annoyed that he had interrupted this memorable moment. "I scouted the place and dug the hole the day before. I figured why risk driving around with that stuff and maybe get caught or getting blood in the car. It didn't seem to matter if it was found, as long as it wasn't found in my car."

Mayo shook her head. "And you didn't mind casting suspicion on Toby's father?"

"I didn't think of that. I didn't even know he was still in Colorado. I figured so what if they trace it back to Toby? He's dead."

Mayo and Gumble exchanged looks.

Maggie looked around and sat on the ground. She began rocking gently.

"I can see you think I'm some sort of devil," she said. "And maybe I am now. The last time I came here, the day I found Toby, I was never the same after that. I wailed and screamed and there was no one here to hear me or help me. Something inside me broke and I can tell you it will never be fixed."

"Why did you scalp her?" Gumble asked. "To make us think it was an American Indian?"

Maggie flashed an unpleasant smile. "No."

Mayo had a sudden memory of Maggie's scalping demonstration. *You get the victim face down, put your foot between their shoulder blades...*

"C'mon," Mayo said. "You read about the Zippy's thing and her claim that it was an American Indian who attacked her and you took advantage of that."

"You're wrong," Maggie said. "I was making a statement."

"And what statement was that?" Mayo asked.

"Didn't I explain it to you?" Maggie said. "It's proof of my courage."

Epilogue

Mayo strolled among the white teepees of the Cheyenne and Arapaho, peering in through openings at the stuff of everyday life—old deerskin coats with elaborately beaded fringes, moccasins and leggings, cradle boards, shrivelled tobacco pouches. The exhibit had a calm, clean feel to it, as though the fear and uncertainty and violence of those days had been expunged from the objects.

She found Monte in front of a glass case full of weapons—a Henry rifle from 1866, a Spencer Carbine, an assortment of tomahawks, war clubs, and bows.

"I want those," Monte said.

Mayo nudged him with her elbow. "I thought it was just Glen who was the family weapons nut."

Monte gave her a sly look.

Mayo felt a little tired, so she found a bench and sat to wait for him. Monte had jokingly referred to their day trip to Denver as a "date," but she wasn't sure what it was. They ate cheeseburgers at My Brother's Bar, which struck her as ironic only when they'd finished eating. They drove to Cheesman Park, where they strolled hand-in-hand among the fading autumn colors. She took Monte out of the park and down the familiar block, where they visited the Victorian she had shared with Glen. He offered to help her pack up her things and sell it.

It felt okay, having a look through the house and talking about her options. Even though she didn't decide anything about the house, going there felt like an achievement.

It was also opening day for the Sand Creek exhibit at the Colorado Frontier Museum. When they bought their tickets at the front counter, she recognized Volunteer: Tilly with the lavender curls, but Tilly didn't acknowledge her. Felix Arkenstone had taken a leave of absence so he could focus on organizing his wife's defense, and Mayo was impressed that he was sticking by her.

There'd been a few other important changes. Dean Mason of History Department at Colorado Western U had suddenly resigned, giving the old favorite, "spending more time with the family" as a reason. Kate Russell gleefully phoned Mayo with this news and also let her know that she and Daryl Sweezy were engaged.

Patrick Hull declined to press charges against Donald Chestnut or Jody Holloway. He wanted to move on, he told Mayo.

After the lab report finally came back saying that Heather had not been raped, Delia Holloway dropped her lawsuit against the Town of Sugarloaf. Mayo suspected this change of heart was helped along by Davy Brown's surprise visit to Delia, an encounter that reportedly involved a dozen roses, a bottle of Dewars brandy, and a lot of Davy Brown flattery.

Back in Sugarloaf, life had returned to its old rhythms. McKern was working at Daffodils, though he did not give up trying to get back on the force. He had told Mayo he was signing up for some sort of refresher course in law enforcement.

Brin Beedle got her scoop, along with a front-page byline in the *Denver Post*. In the weeks since the arrest of Maggie Hurst, Brin had become such an avid admirer of Mayo, Emlyn had begun calling her Brin the Toady. Brin did not publish a story about Mayo's past, but Mayo was aware that Brin was keeping it in a comfortable place for possible future use.

After a bruising altercation that tumbled out the front door of their home and well into the yard—an event that was witnessed by neighbors up and down Rattlesnake Road—Patty Field left her husband Corey and moved into a rental a few blocks away. A rumor was circulating that she had taken up with McKern again.

Patty had made it her new mission to keep an eye on Jody and had visited her at the hospital, where she had been sent by the jail physician. Patty reported that Jody had said little, except that she wanted to donate the diary to the museum and continue her sister's quest to find Alonzo Holloway's grave.

Meanwhile, Mayo, Gumble, and Deputy Nutt were on call a few more hours than they wanted to be, and Mayo had sent out some feelers to find a replacement for McKern. Davy Brown was still officially standing in, but Mayo didn't like to ask too much of him because of his age and his duties as mayor. Besides, not much was going on and Mayo frequently took off early and headed for the high country with Monte and the hounds.

Life was pretty good, she thought, watching Monte gawk at the weapons case. She left the bench and joined him as they headed into the next room, which contained the bulk of the Sand Creek Massacre exhibit.

The display consisted of a sequence of stations, each offering a recorded narrative at the push of a button. The stations featured enlarged pictures of the individuals involved, along with samples of period clothing and weapons, plus a few artifacts found at the site of the massacre, such as flattened tin cups, a cast iron kettle, arrowheads, bullets, 12-pound cannonballs and cannonball fragments.

The narrative told the story of chiefs Black Kettle, White Antelope, Left-Hand, and Lone Bear. These were some of the "peace chiefs," who had tried to work out a compromise with the ever-increasing onslaught of white miners and pioneers. Would-be peacemakers Edward Wynkoop, Samuel Tappan, Silas Soule, Joseph Cramer, and William Bent were outranked and out-maneuvered by John Chivington, who knew the encampment consisted mainly of the chiefs who had been in peace talks with him only seven weeks earlier. On display was a letter from the young Captain Soule to Chivington, dated about a month before the massacre, telling him exactly that.

According to the narration, most of the soldiers with Chivington didn't know and didn't ask whom they were attacking. Some accounts had them drunk. Those who did know tried unsuccessfully to stop the attack and ultimately refused to fire. Nearly 150 Cheyenne and Arapaho were killed.

Monte appeared at her side, pulled on her arm, and pointed at a nearby glass case. "Isn't that the diary you've been talking about?"

She followed. The diary sat in its own case, opened to a page where Alonzo Holloway goes on at length about his admiration for Chivington and his hatred for the "red devils," especially a particular Cheyenne chief named Lone Bear, the "evil-eyed demon of the plains." A small plaque next to the case noted that the diary had been "Donated by Jody Holloway."

"This old world gets smaller every day."

Before she turned around, Mayo knew who had spoken.

Patrick Hull and Joanna Selig stood before her, Joanna's arm linked comfortably through Patrick's.

Hull smiled and shook Mayo's hand. He wore the white shirt and vest that he'd dressed in for Heather's funeral—a fetching outfit that again brought on an unwanted stir of interest in Mayo. She found herself comparing him to Monte—Patrick the wily, unpredictable, and gnarly, versus Monte, cool-headed and imaginative. Both felt dangerous.

"I never had a chance to congratulate you," Patrick said. "I can't say I'm too upset with Ms. Hurst, since she did it for Toby."

"Didn't I tell you there was someone else?" Joanna demanded.

"Yes, you did," Mayo agreed.

She tried to find something in Patrick's expression—she wondered if she had imagined that there'd been some unspoken spark between them. Now, watching his eyes, she decided she had made it up.

"Thanks for helping out with the note," she went on. "Both of you."

"And thank you," Patrick said, "for not swallowing that pinecone business."

"You heading back to St. Louis then?" Mayo asked. To her own ear, her voice sounded overly casual.

Hull glanced down at Joanna, who seemed suddenly preoccupied with an oversized buckle on her garish red purse. "Pretty soon, I figure." He gave Mayo one of his winks.

Mayo introduced Monte and they chatted aimlessly for a little longer before separating. Watching them go, Mayo felt an unexpected rush of relief and wondered if she'd really been drawn to him.

She decided it didn't matter.

She felt Monte's breath against her ear. "Still got a soft spot for that guy?"

She made a face and stepped along to the next exhibit. "What guy?"

"Never mind," Monte said. "Don't mind me, I'm just here to make noise."

Mayo glanced at him fondly. "You're good for a little more than that, I think."

They found themselves in front of a series of portraits showing the chiefs who had been killed at Sand Creek. One drawing in particular looked familiar. The caption said it was "believed by some to be a portrait of the charismatic Cheyenne Chief Lone Bear." She recognized that name too—it was Alonzo Holloway's "evil-eyed demon," the man who had supposedly injured his leg. Lone Bear also had a couple other names. Mayo stopped, felt a queer prickling of skin up and down her arms as she read the rest of the caption:

> Medicine man and Cheyenne Chief E-se-ma-ki, also known as Lone Bear, also known as One Eye, risked his life to travel to Fort Lyon and demand a meeting with Commander Edward Wynkoop. In this single meeting, he transformed this white soldier who had believed that Indians were "cruel, treacherous, and bloodthirsty," with "no feelings," into someone who felt as though he'd been in the "presence of a superior being." (Quoting Wynkoop's autobiography.)
>
> No one knows what was said at the meeting, but afterward, Wynkoop spent the rest of his life advocating for the tribes. The efforts of One Eye and Wynkoop led to two peace councils, but the peace process was unfortunately aborted when Wynkoop was suddenly removed from command. Shortly after, Chivington attacked the camp at Sand Creek, where One Eye was among those slaughtered.

Mayo stared at the portrait of a strong-jawed, handsome man with a bad eye. Chief One Eye stared quietly back at her from 150 years in the past. She felt a laugh rising. He was Heather's "rapist."

"Something wrong?" Monte asked. "You look like you just went into shock."

She took his hand. "On the contrary," she said. "I've just solved the rest of my case."

CPSIA information can be obtained
at www.ICGtesting.com
Printed in the USA
LVHW05s2331100918
589767LV00002B/291/P